keel kissing bottom

keel kissing BOTTOM

BY

Elizabeth de Freitas

RANDOM HOUSE OF CANADA

Canadian Cataloguing in Publication Data

de Freitas, Elizabeth
Keel kissing bottom
ISBN 0-679-30848-2
I. Title.
PS8557.E363K44 1997 C813'.54 C96-932199-6
PR9199.3.D44K44 1997

Cover design: Jonathan Howells
Cover photograph: Derek Shapton
Author photograph: Greg Staats

Printed and bound in the United States

10 9 8 7 6 5 4 3 2 1

part one

The vessel exploded. The anchor was split in two by the force of the blast. The flukes were driven into the harbour's bottom, and the shank was launched into the sky and hurtled like a rocket over the peninsula. It flew over the shredded walls, the shattered glass, the broken teacups, over those who looked up and wondered what on earth, over the only city in the world that had ever seen such sudden annihilation. My mother stood at the helm of her own boat describing the event with disturbing enthusiasm. She rocked to and fro, depicting the shock wave that flung ships ashore, the fire that ran wild through the streets, and even the restless fish who swam near the surface that fateful morning. She swept her arm up over her head to show how the shank had flown from the explosion, landing on the south shore and piercing the thin soil that she had since inherited. She gripped the wheel and grew misty-eyed, and I wondered whether her rapture would unleash a storm of tears. But instead she rejoiced. "We were chosen," she announced and pointed to our house across the gentle water inlet named the Arm, where the ocean reached in as if to cradle the poor peninsula.

My brothers and I sat in the cockpit glancing nervously at each other while our mother flailed about depicting the various horrors reported on that day. The steep streets of Halifax were said to have been strewn with fragmented bodies. Frail clapboard houses were flattened in an instant. Sleeping residents were put to rest permanently. But it was the shank's determined flight that most confused us. My mother often described the famous trajectory, always with awe and admiration, but never before had it been fleshed out with such flourishing gestures, and never before had our family home been the target. The explosion was said to have been an accidental collision between a munitions ship and a relief vessel, and not merely a provision for the sole purpose of the flying shank. "Some say it punctured the house's roof," she whispered. Sure enough, the attic revealed a roof hampered by more than one half-hearted mending, as if the house had received its fair share of falling objects.

"But the monument says it was an accident," my brothers whined, all three at once, packed snugly knee to knee on the starboard bench. They were reluctant to see themselves as offspring in a bloodline made bad by being bull's-eye on that horrific day. They cocked three pouting faces like progeny in mild revolt. The monument to which they referred had been erected to memorialize the landing site of the heaven-sent shank and sat surrounded by tulips in a heart-shaped bed beside our house. The plaque stated the number who had died in the disaster, as if the spot itself marked a massive grave, but there was no mention of our family home having been its chosen destination. My mother frowned and pulled in the mainsail as the wind retreated across the bow. She said the truth had been silenced by Granny. "Your granny was a landlubber," said my mother, who was anything but. "She lied to protect the property value."

The lurid details of Granny's greed, her skewed values and deceit, and the fact that in this instance she had fed lies to the officials, came as no surprise. My mother had been cussing her mother for as long as I could remember and had convinced me, then at the gullible age of twelve, that various conspiracies had buried all local truth. But I was frightened by the news that we had drawn the shank down upon us and that we were to blame for the Halifax explosion. After all, this was no minor crime. It was the kind of family secret the schoolyard would never tolerate. Worst of all, my mother seemed to relish it.

"Can you imagine the power required to split an anchor in two? How could anyone think that it was merely an accident? That shank had our name on it. The Seeburths — we're graced with a legacy of shame." She laughed like a lunatic, and I shuddered to think this was my mother. "Someday, Mary, you'll understand," she said as she drummed the wheel and fixed a fierce gaze on the mansions that lined the opposite shore of the Arm. We sailed past their groomed sloping lawns and out into the ocean swells. A large cargo ship passed us and entered the harbour. A whale surfaced at our stern, its stinky breath unbearable. We turned south past Chebucto Head and other rocky façades, staying close to shore and weaving in and out between the fishing nets. The skin behind my ears tingled with the touch of a morning breeze off the cold, dark Atlantic. My mind raced through the events of the previous few days, but there was nothing to shed light on my mother's behaviour. I wondered if I had done something wrong and her mark of doom was meant as punishment. But she seemed far too exultant for such a simple motive. The truth was we had been chosen, but chosen by whom? If my mother's sudden madness were any indication, then our future was bleak. Her eyes were like those of a fanatic, her breath shallow, her lips trembling. I sat anxiously hoping that gravity alone was the cause of the shank's landing.

Sailing was my mother's passion. She had devoted her life to wind and water. She often bunked on the boat at its mooring, the wind in the halyards her lullaby, while we slept in beds beneath the leaky roof. In the morning she rose early to make us watery porridge. Clumps of brown sugar were added to balance the salt that entered everything she made. It came off her hands, and her breath, and her very being, and having lost the taste of it, she always added more. We shovelled the sticky stuff down, grateful to have our bellies full and feel her love, if only for a fleeting hour of indigestion. She always left us with the breakfast dishes hardening in the sink and went about her ship-shaping chores. The boat was old and wooden and required constant repair. The rigging and the sheets had to be untangled, the wood oiled, the cracks sealed. It was a broad-beamed thirty-three-foot boat that slept six snugly in a permanently damp and mildewy cabin. The lockers were lined with crud and the food always smelled of gasoline. On deck the lifelines and grab rails were rotted with seaspray, and the sails were ragged and too small. Along its bow was the name *Fortune Smiling*. In a world where anchors fell from the sky, the name must have seemed a necessary precaution. My mother swore by it and claimed she had never run aground.

But running aground was the least of my worries. I half-hoped we might scrape the ocean floor if only to secure my mother's sanity and bring her to her senses. The feel of something hard against the hull might have cured her. But the further out we went, the less likely that became. The boat graced the water with a gentle rippling at the bow, until the sea turned suddenly placid and excruciatingly calm. The calm in turn called forth an eerie resignation from my mother. The sails hung and the boom swung back and forth. She sat behind the wheel spinning it without effect, eyes peering up at the empty sails and then lowered, lids almost closed, as she searched the dead calm for evidence of rippling. Nothing gave. Her face grew pale. Her voice was thin as air, her words sucked out to sea. They were menacing words about how a boat balances sea against wind, how the ropes that mediate are so taut they can rip the skin from one's hands, but when these forces are withheld, the boat becomes an awkward hulking hull unsuited to its circumstance. “Like a sitting duck,” she warned us.

My father appeared at the cabin door with a bottle of whiskey and a mug for my mother. “Better booze on the rocks than boats on the shoals,” his anxious voice unfit for the throwaway refrain. Mother stood at the helm, as always, although *Fortune Smiling* was paralysed. With one hand resting on the wheel and the mug of whiskey in the other, she gazed at the horizon, a disclosure, so she later called it, on her burning lips. Liquor worked wonders in loosening my mother’s tongue. It greased and lathered her words and on this occasion it even unhooked her vision.

“Look! Up there! An anchor!” she shouted.

To our credit, we looked. We were inclined to believe in falling objects. We were inclined to believe anything our mother said. We curled our fingers into binoculars and searched the haze for swooping gulls and other explanations. But the sky was empty of suggestive shapely clouds, empty of birds and planes. I found no optical illusions that might account for her observation, and I began to suspect the worst. She was seeing shanks where there were none.

“I can’t see it,” I answered.

“Well you’re blind. Look, there it is!” She took a swig and looked up to check the sails for the slightest sign of wind. I glanced at my father, who drank straight from the bottle. He stood framed in the cabin door, his squinted eyes scanning the sky for falling anchors. I followed his desperate example and stared unblinking above me. I began to see spots. I tried to rouse them into parabolic flight. I tried to invest them with gravity. But they vanished and with them my hopes of denying my mother’s hallucinations. My heart skipped six beats and my blood began to crawl in the opposite direction. I pushed my tongue up against the roof of my mouth and felt the bottom of my brain and the presence of a warped sense of self emerging in the shadow of what I would later refer to as my mother's crisis.

"Could be worse. Could be devoured by fog." She offered this matter of fact as if to bolster her new-found vision. Her ice cubes clinked against her tin mug. She aped the creepy fog fingers with her grappling weathered hands. We shrieked and slid into the corners of the cockpit. Suddenly the fog seeped over the horizon and surrounded us, as though conjured up by her words. Her voice grew weepy, her vision wiped out. "It gets all misty, just like in heaven," she said and seized the wheel and tilted her head back to keep heaven above her. I crouched and waited, suspicious of the quiet, straining to hear the foghorns or the sound of waves crashing, straining to make sense of her phantom shanks.

On a sea vessel, adrift and bewildered, we were meant to rely on buoys with foghorns to aid in our navigation. Each buoy is anchored for life, singing mournful songs induced by the movement of its chain. Each horn has its own phrase and rhythm. I had always believed that foghorns bemoaned their service. Made of rustproof materials and painted with antifouling, they were forever abandoned to the unforgiving fog. And even when the thick air cleared, and the heavy smoke vanished, as it refused to do on this particular day, they always appeared chilled and miserable, locked to the insipid surface, the sea still tempered flat. In the midst of my mother's hysteria they seemed to be conspiring against us, calling us out into thicker fog patches and adding to her confusion. Their sad song was dispersed across the surface and seemed to emanate from everywhere at once, offering no direction whatsoever.

"Better turn the old bugger over," my mother ordered, referring to the make-and-break gasoline engine which sometimes powered our boat. It was an explosive device without clutch or transmission. The angry combustion chamber boomed with gasoline vapour when the cast-iron flywheel was turned. Direction was a guessing game, as the propeller might spin either way. Starting the volatile machine was a dangerous assignment. I went reluctantly, and, as always, the thing refused to budge.

"It won't start," I cried.

"Well, try again."

I was an obedient child. I didn't question commands. No one does on a boat, and boating had always determined our family standard. Being the eldest meant being the first to obey. Even then, when my mother's strange behaviour and words frightened me. Especially then, if my obedience could redeem her state of mind. I would have done anything to ensure she remain at the helm. I carved out a large inner space for prayer and wishes and all the other unfounded ways by which things can come true. I cranked the flywheel a second time and wrenched my shoulder, but I felt no pain for all the dread of failing her once more. I eyed the unlikable Pipsqueak, my mother's constant canine companion, and swore inwardly against all machines.

But my mother ignored the setback and seemed suddenly very cheery.

"What we need is a course of action. A compass direction. A route on a chart," she suggested. The rest of us looked despairingly out at the wall of fog. We had no bearings. The world was hidden, my mother's mind so muddled she couldn't make sense of tide or current. Except for the scent of land, we were without one reliable mark and literally in no position to use the charts. Yet she persevered. "We don't need bearings," she said, her eyes wide with discovery.

To use the charts without bearings was a command akin

to palm reading. If I had known then where it would lead, I would never have squeezed into the cramped quarters of the cabin and mapped out specious routes on random charts. I would never have plotted with such careless abandon and never dared relay the numbers of my reckoning. But what choice did I have? The dutiful daughter scared to death by her mother's faltering reign. She repeated every one of my inconsistent calculations, as if in confirmation. She spun the wheel hand over hand, she unhitched the sheets and pulled the empty sails in. I advised full-circle tacks and other outrageous manoeuvres. I announced buoys, lighthouses, and even islands, all of which belonged in other seas. She didn't care. And her not caring caused a morbid passion to grip my soul. I became gravely attached to the ocean bottom. The bottom was the overriding variable in all my calculations. The bottom was the reference point determining the allowable depths. I traced its uneven tidal-shifting floor on the charts and positioned the always-moving boat above it. I began to think only of that dark underwater world. I imagined it rising from the charts in all three dimensions and saw myself on the briny bottom, watching the underwater landscape grow around me. If majestic rolling hills moulded the floor, I might have felt at ease. But the charts made it quite clear that the sea bottom was riddled with crags and cliffs. There were canyons and giant boulders and sudden drops. Just off the coast the continental shelf collapsed into unknowable depths. And further out beneath the Atlantic was a mountain range larger than any above sea level. Sailing on the liquid surface seemed unsound. I imagined myself among the bottom-dwellers, at the edge of a cliff, looking up at the boat's hull resting on the water's surface. Suppose the density was suddenly changed, suppose the relation was reversed and the boat plummeted down against the jagged bottom.

Whatever fear I felt turned quickly to exhilaration. A butterfly feeling of exultant sea-floor affection, a sudden awareness of how to appreciate my mother's visions. And to mark the revelation, the cold moist climes burned off abruptly, the fog dispersed, and we tacked our way back up the Arm, the Dingle Tower and Hangman's Island. I don't mean to suggest that I fully understood my mother's crisis, nor how my own experience that day would affect my future. For the most part, our twin distempers remained a mystery. But I was aware of a new sense of direction arising from the depths of my navigator's despair. Up and down might seem a simple order to some, but it came to me in all its unexpected glory only on that day, and in doing so it exposed the topsy-turvy world in which I lived. I hung my legs off the stern as we sailed up the Arm. The ocean's ardour brightened the evening sky, and back we were, safe and sound, beside the shank.

We returned to the shank monument as if to pay homage to a founding father, and in the weeks that followed my mother's crisis she grew to love disasters and accidents and sudden reversals of all kinds. She began to put up pictures of destruction, cut from the newspaper and library books. She pinned them up conspicuously on every wall and marked the country, the year, and the number of dead. Many referred to unfamiliar places and were full of wounded, foreign-looking faces. Images of the Halifax explosion were her favourite and decorated the walls of her bedroom. The house gradually became cluttered with floods, earthquakes, and fires. She seemed intent on reminding us of forces larger than life.

One photograph in particular caught my attention. It was pinned to the fridge with a magnet. The picture showed a bleak strip of ruins and smouldering garbage. From where I sat at the kitchen table, glumly stirring my porridge, I could see the picture perfectly framed between my parents' heads. Beneath the image was the printed title, "Bay Street, Toronto, 1904," and beneath that a few words of text about a massive fire that had demolished the street. A fire that had consumed every business and building, but taken no victims. My mother told me that Bay Street was the most high-ranking, influential street in the entire country. She said it was lined with glass towers and paved with paper money. She said that men there wore precious silk underwear, exotic leather shoes, and gold buttons on their suit jackets.

Inspired by the photo and my mother's description, and perhaps a bit desperate to salvage some sense of order, I started a gang called "The Living Fire." My three brothers and my cousin Sarah were the only members. Everyone but Sarah was forced to suffer through initiation rites. Sarah claimed to be an impartial insider and beyond such trifling matters, although she clearly enjoyed participating. Stanley, Mark, Denis, and myself took turns lying naked on a sacred mound of earth located in the middle of Hangman's Island while the others prodded us with sticks and chanted, "We are the flames, from far away, the living fire."

Mark got a stick in the eye and ran smack into a tree. My mother stitched up his nose the way she might a torn sail. Mark was scarred for life, and our gang was forbidden to meet. I carried on secretly, the Living Fire coddled in the cockles of my heart. I read histories of the financial capital, built high-rise castles out of stones and shells and imagined the city rising up like a sanctuary from the rugged sea bottom. I treated the photograph of the Toronto fire with reverence, dreaming of a thunderous Judgment Day when I would be rewarded for my faith.

True, I was confused, but I was only twelve. My mother's obsession with disasters weighed heavily on my heart, as did her strange and sudden conviction that we were branded by the steel shank. All delusions aside, it seemed a forewarning of future persecution. I was haunted by a sense of the alien terrain that lay hidden beneath every surface. I began to believe that Bay Street's very power sprung from those founding destructive flames, and that the masters of the universe wore hot pants and gold buttons.

"Shall I crack an egg over your head?" I asked. My brothers nodded eagerly and lined up to receive the pleasant sensation. On the first knotty head of hair, I placed one hand shaped like a bird's beak, the point pushing into his scalp. With my other hand, I slapped the back of the beak, driving the bill into his head. He leaned forward and pressed his dirt-smeared lips into my shirt so as to muffle his laughter. I repeated the gesture, the second crack just as cool and professional as the first. Then I lightly touched his crown, my fingers fanning outward and slowly spreading as if they were gooey egg yolk leeching over his entire head.

Egg crackings were hardly a means of discipline, but my brothers' behaviour always improved after a little head banging. They delighted in the hard slap at the start that reverberated in the hollows of their heads. They relished the feathery feel of my fingers as they unfurled and advanced, creating an imaginary helmet of yellow ooze. The boys became almost manageable when subdued and sweet-tempered by this soft pressure from above. I perfected my technique until rumour spread and other children came, but it was sedating my brothers that brought the most satisfaction. Mother called them "The Bad Eggs," and called on me to collect them. She dressed them in matching outfits and constantly confused their names. They were similar in size and proportion and thought of themselves as triplets, although this was far from the biological truth. Mark, Denis, and Stanley, and no one leader amongst them. They did everything in unison: walking with equal pace, eating the same portions, rising each day at the same moment. They must have seen safety in their unanimity, safety from their disastrous parents. Even before Mother's crisis, they had developed a way of speaking that ensured their togetherness. Each sentence, request, and response was split three ways amongst them. It was quite a simple feat, considering the obviousness of what they usually said. Their concerns were all practical: how to build things and how to break them.

"Has she gone crazy?" they asked me, as we watched our mother sharpen the scissors and then cut earthquake pictures from an ancient encyclopaedia.

"Of course not," I lied.

"Then why all the disgusting pictures?"

"Because they're true. They happened."

"What difference does that make?"

"A lot," I replied, although I was unsure.

I was inclined to defend her habit, if only to sanction my new-found Bay Street fervour, derived, as it was, from that photo on the refrigerator. Precisely how I was supposed to unlock the fervour and apply myself remained unknown to me. I had invented a new doll game called Playing Exchange, but the rules were much like those of Playing House, and the dolls looked impish in their ragged scrap suits and string ties. The world of high finance was still only a fantasy, a dream I didn't dare overindulge, save my secret reverence to the Living Fire. The fact that my mother collected pictures that depicted real disastrous events was in some degree proof of this world and its destructive power. Her pictures were also proof that our lives could be easily turned inside out and confirmed both her fear that the sky was falling and my own suspicion about false bottoms and rising sea floors.

The summer of my mother's madness was uncommonly hot, the wind so rare we felt graced by its touch. One muggy night I lay in bed tormented by dark sea-bottom scapes, every corner of my room a crack opening into cavernous underwater terrains. I didn't dare go to my mother, fearing she might encourage my nightmare. She slept with arms and legs spread like a sea star, my father curled up in a shell at her midriff. I passed their open door, entered my brothers' room and found them wide awake. I watched their beady eyes glisten and shift in codes only they understood. I said nothing but still conveyed my anxiousness. We left the house barefoot in t-shirts and underwear, skipped across the rocky lawn and through the tulip garden and, under a full yellow moon, we stole away in our neighbour's matchbox sailing dinghy. The night was still and the single sail hung heavy on the halyard. I brought it down with a loud crumpling as it puckered at the base of the mast, and we drifted, pressed together in the tiny cockpit. We leaned back against the gunwales, staring up at the night sky and listening to the mild lapping of the sea against the boat's hull. I felt comforted by how impossibly remote the night was. A mist veiled and unveiled the bright August stars. Venus had already gone to bed. Vega, the brightest vertex of the summer triangle, shone directly above us, while its two companions spun around the mast. We lay there for hours, the tiller knocking against our legs, the boat slowly turning. Being on a stolen boat, without my mother at the helm, was the most disobedient, the most delinquent, and the most sensual thing I had ever done. I felt a deep bond with my brothers, which I had never felt before. But the bond was broken by the sound of trumpets. The notes were woolly and full of wet air. Images of fat lips around brass mouthpieces replaced the triangle of stars. The boys sat up, their trance broken, the boat rocking from their sudden movement.

"What's that?" they asked. The four of us looked at each other, at our pageboy haircuts and our aquiline noses, at our ridiculed elephant ears, and our unsmiling lips. By all counts, we were ugly. There was no denying it. Something about the music sabotaged our romantic illusions and was intended to do so. I believe my mother chose to play her baroque records for that express purpose, for I'm quite certain stolen property was not the issue. My guess is that she wished to inhibit any intimate filial bond, not for the sake of incest taboos, for which she had little regard, but because she hoped we might foster better standards than what we offered each other. She had grown very critical of her family in the weeks since her crisis and prayed that we might save ourselves from each other.

Without exchanging a word, we tillered back to shore, the water dark and deep since the moon's setting. We rushed back over the lawn and into our beds, but each ensuing night of the heat wave we repeated our escape, slipping the dagger board into the dinghy and pulling up the glowing white sail. And each night the trumpets ended our communion. Perhaps the stellar triangle was especially magnetic that summer and the high temperatures especially sensual, for what else could explain why I wooed my brothers, who were no prize by any standards? I was divided between myself and my fair judgment, and whether I blame the shank or the sea floor is irrelevant, although I am inclined to blame the sea floor and its nightmarish haunting for driving me into the boys' room to begin with. At any rate, the sound of the trumpet was sufficient to keep me frigid and loyally bound to my mother.

As if she knew precisely how to end our growing alliance once and for all, she gave the boys one toy boat to share amongst the three of them. It was a self-righting single hull painted dark blue. They tied its bowline to all three of their wrists and pulled it along while wading through the water. If any other children came to inspect the toy, they were rudely ignored. My brothers kept to themselves. I wrongly believed that I had breached their insularity, for I regarded our star-gazing as a sort of engagement. When they carefully attached one of my Bay Street dolls to the immovable toy tiller, I assumed the gesture was affectionate and meant to include me in their game. I sat on the warm beach burying my legs in the sand, watching the miniature boat pitch and plunge and then right itself. The boys grew bored and plonked seaweed, rocks, and their sandwiches into the boat. They let the line go and watched it sail across the Arm. They jumped up and down with rapture, cheering on the white-breasted greedy gulls who dove down to peck at the food. It was then that I realized my error. I watched in horror as the birds' gnarled claws scratched desperately at the slippery hull. Their enormous orange beaks shredded my doll's arm, tore at the plastic sail, and caused the boat to list and then submerge. My brothers threw rocks and screamed with triumph when the toy boat finally sank. Down went my little plastic doll, who might have survived if he hadn't been so judiciously tied to the tiller. They turned their ratty faces in unison toward me, and I saw the evil pride they took in double-crossing me.

"You'll regret this!" I yelled.

"No, we won't," they yelled back.

"Yes, you will!" I assured them. "When I'm queen of Bay Street!"

They laughed at what must have seemed the idle threats of a wounded sister, but I never forgave them, and my heart hardened against them. They, in turn, diligently betrayed me. My other dolls met similar ends. The poor creatures lived in a constant state of dramatic upheaval. They were often stolen and tied up, their faith strong through blindfolds, rope burns, and torture. On kinder days, the boys put snails on their legs and watched them slither up over their knees, but more often, they tore my dolls limb from limb, always poking their fingers into the holes where legs had once been. My father tried to fix them with glue, but it made their joints rigid and their limbs inflexible. I realized that my brothers loved only themselves and that the summer triangle was closed to me.

The weather became wet and chilly. My mother began wearing rubber raingear and refused to remove the slick bulky suit when indoors. The sound of crinkling rubber followed her everywhere. Visions of flying anchors continued to cause us consternation. Mother often pointed two fingers at the empty sky and grinned with satisfaction. My father suggested a rest holiday at the Joggins Cliffs of Chignecto Bay, but the rough-hewn crumbling cliffside only confirmed my mother's fear of natural disaster. My experience charting the sea bottom had inspired an interest in topography, which meant that I read avidly, mostly about geology, and knew a great deal about the Joggins Cliffs.

We arrived in the morning and found the pebble beach deserted. I stood beneath the stacks of shale ledges and slippery wet siltstone and listened to the choppy waves slap down, one on top of the other. I listened to the sea shuffle stones about, knocking them against each other, splashing over them and then licking their curves and drawing them out. I felt the fuzzy dampened rays of the sun on my forehead. I could hear my brothers collecting rocks nearby and filling their pockets. Sounds of triumph erupted whenever an especially exotic-looking stone was retrieved. My parents sat together, closer to the water, sipping hot coffee from a thermos mug. My mother had developed a nervous tic as she constantly threw her head back and glanced upward. I watched her sip and swallow and shrink from the phantom shanks.

I rested my head on a library book entitled *The Earth* and dreamt of distant worlds buried in time. The crumbling cliffs stretched for miles up and down the coast. I felt oddly at home where the land had been torn open, cracked wide open, to reveal the simple traces of trapped reptiles and lifeless tree trunks swallowed by the rising bottom sediment of a primeval sea. Bare-ass naked cliffs told the stories of early rivers, deltas, and floods. A curve in the edge of slate, like a puddle stain on linegrained sandstone, indicated that a river had once cut down through the soft sediment, its profile unmasked in the cliff face. While other kids imagined magicians hiding in their closets, I imagined the world unhinged by giant geologic upheavals. Without friends, trustworthy siblings, or sane parents, my early adolescence was a lesson in isolation. I was alone in a dangerous world, a world that my mother insisted was full of disasters. I lay beneath a protruding ledge and wished an avalanche would bury me in the ancient rubble and crush me with fossil fragments. Anything to escape my loathsome, indistinguishable brothers, whose recent betrayal still oppressed me. I had watched them go exploring along the jagged shoreline and now saw them racing back chased by the tide, hardly a dry stone to trust their step. I wanted them to slip up, fall, and crack their heads. I closed my eyes and heard the horrid sound of their skulls splitting open, but then looked and found them safe and sound, taunting me with hammer-shaped rocks and broken shells.

We stopped to picnic later the same day during the afternoon calm. A hardscrabble road on the other side of the Chignecto peninsula led to an impressive view of the flat Bay of Fundy. The water brooded beneath the sun like a massive mirror made slightly foggy. Five tall and eerie islands rose up from the warm mist and the oddly even sea. Their dark still figures were so ominous and inviting, so strangely shapely against the flat expanse. The tide had carved a hole in one island, creating an eye into another world. My mother explained how all five were the result of an angry Mi'kmac god. Thundering bad-tempered Glooscap had thrown sod at Beaver and there the sod remained. Not knowing the full legend, we knew nothing of Glooscap's reasons, nor did we ask whether Beaver had deserved punishment. My mother said it was simply one more explosive moment in the making of the world. I never doubted her words. I felt speechless before the sacred landscape and imagined the god's giant fingers sculpting hollow pits in the earth, laying hold of the land and hurling the soil. Those mounds seemed animated with spirit, the kind of spirit that comes from a mud-slinging god, the kind of spirit who speaks to bitter, lonesome children obsessed with lunar landscapes.

We took the steep road angled down into the cliffs and reached the spongy orange silt. Thousands of minute white barnacles crunched beneath our step as we walked out toward the islands. When our way was blocked by the incoming tide, we laid our picnic out on the smooth incline of a rising sandstone. My brothers rolled up their matching blue corduroys and commenced rock hunting. The stones were brightly coloured whether wet or dry. Many were composed like patchwork, displaying faults of feldspar or quartz or marble. The boys filled their pockets greedily, grasping after rocks whose shape suggested jewels hidden within. That jasper, agate, onyx, and amethyst might be contained was an inspiration to collect almost anything. They tried hammering open these rocks in the hopes of discovering the crystalline beauties.

There was no good reason for my despising them as much as I did at that moment. They were just typical boys after precious stones. They hankered after what the market deemed valuable. We may have had nothing else in common, but we shared this fascination with the mystery of monetary worth. Perhaps I knew then that concerns of that sort were more cutthroat than binding, for every living cell in my body was sending hostile messages in their direction.

I stood beside a small pool full of hermit crabs busy bumping into each other and fighting brief duels at each encounter. One crab, too large for his current drab shell, fought mercilessly with another who had recently acquired a rather ostentatious blue spiral. I picked up the glittery shell and the crab withdrew. I rolled the shell back and forth in my palm, wishing I had one of my own so as to fend off my cruel brothers. I dropped it back into the pool and the crab instantly reappeared, lashing out at another as if nothing out of the ordinary had occurred.

I walked away from the incoming tide and climbed back up the cliffs. I sat on the edge, which smelled of clover and wheat grass and ripened blackberries, and stared at those five enigmatic islands. They invited me and dared me to swim out against the dangerous undertow. Their dark outlines drawn out of the mist promised a kind of sanctuary. I longed to be there and to hold them in my hands the way that Glooscap did. I imagined fitting my fingers between their summits, pressing the heel of my hand into their clay beaches. I looked down at my little family scurrying about on the mud bed, and then thankfully returned my gaze to the god-slung oasis.

Crystal Crescent Beach was surrounded by sloping hills dressed in blueberry bushes. The lush rust-colour of a burnt-out car body rested reverent and rich against the porous white sand. The path down to the beach passed through shallow sand dunes where beer bottles lay scattered about the remains of fire pits. A recent storm had torn up and delivered mounds of seaweed along the shore. Sarah and I jumped over the green and black bobbled muck and ran in and out of the cold Atlantic. We stayed in the frigid water just long enough to relieve our bladders. We shivered uncontrollably, our teeth clattering, our flesh shaking like the chugging jolts of an old engine. My urine felt like warm tea between my icy legs. The act of peeing in such cold water required deep concentration. I tried to ignore the waves that rolled frostily into my armpits. Our legs grew so numb that it was difficult to know when we were done, but out we ran all the same, out of the heartless ocean and back to the warm sand, where we rubbed each other's blue legs to get the blood recirculating.

Sarah was my cousin and bosom-buddy. I might never have survived that dreadful summer if it weren't for her friendship. My brothers' betrayal paled beside her radiant power. She saved me from the horror of family gatherings, including the summer picnic at Crystal Crescent Beach. Nourished with tuna sandwiches and ginger ale, bored and bikini-clad, we took off together down the beach in search of odd abandoned objects. We scavenged the surf for trophies worth salvaging, but found only the glutinous remains of dead jellyfish. We traipsed over the outcrops of slimy rocks, amazed by the giant granite boulders that stood so unstably on the slick ledges. We jumped over the incoming water where the rock had fractured in two. And when we followed the fault and traced the striations, we dared each other to put an arm into the cleavage. Sarah did, I didn't. She was brave, I wasn't. My unwilling arm was governed by the fear that such crevices opened onto darker worlds not to be toyed with. I followed her as she walked on the balls of her feet, carefully avoiding the dead crusty weeds and dried barnacles, out to the wetter rocks that eventually gave way to the sea and its flora.

"At least your family ignores you," said Sarah as she crouched near a pool of water. "My mother never leaves me alone."

The notion of vigilant maternal scrutiny was utterly exotic to me.

"What does she do?" I asked and lay down on my belly beside her.

"I don't know. Nothing, I guess. She just bugs me."

We stared into the pool. Spiralled snails clung snugly amidst the algae. Blue-ridged mussels lined the rocks and were oblivious to the predatorial whelks that inched toward them. Sarah pointed to a six-legged sea star. "Look, it's got one too many legs!" she said with enthusiasm. She peered down at the studded carnivorous creature as it wrapped its legs around a blue mussel and began forcing the shell open. I had seen this sort of slaying before. "There's no stopping sea stars," I said, trying to sound informed. My father had explained to me how the sea star has the strength of the sea; water circulates like blood through its rays, pumping and pressurizing suction cups that enfeeble even the most resolutely sealed bivalve. The world seemed full of slow deliberate predators like this one. Predators without much ingenuity, but driven by a plodding implacable instinct. And always driven toward the same victims in a cruel but well-established order. We watched the mussel struggle to keep itself closed. Then it slowly surrendered and was eaten alive in its shell.

The sun felt warm on my back. The heavy heat pressed against me and weighed me down. My skin tingled. The heat moved deeper, penetrating every pore and reaching the very marrow of my bones. I grew dopey with the lulling sound of the waves rolling in and out, the rhythm on the nearby beaches like a slow stroke over the shifting sand. We were both drowsy. We lay on our stomachs, our shoulders touching, our heavy heads resting on our hands. Face to face, my face, Sarah's beautiful face, our bodies baking in the luxuriant sun. I watched her black eyelashes lightly shift against her freckled skin. I struggled to stay awake, to keep her in focus. Then I lost sensation, lost the feel of my body against the rocks and dropped off into sleep.

Sarah was a great source of comfort. She was two years older than I and better at almost everything. I felt graced by her friendship and attached myself to her, like a barnacle to a boat. She often demanded oaths of allegiance, which I freely gave. "Will you follow me to the end of the earth?" she asked, and I swore that I would. My loyalty was unwavering. The end of the earth was hung and pasted everywhere on the walls of my house. If Sarah managed to escape, then I would follow, for she alone offered refuge from my family. As to what I offered her in return, I can only guess. I suppose my absolute devotion was difficult to refuse. I doubt very much that she was ever driven by any altruistic passion to relieve me of my woe. But who knows the true thoughts of those they adore? I do know that I would never have risked the pure physical joy of baking in the sun beside her.

When I awoke I was dizzy from the heat, my vision

blurred, and Sarah was gone. I sat up and spied her tomato-red bikini in the distance. She was lying down on a ledge that looked out over another secluded beach. When she heard me approaching, she picked up her walking stick, normally used to poke and prod at the unknown, and waved it frantically, meaning I was to keep down and out of sight. I quietly crawled to her side and peered over the ledge. Two naked men, greasy with oil and fairly bronzed, lay on top of each other. They were perfectly still. Their faces were buried in the sand. Three ass cheeks, one hidden from view, lay serenely exposed in the sun, glistening like the smooth valves of giant clams. Their limbs were sprawled at their sides, as if they had fallen out of the sky.

I had never seen anything so strange before.

"What are they doing?" I asked.

"They've just had sex, silly," she said, admonishing me in her mother's voice.

"Are you sure they're not dead?" I whispered. But she didn't bother to answer. "How did they do it?" I asked, knowing this was the dangerous question.

"You don't know?" She raised her eyebrows.

"No, I don't."

"They poked it in the bum, that's how!" She scowled at my ignorance.

I was angry at myself for being such a dolt. I picked up a small stone, swung with all the strength I could muster and threw it at the pair on the beach. My aim was surprisingly accurate. The stone sounded a *chink* as it ricocheted off a half-buried bottle of wine beside them. They leapt up, their chest and legs and hairy crotches patched with white sand. They spun madly about, swearing and scanning the rocks for the culprit. But Sarah and I were already hurtling back to our family, our bikinis sliding insolently all over our prepubescent bodies. The sand trapped in the lining of my bathing suit bottom had hardened into a cement-like pad between my legs, which scratched my inner thighs as I ran. Sarah, the faster runner, was ahead. I chased after her, sprinting over the fine-grained sugary granite that scraped the dead skin off the bottom of my feet. Finally, I caught her arm.

"Is that really the way it's done?" I panted. She spun around, enraged by my stupid questions. She plucked each of my fingers from her arm and then replied with the wisdom she had been granted as my superior.

"Yes," she said and turned away.

Aha, I thought, sex was something between men. It was a kind of fraternizing on the beach that involved remaining perfectly still. The asshole was obviously the way inside. I had never given the topic much thought before that day, although the idea that my parents' relationship was sexual had always struck me as absurd. But beyond this simple observation, my mind was on the cracks and crannies of the planet, not of the human body. I was shy about my own, but I had reasons to be: my behind was as big as the morning sun, and my legs were as thick as tree trunks, of this my brothers often reminded me. Sarah's answer confirmed what I had suspected all along — that sex was not meant for me.

We launched a full season of serious spying. Human beings, particularly males, became a source of fascination. We relished the intrigue of watching without being seen. We hid inside rooms and eavesdropped, we secretly observed through windows, and we followed and stalked without restraint. My brothers were easy prey. We dogged them to Hangman's Island, where they had carved holes into three dead tree trunks.

To our delight and disgust, the rascals dropped their pants and poked their little penises into the tight triangular array.

Tree-shaming was blackmail material.

"What shall we make them do?" asked Sarah.

"Let's make them do it to each other," I suggested.

"No. We can't do that!"

It was always she who upheld the moral statutes. I seemed to lack all sense of propriety, except in those cases when I was driven by fear.

"Spankings?" I suggested instead.

"Boring," she sighed.

We decided we would hold a "spectacle." Wearing dirty sheets wrapped like togas, we danced a combination of ballet, theatre, and opera. We played my mother's baroque records and leapt about the room, embracing, kissing, stabbing each other with lustful vengeance, and weeping. The boys were obliged to applaud. Sarah's intrepid temperament kept them from seeking revenge. She was a bully, no bones about it. But she was so multi-talented, there was no reason to resist.

For years she had coached me on self-improvement. She offered dance and etiquette lessons and much more of her mother's dogma than she would care to admit. She was determined to reach adulthood as soon as possible. We often burrowed into Sarah's closet and sat pinching our tiny nipples because she said this encouraged growth. I followed her instructions, but I didn't share her passion. Being a woman seemed a rather bleak prospect. I far preferred the romantic visions of the cowgirls that I read about in Westerns. I often rode our neighbour's horse, JoeHow, at sunset, and imagined the thorny desert on the horizon. Becoming a full-fledged female brought along too much baggage. I felt an itchiness crawl over me whenever my reflection revealed the inevitable. At those moments I wanted nothing more than to be a pyromaniac, in tribute to that great founding fire. Sarah thought my Bay Street ambitions were laughable. She had quit the Living Fire and said there was fat chance of my ending up in the arms of a financial wizard.

"Grow up!" she demanded the following summer. "You don't have a penny to your name."

"It's not a matter of money. It's just know-how," I answered.

"But the point is you don't know how."

She spoke the truth, and I felt obliged to shelve my aspirations, at least temporarily, and adopt hers once again.

She was determined to become a champion swimmer and insisted that I also enrol in swimming lessons. She was, as usual, better than me. I swam in her wake, watching her legs scissor-kick and her slim hips roll. But my breathing was so erratic, my coordination so poor, that I swallowed water at every turn. I could hardly keep up. The spluttering swish of her body dissolved into blue as she vanished from view, her splash a blur of reflective bubbles nearing the end of her length. A dip and somersault turn sent her ploughing through the surface toward me, her yellow-capped head rolling from side to side as she gulped a lungful of air and let the bubbles stream from her nostrils. She had marvellous style. I loved watching her carefully cupped hand cut the water and push a fistful along her belly and out behind her. I loved watching her twist and stretch and crawl. I tried to pinch her toe whenever she lapped me, but I was always moved into a slower lane and had to watch her from afar.

Many early morning lessons began with a dense fog hugging the warm water surface. The fog often thickened with our hot breath. Outlines of bobbing heads approached and retreated; a splash or choppy wave announced their proximity. Wolverine echoes of playful hollering saturated the chlorinated air. Swimming in those conditions was a lonely endurance test, a marathon of length after length, waiting to share a precious moment with Sarah.

"I think I feel the big rollicking wave of Mary Seeburth beside me," said Sarah from the misty adjoining lane. She dove under the partition, through my legs, and up behind me.

"It wasn't my wave," I said, for I had been skipping lengths and shivering in the shallow end for at least five minutes. We ducked down into the fog when the swimming coach walked by.

"Look at his rotten swimsuit. It's so see-through, you can see his crack," she whispered. I could hardly see his outline, let alone his behind, but once again Sarah had shed a little light on male tectonics.

In the corner where we stood, two jets of warm water shot into the pool. We pressed our bellies against the hard rush, an endless barrage of soft-gloved water. Sarah liked to duck under and push her face into the heated stream; she liked to feel it flatten her nose and rumble in her ears. She always wanted me to go under with her. "Let's have a tea party," she suggested, and cross-legged we sat on the bottom, our arms churning to keep us down, our chitchat garbled in hysterical bubbles. Beads of breath that abandoned us clung to an arm or finger or forehead before rising. I felt vaguely troubled as the air departed from me but remained fascinated by the submerged Sarah, her skin pale green in the underwater light. She seemed so otherworldly and beautiful.

Her skin-tight swimsuit was an alligator green. She said it struck fear into her competitors and doubled her speed. At competitions she won all the prizes. But Sarah always won prizes; her drawers were crammed with trophies. She excelled at everything except sailing, which had become my forte through years of enforced service. Sarah couldn't sail herself out of a bottle. She suffered from motion sickness. I was glad she suffered from something. My mother said she was the exception, as superior sea-legs were a family legacy. The rest of us were immune to the nauseating effect of sea swells and storm waves.

Or so I thought, until one windy day on the boat I grew miserably impaired. I clung to my unstable seat while butterflies flapped their unsettling wings in my stomach. I stared at the horizon, the steady line between sky and sea, desperate to achieve some measure of level-headed perception. On land my condition strangely worsened. I could barely walk, my balance was so severely skewed. A mortifying nausea took hold, and finally I fainted from dizziness. The doctor said that I had an inner ear infection, which put an end to swimming. I remember his chubby pockmarked face and his pumping hand gestures as he described the small sac inside my ear that affected my sense of balance. "Shaped just like a bagpipe, my dear," he grinned, "filled with little hairs and crystals. And the two together distinguish between up and down." It was hard to imagine that the centre of the earth was established in a small sac inside my head. Up and down, top and bottom, were mere tentative precepts. Infection could easily obliterate them. I struggled to make sense of this fact. My mother's mania about heaven-sent shanks had only recently driven me to the sea floor. My sense of being on the bottom was suddenly put into question by the doctor's news. But how could the world be contained inside my head, when the size of my cranium was exceptionally small? The encyclopaedia entry on the inner ear added to my confusion. The little sac, I learnt, was like a tidal pool filled with an ancient sea. It had developed from the lateral cells of the primeval fish from which we all evolved, cells that sensed position in relation to the rest of the aqueous world. I lay in my undulating bed, disoriented and dizzy, my crystals having floated away. Asleep, I dreamt of swimming.

When Sarah came to visit, she clenched the bedsheets, and her eyes grew watery.

"Will you recover?" she asked.

"I don't know," I replied in a wavery and highly dramatic voice. "If I die, will you bury me?"

"I'll give you the best burial ever!" she promised. "I'll give you a burial at sea!"

But two days later my nausea subsided, my sea legs returned, and I sailed with my family through another dead calm.

Mother suggested flogging a cabin boy on the starboard deck. It was a time-honoured practice meant to encourage the wind.

"Which one of you three ill-begotten boys will be the one?" she bellowed.

My brothers ignored her. They began whistling and tapping their perfectly parallel feet. Their heels whacked the wood planks to the disciplined rhythm of their song. The thumping sound was diffused across the sea. My mother glared at them. "Whistling only mocks the wind," she grumbled. And she was right. Whistling kept the wind far from the hanging halyards and the saturnine sails. It mocked the dead-pan sea and the breathless day. The saucy sound of pursed lips riding a lungful of blow kept the ocean calm and ungiving. My brothers were fully aware of this fact and increased the volume, until she could stand it no longer.

"Stop the racket!" she yelled, her wrists resting on the aimless wheel, her eyes bloodshot, and her hair thick with salt. Two years had passed since she had turned our home into a gallery of disasters. Two long years during which family rapport had completely degenerated. My mother's morbid fixation had hardened my brothers against her. Stanley, the eldest, spoke only gibberish when she was in earshot, while Mark and Denis made gruesome faces behind her back. I had grown brutally shy and sought escape in our outmoded encyclopaedia, reading obsolete accounts that would handicap me for life. A difficult period of adjustment, said the guidance counsellor at school, as she eyed my widening hips and disappearing face. Sarah's company was my only asylum, but it seemed more and more infrequent.

And since sailing was her one failing, she never joined us on the boat.

Mother looked haggard in the ruthless cold grey of early morning. She apologized to the boys. "Bit anxious today. I had a bad dream last night. Bowled me right off the bunk!" she offered as explanation. No one asked for details. No one wanted to know. My brothers stopped their whistling, slouched over and dropped their heads into their laps. The dark glass surface of the sea was silent and morose, as if the water itself was in prayer. Our patched sails hung like giant death shrouds. We were drifting toward shore with the tidal current, the make-and-break engine long since forsaken. I'm not sure which I feared more, the rocks or my mother's delusions, but both seemed imminent.

I climbed onto the deck and over to the mast where a dew-covered spider web was attached to the mainstay. A thick seam of hardened silk showed where the spider had mended its broken web radials. It was a sloppy remedy, the kind conceived by a desperate soul. The heavy seam had pulled away from the other threads, leaving gaping holes. The entire web was muddled, as if hastily spun. The exaggerated zigzag in the outer loop of sticky spiral was too long and delicate, stretched between too few anchor lines. A gust would easily destroy it. Even a gentle breeze might unfasten the four hook lines and send the fine mesh out across the water. I leaned closer to examine the adhesive network. The silk smelled fishy, as if coated in the estrual scent of the enormous female spider that hung in a cryptic posture beneath the hub of the web. She was a garden spider out to sea. A castaway, hoping to leave land behind. I assumed she was on a suicide journey and yearned to parachute out over the hull, carried by the wind, her web a magic carpet. Her body was a series of knobs, spikes, and spurs, all of which were hairy and plastic-hard. She was already too large to attract the significantly smaller males, who feared being eaten by their mates and preferred coupling with the more immature members of the opposite sex. I had watched them all over the sides of our house, stalking female juveniles. And I had watched them, still unsure of their safety, wrap their lovers' jaws with silk and hobble their legs with a few sticky lines, just in case.

The castaway tapped the spokes of her web to test the tension of each. A wasp flew out of the boat's air vent and directly into the trap. The spider rushed out to capture her prey, wrapping it in thread as strong as steel. She hung from two legs, spinning around and around, working a series of pulleys and swivelling and trundling her victim into a ball of smothering silk. I watched, fascinated, as she and her prey became a dizzying blur of spigots, spinnerets, and hairy legs, a spinning orb, the wasp at the centre incarcerated, its sting no longer potent.

"Visitors," announced my mother, as she looked out across the soup in which we were stranded, our sails hanging to no purpose. I expected visions of shanks at any moment. But I was wrong. The whining sound of a small boat engine, revved to breaking point, spread across the water and stirred the air with its high pitch. The thin noise stretched for miles in all directions; a rudderless, sourceless whirring that chilled me to the bone.

Some of the locals behaved like pirates, and many disliked my mother for reasons unknown to me. I rose from my crouch, my knee puncturing the web and severing one of the mooring lines. I searched the horizon for a boat but saw nothing. Only the black sea and the deserted shoreline, the sky still heavy with the slow dawn. Only shrubby trees grappling the granite rocks, and the devilish terns that flew a wing's breadth above the surface. Only the nasty low tide peaks of stones and ledges, which reared their ugly heads before us. I held my breath and scoped the horizon a second time. Gradually the pinched and narrow whining increased until finally the bow of a small motorboat appeared near the mouth of a cove. It was low in the water, crammed with hulking torsos shoulder to shoulder, each capped with a slug-shaped head. I crouched again behind the mast; the spider already repairing the damage done to her web. In the cockpit, at the helm, my mother stood suspiciously eyeing the barrel-shaped motorboat. The rest of the family was down below in the cabin. "Stand guard at the grab rail," she said quietly. I crawled over and kneeled beside it. Together we watched the boat change its course and head directly for us, ploughing through the water, its bow slicing a deep crack and splitting the calm in two. The piercing engine noise shattered the placid, still morning and increased with intensity until every damp moment was spiked by its shrill reverberations. The passengers wore thick raingear and rugged chins, their arms resting on the battered gunwale. They dropped their jaws and hollered, their breath a squall, their words toothless and lost in the din. The man in the stern, his hand firmly on the engine's vibrating throttle, nodded his head in our direction and said something to the others, who laughed uproariously and slapped their knees.

Needless to say, I was confused by their show of disdain. What had my mother done to deserve such derision? They poked their fingers in and out of circular rope ends, but I made nothing of the gesture until later. "Put a sock on it, you old fart," muttered my mother. I looked from her to the men, and then back. Was this a friendly visit? I wondered. The motorboat surged through the wet morning, scudding over its own wake and barrelling by beamside. The skipper raised his bottle and cheered us, then turned his throttle and tore off double-time. The first of their waves gently rocked our hull, but with each succeeding wave the surge was heightened, the roll compounded, and our boat pitched back and forth. With no wind to balance the impact, we lurched shamelessly, our cabin rattling its contents with every swing and toss. Suddenly the boom swung from the far side of the cockpit, swung with the roll of the boat and snapped me in the back of the head. I flew forward onto the lifelines and collapsed, unconscious.

I had an uncanny knack for finding sharp corners and falling blunt objects and swinging booms. I was, as they say, accident-prone, as if, in some small measure, I hoped to live up to my mother's expectations of disaster. My skin was tattooed with the traces of these various incidents. The snap at the back of the head that day was significant only for the seed of suspicion it planted concerning my mother and her extramarital relations. I realized upon waking that the men and their rude rope gestures could only mean one thing.

I came to with a burning sensation in my esophagus, my mouth around the lip of a bottle of whiskey. My eyes were watery with the sting at the back of my throat. Mother's blurry face peered down into mine, her features smudged, her smeared concern offered in the tilt of a bottle. I sat up slowly, wiped my eyes and touched the throbbing lump at the back of my head. The pain was still rapidly beating up and down my neck. My balance and vision were slow to return. The sea sloped on an unlikely slant, the mast spliced in two, the boys a three-headed monster. My sense of direction shifted from one bent version to the next. Mother pulled me to my feet and slapped me. "Wake up girl! We're almost on the shoals!" she cried.

She had never insured the boat, the cost being too exorbitant. But at moments like this, she called out for a banker or an insurance agent, promising everything, her first-born and her bad eggs, if only he would save her fortune. But the pinstripes of business suits were never seen at sea, and the wavering water ripples were liable for nothing. The ocean lay taciturn and smug, withholding all security. The motorboat had vanished, along with its wake and its whining engine, and we sat ensnared in stagnant water, the wind concealed beneath its surface. I found myself wishing a banker would sweep down and rescue our soon-to-be-damaged boat. I imagined his comforting arm around me, his words of assurance, his generous indemnity. But my mother had a better idea.

"Get in the dinghy. Quick. You and your brothers. You're going to row us off the rocks."

She retied the dinghy to the anchor cleat, and our father helped us climb in.

"They don't have life jackets," he said to my mother.

"It's too late for those," she replied.

We hunkered down on the dinghy's wet benches, fit the four oars into the oarlocks and began a rampage of rowing. The rope connecting us to the bow was taut with our effort. If we glided for a moment and then pulled in unison, the rope cracked like a whip. *Fortune Smiling* was a heavy load. Our hands blistered, and still the boat seemed stuck. We rowed furiously against the unflagging tide, Mark and Denis behind me, driving their oars into the small of my back. Stanley beside me, cracking my knuckles or my knees whenever he thrust the shaft down and raised his paddle up out of the water. My head was still throbbing from the knock of the boom, and my palms were chafed, my knuckles bruised. Mother pointed whenever our little prow swayed from its course. I tended toward the deeper pull, while the boys dipped their paddles quick and shallow. The little dinghy veered from left to right. We worked like devils, churning the water for all we were worth. We sat level with the boat's waterline and looked up at the menacing unmoving bow above the calm. I fixed my eyes on the bowsprit, and suddenly I was on the sea floor instead of the water surface, looking up at the massive hull above me. Submerged mountains were rising up around me, quiet and otherworldly. A full-fledged phobic landscape arose, an impression so strong that I stopped rowing and sat spellbound, and I was only released some time later by a gentle breeze against my brow. The wind had sprung as if from nowhere, and *Fortune Smiling* sailed smoothly into safety.

By mid-morning the sea had radically changed. The breeze that burst through the calm had grown steadily since its appearance. The almost imperceptible swells had turned into gentle tumbling waves, the surface alive with curls and ruffles. The boat plunged and rose through the purling water, bubbling foam and hissing spray as we moved with the cold constant wind, a wind no longer doubted. My faith in the obstinate sea was restored, my faith in the boat as well. The sound of the gale, its steady broadside barrage, was deep in my ear. The sail thrummed along its edge. I looked up at the mast. The fugitive and her web had flown.

"Did you know that the world is nine-tenths water?" I asked my mother.

"Yes, I did."

"And that human beings are born ninety percent water?"

She nodded and turned the wheel against the pull of the boat.

"I have heard that before, yes."

"Then why do we live on land?" I asked in earnest. I asked because I couldn't ask the more pertinent questions, the questions about her sanity and my sea-floor sanctuary, the questions to which she would never give a straight answer — not because she was a liar, but because she was evasive. She had perfected a kind of absence that drove all of us crazy.

"I don't know why we live on land. Maybe we like the feel of something *hard* against us."

Her bawdy laughter and sloppy wink made me nervous. I hated her humour. I never understood her jokes, but I knew they were dirty. Although to be fair, I found almost nothing funny at the age of fourteen. I was too sensitive for my own good. Mirth seemed the domain of those above me, of gods, and mothers, and popular girls.

I changed the subject.

"Are we out salvaging today?"

"You bet we are! Should be a good day. A ship lost some wood in an offshore storm last night."

Mother was intent on recovering some of these valuable parcels and stationed all of us on deck as look-outs. All except Dad, who was down below preparing cocktails, chipping an ice chunk and lobbing small shards at my mother's dog. We sailed south toward a shady group of fishing boats that had gathered where no nets were set. The water was shallow and churlish. The boats' pointed prows and wide transoms see-sawed over the waves. I wrapped my arm around the mast and searched the rolling sea for offerings. "Over there!" I shouted, and pointed amongst the boats where the dark, bound planks bounced up out of the water, nodded with each cusp and disappeared for a moment in the downswell. Fishermen hooked ropes into the floating cargo, tied the ropes to their stern and ferried the wood ashore. We sailed toward the boats, my mother eager to claim her prize. We salvaged one bundle of storm-given gifts with the spare grapnel anchor by snagging the bundle's binding with its sharp points. The wood was a rich coffee-brown, beautiful and slick in the water, and glistening red when it surfaced. We towed the bulky catch behind us. It surfed on our wake like an unmilled sled.

These ocean endowments, as Mother called them, came frequently to the eastern shore. Trade winds, currents, and bad weather guaranteed a bounty of unbound and unregulated cargo. Otherwise unemployed fishermen, hunched over their radios like vultures, waited for the storm and the distress signals from freight steamships. Harvesting the outcrop of sea disasters seemed a natural way of life. The gifts came with the benediction of currents and tides, free of taxes and nosey inspectors. In the minds of maritimers, their poverty justified it. If the ocean saw fit to redistribute the wealth by tapping, on occasion, the mercantile shipping lanes, then so be it. None of us was greedy, and took only what we might use or trade. Staples were preferred, as luxury items were usually damaged. Rare exotic foodstuff was circumspect; crates of tropical fruit once littered the rocky beaches of Bootlegger's Point, the strange fruit left to wrinkle into sodden raisins. Only low-risk items were salvaged, items that the community was certain to trade in. Legal tender was scarce, and trade and barter were common.

Ours was a system of commodity exchange that worked surprisingly smoothly. People always needed what others had. It was as simple as that. Fish in return for bread, milk for eggs, linen for soap...Hoarding was frowned upon and unlikely, given the reciprocal nature of most needs. There were no favours or open arrangements, every swap was a closed and final agreement. There were no empty promises that the value of some object would increase over time. The worth was measured at the moment of exchange and determined by the locals who had run the grocer out of the area, destroyed his price tickets and cash register and boarded up his building. In truth, most people still went into town daily, and there were rumours of bank accounts. And to be perfectly honest, most families would never have survived without their unemployment insurance.

My mother traded in salvaged goods, and we fared quite well, better than most. I suspect she also traded in contraband, for she alone was often informed of potentially free loads. We frequently sailed into the deep coves of deserted islands and dug up barrels and small, suspicious packages in the rough-hewn sand of secluded beaches. When I asked how she knew where to look, she spoke of our family heritage and how the Eastern shore had been a rum runner's paradise. Most of the men in her family had worked on rum row, a far more profitable profession than fishing or carrying ordinary cargo. She remembered as a child uncovering the occasional stash on Horseshoe Island, abandoned by smugglers after prohibition. The coastguard had often chased her uncle's boat, its freehold full of whiskey. But those days were long gone. I knew for certain that our freehold was empty because of the boat's draft — *Fortune Smiling* had always needed ballast.

"The wood isn't holding," cried my father as he pointed over the stern.

The anchor hook was slipping, our bundled mahogany unsafe. We sailed up into the wind amid the other boats, our flapping sails noisily buffed by the advancing tempest. Mother waved at the crew of a fishing dory. "Hey boys!" she shouted and pointed to the wood. They bolted over, released our sled and filled our cockpit with a fair exchange of iridescent fish. The shingled scales were flexed and radiant as the fish writhed, their silvery blue tails flailing at my mother's feet. It was a mishmash of species. They fluttered their fins, thrashed about and knocked their still luminous snouts against my mother's legs. The shining white belly of a nearly dead mackerel was squeezed between her knees.

"I hate mackerel," she muttered, and took a swig of whiskey.

I was still standing on the deck, mesmerized by the mass of fish in the cockpit. The wind had grown to gale force, and the sails filled as we pivoted, the sheets running out through the cleats. It blew hard from behind us; we were carrying too much sail. Our bow was driven down by the sheer volume of the gusts. My brothers and I scrambled over the squirming mass of fish and sat as far aft as possible to keep the rudder from lifting out of the water. Mother now regretted trading the mahogany, as it would have worked well as a drag anchor. Our boat was of poor design. It was too narrow in the bow and too broad in the stern, much like my own shape. Running with the wind was tricky in the best of weather conditions, and it was downright dangerous in rough seas.

Pipsqueak, my mother's dog, smelled the bounty of fish and jumped out from the cabin. Although poodles were known as good water dogs, this teacup copy, bred beyond even the miniature scale, had lost the water legs and the seaside sensibility. She was a nervous, bad-tempered dog, so tiny she was grotesque. My bored brothers had aggressively sheared her light apricot curled coat, leaving only corded dreadlocks around her head and an explosive tuft of orange fuzz between her pin-sized ears. Mother had traded two chickens for the dog, thinking it might guard the boat and keep thieves away. Her midget proportions were a frightful sight and had probably deterred local hooligans from stepping aboard. But whenever we set sail, the little guard dog abandoned her post, scampered into the cabin and hid beneath a pile of old sails.

The hard wind and steep plummeting that day had rearranged her roost and ruined her hiding place. She climbed from the cabin and fancied a nibble. She leapt up off her hind legs like a hysterical circus dog and barked at the inclement weather and the heap of smacking forked tails in the cockpit. The boat surfed at high speeds down waves, the narrow bow diving down into the trough, the buoyant broad stern rising up on the cusp. The rudder lifted out of the water. My mother spun the weatherhelm wheel, but the wave had its own direction. "I can't hold her!" she yelled. The boat suddenly swung, broaching windward and rolling leeward. We held on for our lives. Pipsqueak, the rotten cur, went berserk. She bolted up and down the deck, barking and growling and snapping at our feet. The boys ran forward and jumped up onto the gooseneck. They clung to the sheets, kicking at the yapping animal. My father defended himself with the boat hook; my mother was protected by a slippery goggle-eyed moat. Pipsqueak's apricot dreadlocks flopped across her glassy brown eyes, the tear ducts plugged with gunk. Whiskers puckered up around her nose, the barmy froth of fear on wet lips, the yellow teeth gnashing. The damned teacup was sick with hydrophobic fever. "Look out! She's got water fever!" warned my mother, too late. I ran from the tiny snapping jaws, but the monster cornered me against the jib halyard. She howled with fear and scrabbled against the deck when the boat plunged off a wave and soaked us. She shook the spray from her knotty braided fur, fixed her eyes on me, the enemy, released a growl from deep within her throat and leapt onto my arm, sinking her sharp teeth into my flesh. I screamed. The pain was salted and extreme. I looked down at the mangy bitch, her jaw clamped around my forearm, her body stiff with terror. My father stumbled into the periphery of my vision, grasped my shoulder and booted Pipsqueak so hard the dog flew over the lifelines and into the Atlantic. Her midget mug, fur and all, bobbed about in the swells. A few teeny-weeny yelps were heard before she vanished, swallowed in the belly of a wave.

My mother's dog, fatally afflicted by hydrophobic fever, punctured the skin of my forearm and left behind a mottled scar of tooth craters. It was impossible to forget with those nicks and dimples as reminders. That moment of intense fear and pain and panic was fixed forever in time. With slow-motion clarity I imagined the little dog flying out over the rails in a perfect parabolic flight. Pipsqueak's assault confirmed my sense of self and persecution, kindred apprehensions during my tender teenage years. And yet I felt a certain triumph at being beholden to my father, who had never done anything so brave before. But the joy was brief and sank like a deadweight when my mother realized what had happened.

"You didn't have to be such a brute about it!" she cried, and then cursed him, "I hope that sea poodle gets you back some day!"

Her words stabbed at my heart, the heart of a daughter loved less than a favourite dog. My wounded arm was nothing in comparison to the loss of the poodle. My father, fearful of her curse, reproached himself and regretted booting the mutt overboard. I felt like a fool for lauding his courage. I ranked lower than a teacup water dog and could barely muster the self-respect required to lift my head and watch as they made their peace.

"Sorry, love," he said to her, later on land, and pressed a bouquet of tulips against her breast.

"I forgive you," she answered, and buried her face in the silken petals.

At that moment, mercy seemed to me a very strange thing. For, if I was not mistaken, there were two victims, myself and Pipsqueak. The dog, no longer with us, had been the villain and would be damned, which meant that amends should have been forthcoming to me. But no one was begging for my pardon; my parents seemed determined to absolve themselves in each other's eyes only. Eating humble pie was not in my mother's repertoire, but I didn't dare interfere in what seemed to be a tenuous accord. For how, I wondered, could you bury the hatchet with a bouquet of tulips? Surely reconciliation would require more than a few flowers, some of which would be dead before the following day. I tried to invest the gesture with significance. I tried to imagine the bulbs bursting with emotion. I went regularly to the garden surrounding the anchor shank, sat cross-legged and mystified, and studied the tulips with rapt attention.

My father had recently rescued the garden. It had been blind for years; the buds emerged from the sandy soil, reached up an inch or so and promptly withered and buckled. Whether it was lack of sunlight or proper drainage, or simply my mother's neglect, every year they drooped and fizzled and failed to flower, their bed long overgrown with weeds and grass. My father knew a great deal about gardening and tended to the ill-forgotten tulips. He dug up the intruders and planted new bulbs. He mixed fertilizer, peat and sand, packing the bulbs deep beneath the surface. And in the spring the buds wrenched free and rose skyward. The array of blossoms was spectacular. A virus had infected every bulb and caused the colours to streak and splotch. Some were marbled, speckled and striped in deep purple or blood red. Some had black-edged petals and yellow seams or double heads on stout stems. Others had fringed and jagged petals, and still others twirled and twisted. I relished the odd variations, the upshot of some viral disorder. I admired their accidental beauty and began to see how they might be a gift of faith and reconciliation. The promise of the unknown found tribute in their freakish appearance. They flourished not through health, but through sickness, their scent invisible and yet persuasive. Their lives were short, but not cheap, no, not at all cheap, for it was their fleeting glory that made them so precious. It was their freakish fleeting glory. Finally, I knew why my father prized them as much as he did. One morning at the heart-shaped garden bed, together we watched as the tulips curled open under the sun, their swagging leaves hanging down from arrow-straight stems.

"What colour do you think?" I asked and pointed to a large bulb.

"Hard to say. Maybe orange. Maybe not."

"Is there really no way of telling?"

He rubbed his flat palms together. In the morning light he looked to me like a wiry miser mulling over his booty.

"It's one of those secret forgotten sciences," he whispered.

The story, which he shared with me that morning, concerned the mass hysteria of so-called tulip mania. A virus had also infected the first tulip bulbs to enter central Europe and caused them to bloom with fantastic colour variation. People were unaware that disease was the source of such diversity. They speculated about the unpredictable exotic blooms, their sudden short-shrifted prime, their unexpected brandings. "This was the seventeenth century, after all, and they had savage ways of thinking," my father explained, peering suspiciously over his shoulder and speaking fast and furious, as if he might be silenced at any moment. Fanatics, he nodded assuredly, gambled on the flower. Prices soared. People sold livestock and invested in tulips. They mortgaged their homes and belongings to buy and sell bulbs that were still underground. Tulips became the junk bonds of the first ever futures market, and fortunes were lost when it crashed. Puritans and ascetics saw the evil of wealth in the soft rounded petals. Others, reduced to financial ruin, resented even the unblemished bulbs. I committed every word to memory. I believed that my father hoped to encourage my Bay-Street ambitions with this fine example of how hysteria was at the heart of economic upheavals.

"Nature is a wild card," he added solemnly, as if this summed up everything. It was a dubious pronouncement coming from someone claiming to be a scientist. Although his gardening skills were exceptional, he swore that science was his true calling. But until this tulip confession I had always assumed he was devoted to taming nature. No one paid him to do so, but he studied the ocean with obsessive love, collecting and cultivating all and sundry sea creatures. If nature was some sort of wild card in a betting game, then his was a stranger vocation than I first supposed.

His laboratory was in the basement and lacked all sophistication. It was really no more than a giant aquarium, glowing an eerie sea-green both day and night. The air resounded with the sound of oxygen-pumping engines. The walls were lined with glass cases, each with a lounging invertebrate entertained by a few small fish. In one was an arching skeleton shrimp, in another a greenish-black lobster swinging his stalked eyes, and in a third an old snow crab scrambling sideways. Everywhere barnacles sucked at the glass, clams clustered in corners, and urchins shuffled through the sand. I often snuck down the stairs to spy on the pregnant seahorses flapping their flimsy fins. I especially hated the flat flounders, their two eyes assembled on their scaly side, and their white belly blind on the bottom. But it was the ugly mottled monkfish, who swam alone, its hinged teeth hidden from view, that my brothers claimed I resembled.

It was an odd collection by any standard. My father had erected a wire fence and partitioned off his laboratory, not because he expected any attempted escapes, for that was out of the question, but because the boys had a fancy for fingering the trapped darlings. He also installed extra-strength sprinklers, which would spray automatically in the case of a fire. The sprinklers were capable of flooding the entire basement to aquarium level, allowing all mobile marine life to evacuate their tanks, follow the current created by the floor's incline through a trap door where a tunnel led to a bucket of safety, and where my father could then attend to them. He had never tested the procedure, but would often emerge from the basement with a doll or book in his hand, exploding with anger at the delinquent responsible for blocking the essential outlet.

He did a lot of exploding for a shy spineless man. He burned with frustration at the sight of leaking roofs and rotten wharves. He hated broken things and faulty reasoning. His bad tempers seared through his frail body like wildfire. He cursed and swore and flailed his arms about. Suddenly he would shake with fury and come at us like a meteorite falling out of the sky. It happened when we least expected it, when things seemed most calm. In a flash, without rhyme or reason, he would tear open the quietude and scream at my mother. She endured the torrent time after time and always forgave him. The tulip exchange was only one instance. I suppose his sudden bad tempers caused her to expect explosions behind every peaceful moment, and may have had everything to do with her morbid infatuation with disaster. But she retaliated by eating shellfish and scallops and lobster that had often been stolen from his laboratory. She sat at the kitchen table, dipping them in butter and dropping them into her mouth. Her eyelids quivered with pleasure at the taste sensation. She licked her salty lips and smiled teasingly over at my father, who always refused to eat the sea creatures, even when they came from a neighbour and not his collection. He claimed his squeamishness was caused by one too many dissections. But I'm positive he identified with those cracked and swallowed crustaceans, so utterly helpless on dry ground. He would always limp away from the shell-strewn dinner table, labour down the stairs and scatter little nibbles in the tanks of his aquatic assembly.

He was a small man, much smaller than my mother, and had a bad limp, the result of a criminally careless nurse, so he told us, who had dropped him down a staircase when he was just an infant. When he learned to walk, he began to drag one leg. The doctors, called on much later after various herbal remedies failed, said it was a nerve injury that had fixed itself with twists and imbalances. The limp soon became second nature, as primary as the need to walk. His body seemed to sustain the memory of the original shock, maintaining only a cautious and fragile skeleton. He felt instinctively drawn to the sea, to a world where walking was not esteemed, where the simplicity of one foot in front of the other was overturned. Gardening was nowhere near cherished as much as his basement-world of gracious monsters. He often said he dreamt of living in the Devonian age when shellfish and trilobites swarmed the seas, and the land held only plant life and a few ambitious amphibians. "Gravity is depressing," he said about the bipedal world.

It was quite clear to me that without gravity Pipsqueak's flight would never have ended. Instead of drowning, the mutt would have permanently orbited the world, a far less desirable outcome, in my opinion. I can't imagine that my father truly wished the dog back, but I do think he honestly regretted drowning it. Not for its own sake, however, no, not to save Pipsqueak from the sea, but to save the sea from Pipsqueak.

He began, as if in penance, a new study of plankton, the bottom of the food chain, the amoeba-like beginnings of everything. The ever-widening Atlantic was saturated with rampantly breeding plankton, especially where the Great Labrador and Gulf streams collided and swept up mineral salts from the bottom. It was an ongoing collision that brought the upheaved water right to our doorstep.

He trailed micro-mesh nets from the stern of my mother's boat, carefully controlling their depth to secure a good catch. When he pulled in his noose, he poured the squirmy plankton into the rows of cocktail glasses that I had lined up for that purpose. Later he siphoned them through a funnel into the empty whiskey bottles we had collected. My brothers refused to assist and sat playing with their fishing lines. My mother stood at the helm chatting curiously about some recent horror she had heard about.

One fall weekend we sailed south to Mahone Bay in search of some particular brand of plankton my father required for an experiment. My mother salvaged a few mysterious crates along the way. We moored at Rafuse Island, which was really two islands joined at low tide by a sandy beach. My brothers and I left our parents on the boat and traipsed over miles of shore, collecting beach stones smoothed into soft gems by the sea. We ran, myself in the lead, carefully leaping from flat stone to flat stone. The trick was to stay on the balls of one's feet and never step on anything that appeared unstable. The rapid flash of stone and bubbling sea beside me kept my mind focused on only one thing, the next safe stone. We ran the entire island perimeter, coming around full-circle to find the tide was in and our dinghy had edged out into the bay.

We had our snorkel gear with us, and we wore it as we swam out to the boat. The rocky bottom was dark with sea-weed and showed only mussels and limpets and scampering crabs. Small schools of fish darted about, but nothing spectacular appeared. In fact, the bottom seemed rather bleak and uneventful, although I did enjoy the odd sensation of floating above it. But then, quite suddenly, the water surface rippled against my skin as if a squall had come. I raised my head and unplugged my mouthpiece. The boys' three breathing pipes remained erect. I looked up at the clear sky and then at the boat. My mother sat busily burning the end of a rope to arrest its unravelling. I could hear the shapes of his screaming as they travelled across the surface. My father exploding. He wailed as if tormented by the very world. He thrashed about because the dinghy had been swept away. Treading water, I watched through the puddle trapped in my mask. I watched for one long moment and then dove down and tugged at the boat's anchor until I was blue in the face.

Later, when he had calmed down, we climbed on board and examined osprey nests through his binoculars. And much later, when the sun had set, and my mother had forgiven him, we pushed aside the bitterness and laughed at the moths that flew into our lantern and combusted.

The earthworm lay laced with formaldehyde on a spongy mat in the dissection pan. I had kidnapped the hapless nightcrawler in the name of science, stolen it from its burrow where it quietly foraged for food, and then thrown it into a jar seething with others. I'm quite certain that its feeble mind never knew its fate. Unless before dawn, one last little neuron fired, and it briefly understood the meaning of its life, and felt the injection and the preservative pumped through its body. Rather unlikely, but one could never be sure. Some of the most wide-eyed and innocent had a strong sense of their destiny. They called it second-sense, and it was sometimes a release and sometimes a curse, depending on the circumstances. I knew for myself that funny unwelcome feeling that the future was already determined by some external power. A feeling too imprecise to allow for any advantage in its recognition. I wondered whether the worm, whose corpse rested before me in a pungent bed, had known or cared to be one among many dispensed to our science class.

I peered down at its mouth and anus, which were indistinguishable to the uneducated eye. We had pierced both with pins at either end of the pan. My lab companion, an unlikable girl named Marly, pointed to a swollen segment, a thick collar near the head, crumpled up her face in horror and said, "That's where the babies are." On either side of us, along the sleek black counter, pairs of students had already begun probing the lowly worm. My father's science had done little to prepare me for the mean butchery of high-school dissection.

His study of plankton seemed like nothing more than a harmless sampling from the sea. Stalling, I shifted my cowardly gaze up and down the counter and saw the unflinching faces of my peers. Their complete lack of compassion was almost inspiring.

I picked up the razor blade and made a small incision. Then I picked up the dull scissors and cut lengthwise through the ribbed skin. The trenches nearer the mouth were wiry and difficult to cut. As I drove the scissors hard through the segments, the protracted worm was pulled up off the mat between its two pinned extremities. My wrist stiffened, and I stopped for a moment, but not because I was squeamish, and not because the worm arched as if it were rising from the dead. I stopped because the feel of the scissor blades hooking on the tough segments made me wonder about my own thin skin. Mine seemed to offer no resistance whatsoever. I wished it was as thick and intractable, as rubbery and protective, as the worm's cozy jacket. I stood there deep in thought, my hand frozen and yet languid, as if itself soaked in formaldehyde.

"Finished?" asked Marly, whose morbid curiosity had ousted her earlier horror. I nodded, although it was quite clear that I wasn't finished. She bent over the pan and applied the forceps with surgical precision, pulling the rubbery skin off the digestive track. Together we stretched out the poor worm's husk and pinned it down. Buzzing fluorescent tube lights lit the exposed organs. They glowed with an eerie lustre. There was something very satisfying about cutting the skin and seeing beneath the surface; it felt as if one had conquered a deceit and were delving deeper to expose the truth.

The smell of stringent disinfectant made me giddy. Flies, made skittish by even sanitized death, flew into my eyes and buzzed in my ears. I poked at the muscular gizzard and pharynx, felt my own throat constrict, then washed my hands immediately. I could hardly believe what I'd seen. The vital organs were simple and straightforward objects. Their careful arrangement was nothing like the chaos I had imagined. For although the walls of the laboratory were decorated with posters that showed the interior design of the world, I had always assumed they were propaganda meant to keep us calm and composed. I looked up at the vividly coloured cross-sections of the human brain, fish gills, insect eyes and flower genitalia, every internal part labelled and given its own splendid hue. I looked down at the worm, its grey inner complexion turning ghostly white in the toxic formaldehyde.

"That is probably the most incompetent dissection I have ever seen," said the teacher, as he examined the jagged cut and the glands lanced by the blade. I had completely destroyed both the sperm sacs and the ovaries of the ingenious hermaphrodite, who had the forethought to carry both.

"Death is precious, and you've wasted it!" he scolded. My cheeks went crimson automatically, but, in truth, his grim appraisal appealed to me. At the age of fifteen, life does seem to drag on forever, while the dead decompose all too quickly. I liked his upturned adage. The teacher often inverted proverbs and denied the truth of commonly held beliefs. Science, he said, must stamp out misguided clichés. I imagined the question on our next test: "Which is more precious, death or life? Explain."

"I could salvage the remaining organs," I suggested.

"We don't salvage body parts here," he chided, and I felt judged for both my poor skill and my mother's livelihood. I glanced at Marly beside me. She struck an innocent pose and smiled, all sweetness and virtue.

"But, sir, life is a gift," she said, although I knew she

thought no such thing. Marly was irrevocably cynical. She scorned the sunny, cheerful girls and always chose me as her lab partner. She was the most malevolent among us, and her attentions did me a disservice. My popularity plummeted below point zero, while Sarah disappeared from my sight and soared through the ranks of high-school society.

"Couldn't we work with the live worms?" asked scheming Marly. The teacher groaned and pushed his fists into the pockets of his white lab coat before consenting.

"Part two: the beating heart. This time read the manual."

We sat down beside the writhing tray and read the manual instructions. Then, without exchanging a word, we stuck our fingers into a bulk-sized canister, scooped out globs of petroleum jelly and smudged the grease on the edges of a glass plate. From the tray of live worms I chose one that caught my eye and placed it lovingly on the glass. The ringed head rose up and swayed as if under a trance. With sticky fingers we pressed another glass pane against the first until the framed worm lay flat and slightly sandwiched. Marly held the glass panes and the now oval-shaped creature up to the light. I peered through a handheld lense and saw magnified the throbbing hearts, pumping vermicular blood into the arteries. The five pulsing loops contracted and expanded at a slow, world-weary pace, the pace of an underground existence. It was beautiful and hypnotizing. I couldn't prevent the hope that glimmered in my own heart as I watched the pounding rhythm of life. Even this most vile of creatures with its thick skin and its artless interior had a driving force within. I couldn't help but admire its candid determination to live, and I surprised myself with the thought that maybe life was precious after all. I leaned closer, all the better to see the action of the beating hearts. My eye was practically against the lense when suddenly the beat stopped, the oval shape flattened, and the bristly ringed skin blackened with blood. Revolted, I quickly pulled away.

Marly giggled, her bad teeth revealed. She had tried but failed to resist the destructive urge. She had squeezed the glass panes together, squeezed them tightly so that both the worm and the vaseline oozed. The rows of skin segments had ripped open, and the guts had spewed out into the surrounding grease. Another wasted worm. Fearing the wrathful instructor, we swiftly scraped the lifeless rind off the glass and into the garbage.

"You didn't have to do that!" I cried.

"Things like that deserve to die," she said nonchalantly.

"How do you know?"

"My father owns a bait farm. Believe me, I know!"

I hated her intensely at that moment. She had squelched whatever resolve I had glimpsed between those glass panes. I imagined the sweet revenge of doing the same to her face. I watched as her eyes popped and her miserable grimace stretched from ear to ear.

"Girls! Girls! Over here!" beckoned the teacher, who stood beside a maze where three worms were being tested for learned behaviour. The other students had skipped the second station and were gathered around him. I turned my back on Marly and walked toward the huddle. They were cheering as if at a sports game. I peered over their heads and saw a worm rapidly advancing down the main aisle of the maze. It reached the end, turned left, shimmied over sandpaper and then received a small electric shock. The crowd cheered. The same worm was retrieved and placed once again in the main aisle. But again it turned left and chose the electric shock over freedom and food. The results were contrary to what the lab manual predicted. The group hooted and saluted the worm's unnerving choice of punishment. "Sadists," I muttered under my breath, but Marly, who was suddenly beside me and within earshot, heard my complaint and stuck her tongue out at me.

My father accused the science teacher of being a fraud. The man, he said, was a failed surgeon, zealous with a scalpel but ignorant of science. Class experiments were ill-conceived; our conclusions derived from cockeyed premises. Our study of behaviour, of dynamic life, was cursory and always murderous in the end. There was no denying any of his accusations. We were cultivating a kind of nihilism and had advanced to frogs and fetal pigs. We learned to identify defunct internal arrangements of all kinds, a skill to be used at the sight of accidents, the skill of uncovering victims and recognizing body parts. "Why bother?" asked my father.

"Because the teacher says death is precious," I answered.

"And you believe that?"

I wasn't certain. My dissections improved, but I was hard-pressed to enjoy them. My dreams were full of writhing, pulsing nightcrawlers whose heartbeats woke me repeatedly. I watched the already-fat vein on my father's forehead fatten, and decided against a candid reply. "Sure," I said, and shrugged my shoulders.

"Well, you're a fool for thinking that!" he roared, and staggered across the kitchen to the basement stairs, his wrath, as usual, sudden and savage. His rage was a disturbing mystery that stripped me of my paltry courage. For even though his words weren't sharp, they were branding hot and easily made me feel the fool. I stood alone and wondered how I might redeem myself. I didn't know that my casual approval of the teacher's dictum threatened the very premises of his last and most lofty experiment. An experiment upon which, so we later learnt, his life depended.

He had been toiling away for weeks. On those brief occasions when he joined us for dinner, his eyes burned with the brilliance of his secret enterprise.

"I do believe that your father is possessed by an entrepreneurial spirit," said my mother. "I hope it's not that tulip business all over again." She rolled her eyes and sent her tongue scavenging along the backs of her teeth.

"I've been crushing the larval brains of caterpillars," he announced out of the blue, "mashing them with mortar and pestle and mixing them with plankton and a few other things." The rest of us fell silent. This was not the simple plankton retrieval we had come to expect. This was not gentle science. My father glanced up defensively. "It's not killing for its own sake," he added.

"Sounds like it to us," said my brothers with much excitement.

He then explained how he had separated the heavy particles from the growth hormone, a golden liquid so potent with juvenile juices that it resisted adult metamorphoses. He had dipped paintbrushes into the golden concoction, painted the bellies of crickets and had watched them grow enormous and remain wholly immature. "This may mean indestructible giants, their strength undiminished with age." He whispered his secret, as if there were someone listening at the door.

"Frankensteins?" My mother asked precisely what I had also been wondering. Did he hope to create monsters? Was it a last-ditch attempt to secure his wife's love? Surely his children were sufficiently monstrous. I wondered if my brothers had been early recipients of this golden concoction, and I feared that instead of spankings I, too, might have received a swab of the stuff. The giant infantile crickets left no doubt in my mind as to the powers of this potion. I saw the world plundered by beardless, puerile monsters. I was certain that no other scientist would sanction what seemed to be a recipe for disaster. Although for that reason, if for no other, my mother did nothing to stop him.

It seems to me now like an idea dredged up from the pit of his despair. I wonder if his studies of fragile marine life had begun to disturb him, or if his faith in the ocean floor had been weakened by findings he never shared. I think he hoped for a more docile world, where his anger was obsolete and his tantrums a distant memory. A world full of gentle giants. He must have blamed the adult world for something, but I never dared ask.

My father wanted funding for large-scale research and hoped to obtain a loan. Costly kennels and cages were needed to keep the giants separate from the control specimens. Abundant supplies of caterpillars and butterflies would be required. Participants would have to be paid. The local trade was too small-scale. He needed cash to cover the expenses and insisted that I come to the bank with him, as if my broad behind and stupendous ears were proof of his powers. "I've made an appointment with a loans officer," he said, as he combed his hair and picked lint from his trousers.

"And he's going to give us money?" I asked, doubtful but very excited, never having been to a bank before. I imagined the banker to be handsome and brawny, a man made in the mould of Bay Street, a pillar of our society. My desire to meet the local financial pundit prevailed over all my scepticism concerning the project.

"He just might," said my father, full of hope and sweating buckets, as we drove the shore road to the bank. His whole life seemed to be riding on this one pursuit. We parked the borrowed diesel truck between two sleek bullet-shaped cars. The parking lot had been freshly paved, and the smell of asphalt continued to linger. The women at each of the wickets glanced suspiciously at us as we pushed through the revolving glass doors. They hammered their date stamps with a resounding thump and counted bills from one hand into another, their sticky thumbs pushing each slip of paper, their lips silently enumerating the sequence. There was an aura of intimidation that seemed to emanate from their well-coiffed heads, brightly painted lips, and respectable blouses, and the fact that their bottom halves were a mystery hidden from view. I watched their exceedingly long nails punch at adding machines and knew that their hands were the object of much worry and wanton glances. When we reached a wicket, we were told to wait elsewhere.

"You should apply for a job here, Mary," said my father, as he sat down on a stiff striped sofa near the loans office.

"They wouldn't hire me. I'm not sixteen yet."

"You're not?"

He had never had a good grasp of his children's respective ages, but I had grown immune to that sort of neglect. My interest at that moment was with the bank manager, who was then opening the thick vault door to our right. He spun the shiny steel wheel with its short chubby spokes until the inner bar lifted and the door jolted free of the wall. Another door composed of forged steel bars was unlocked and slid open. I leaned from the sofa and peered into the safe at the interior walls fashioned from numbered safety deposit boxes. Another safe within the first was visible near the back of the vault. Perhaps there was another safe within that safe, for all I knew. Not yet initiated into the surrealism of finance, I assumed that material mounds of real, tangible money existed somewhere on the premises. I watched the tellers arrive at the safe and deposit slips of stamped paper. My father sat staring at his hands.

Finally a big, blustery man with rosy cheeks opened the mahogany door of the loans office. He motioned for us to enter. His shirt was stretched at the button holes, and his narrow tie was slightly off kilter. "Pleasure to meet you," he said, firmly shaking my father's hand. On his desk, facing out for others to see, was a framed photograph of himself swinging a golf club on a green sculpted Floridian lawn, below him the small, white puckered ball supported by a tee — his ball, the ball he would hit and chase after the rest of the day, the ball that matched his commitment alongside his colleagues. Needless to say, he was not the man I was expecting. He was large, but brawny and handsome were not words that came to mind. He was a roly-poly person all the more frightening for his numbed and frosted veneer. I took comfort in thinking he was only a front man, behind whom hid the true powerhouse. I sat obediently at my father's side.

"I'm sorry, sir, but it's out of the question," the banker apologized. He showed us his flat wide palms as he leaned back in his chair and shook his head. The bank, he said, could not possibly fund such a project. Corporate giants were hot, organic growth was hot, but my father's idea was not. There was simply no potential payoff, no market for his magic potion. We had barely sat down before the rejection was put forward. My father made one last plea. He begged the man to reconsider. The banker thumbed the tissue paper in our file, our featherweight financial profile, and shook his head. No.

I had heard the man's condescension and seen him smirk at the mention of colossal chickens. I knew how to interpret both that and the hushed silence that escorted us to the door. We bowed our heads and dragged our feet over the pristine floor. I blamed my father for everything, for the shaming of tellers and obese bankers, for the disgrace of being broke but ambitious and, finally, for being barred from that teasing series of nested safes. He hobbled in front of me, this small man of science, crestfallen and beaten by the bank. "Now who's the fool?" I muttered under my breath, watching the back of his head.

He pushed through the door and onto the sidewalk, but accidentally stubbed his shoe on the ground. His ankle curled, his body pitched, and then over the curb he went. I watched as he stumbled onto his hands and knees in front of a parked Brink's truck. The armed guard, suspecting an ambush, put his hand on his holstered gun. For one small vessel of time, I wanted to see my father blown away. I imagined the sound of the bullet, the colour of the blood, and, yes, the welcome grief. The image came complete with consoling witnesses and generous compensations from the Brink's truck booty. Then it skulked away and disappeared down a corridor of guilty thoughts. I leaned over and tried to help him up, but he pushed me away, cursing and spitting at the rotten institution. "You'll regret this, you bastards!" he screamed, his fisted reflection in the mirrored windows. The second guard folded his arms across his bulletproof chest and shook his head. My father's composure had cracked, his last-ditch dream had been trampled, a dream which I only then realized was about his own physical weakness and not about a potential market for giants.

Black smoke from our diesel engine retched from the cheap crusty muffler as we drove out of the city. My father gripped the steering wheel with a new-found menacing strength, his veins bursting and his knuckles white. On his wrist hung a gold watch, a watch I had seen on the wrist of the bastard banker when he had patted my father's shoulder and wished him good luck. He must have slipped it off the man's pudgy wrist when they shook hands. "Nice watch," I said, glad to see any sign of ongoing struggle, no matter how delinquent. He ignored me and drove at top speed, leaving the city and its safes far behind him. The road curled off the peninsula and back up the other side of the Arm, past bantam-bush forests and cliffs of detonated rock. We veered onto the gravel shoulder when manoeuvring tight curves and heard the ping of pebbles against the truck's cab. He drove like a maniac and I feared for my life. When we stopped at a local gas station, I was shaking and breathing heavily.

"We need gas," he announced gruffly.

"How will we pay for it?" I asked.

"How do you think?" he chided, and once again I felt the fool.

He rolled down the window. The watch strap, which was large around his wrist, knocked against the door. A girl, the gas attendant, sat smoking between pumps. She looked over at us, her acned face apathetic. She didn't budge. My father dangled the gold watch. The smooth curved links, hinged like reptilian scales, cockled and glinted in the light. The clasp was a wider plate of gold and engraved in elaborate script. The yellow of the face shifted in the light, like sand moving in the wind. He swung the watch out the window, his elbow resting on the door. The gold was a magnet for light, pulling it out of the sky. The attendant stubbed out her cigarette, casually shuffled over, took the watch without hesitation and filled our tank with gas.

"Only you would think of something like that!" my mother said when she learned of his proposal. She laughed at his failure to secure funds and laughed at the luxury of the gold watch. Her lack of compassion was like salt poured into his wounds. He sat, wayworn and empty. He looked up beseechingly, but she gave him no sympathy. "Why would a bank bother with us?" she asked, as if he should have known better. I watched him further humiliated and swore to bring the banks to their knees, if only to bring him justice.

"Your father wants to be alone. Let him stew," my mother said, not knowing how she tempted fate.

She dragged me and the boys to a party in a nearby home. From the shack on the hill came the sound of scratchy shrill singing, strident piping, and warbled fiddling. It was a musical imbroglio, a mess of local talent. We climbed the cracked stone steps that had shifted over the years and didn't quite reach the house. The door was wide open and through it came the smell of spilled sweet liquor and brown sugar baked apples. We joined an already booming carousal. The hot air was thick with smoke from the fire, with the tart smell of sweat from dancing, and with the clabbering sound of too many instruments. The first of two rooms was lit with oil lanterns that cast shadows on the rose-patterned wallpaper. I recognized our neighbour, the wizened bag of bones in the corner, wanking on an old weathered fiddle, the varnish worn off, the bow a creaky, twine-wrapped stick. His stubby fingers nudged at the oily strings and managed a low lament during the mournful songs, but it rose to a screech during the lighter dance tunes. His wife, an elderly upright woman, plonked the keys of a piano, her stiff fingers landing like bricks, her odd chords a tribute to her senility. Her foot pumped away at the pedal, jouncing the plastic Jesus that beckoned from atop the stricken piano.

I leaned against the doorframe between the two rooms, the children in one playing in front of the fire, the adults in the other. I stood cautiously between the two worlds. I wondered why my father never came to these parties, which were chock-full of the same locals who had snubbed my mother on many occasions. I watched her guzzle from the punch bowl and get drunk. She swung her wide hips in front of a fat neighbour who sat blowing deep foolish tones out of his tarnished trumpet. She loved the sound of the trumpet, its proud and prankish melodies. She tipped her chin from shoulder to shoulder, bending her knee and sinking with each sway of her hips. I turned and watched the children clasp hands in two concentric spinning circles, singing "Fire on the mountain, run, boys, run!" A boy in the outer ring cried, "Fire's out!" and all scrambled to reach a child in the inner ring. I turned and watched my mother careen into a seated yardarm who had mended our boat earlier in the week. She leaned forward from the hips, her hands clutching his thighs for balance, her face close to his. I couldn't make sense of what she was doing. I stared at her already tousled hair, the back of her skirt puckered and pleated across her bottom, stared hard at her bent body, the clamour coming from all sides.

The hostess noticed my curious gaze, poked my mother and said something to her that I didn't hear, which caused her to spurn the yardarm, list from side to side and then stumble toward me, saying "Gotta tend to my surly girly." She grabbed my wrists and dragged me into the centre of the room. She seemed like a giant below the shack's low ceiling, her dark shadow skewed and stretched across the walls, her heavy heels bending the wood planks beneath her weight. She jumped from one foot to the other, her head almost touching the crumbling plaster. She held my wrists tightly as we turned and twirled about the small room. I wanted her to let go, but at the same time feared being released to rocket through the room. She pivoted and spun, she the axle and I the spoke. Faster and faster until my feet rose off the floor. I heard the fiddle buzz like a saw, my flying shadow flit from wall to wall, my ankles knocked against the chair legs. Her tight hold hurt my arms. I heard her horrid singing voice through the dizziness, the mean song she sang to goad me:

Chaste Mary did ride his rage
And rocked away her weary
But cold's the sea around the shoal
That wrecked the maiden Mary.

The last verse was recited from another's lap where she collapsed, myself swung loose and hard into the opposite corner, the corner where I remained, with my eyes tightly shut, for the rest of the evening. My thoughts escaping into the rose-patterned wall and wandering through the quiet maze of flowers. I tried to teleport myself to a sanctuary somewhere else, but still the teasing verse tormented me. I had heard the song many times before on similar occasions. My mother's bad behaviour was customary at parties, but she was worse than usual this time, and her song scared me. I opened my eyes a sliver and saw her monstrous shadow flickering at the edges and rising up the opposite wall. For the second time that day, I longed for a stray bullet to end another tyranny.

The next day my father disappeared. He had gone collecting specimens of rockweed and seaweed from the rugged rocks of Chebucto Head, an outcrop of land where ruthless waves batter the shore. He often went there to harvest the creatures encrusted in the cracks. The salt and pepper walls of granite slope down into the water, where tenacious algae cling to rocks and move like the lash of a whip with each explosive wave. Perhaps he went too far in search of hidden limpets and periwinkles, and one big wave reached over the rock and washed him away. Or perhaps he went over willingly, having decided he would join the crooked world beneath the surface. I suspect he went over without a scream. We formed a search party and slogged over those old wrinkled stones, sidestepping the blue feces of blueberry-gorging birds. His path led to a particularly sullen promontory where the sea banged the rock unremittingly. We found his weed-extraction devices trapped in a crevice, but we never found his body.

When his loss was finally indisputable, my mother demurely inclined her head. Our world had suddenly changed. I tried to be hardnosed and stoic, refusing, at first, to admit the tragedy in his death. I assured myself that he belonged in the sea where the medium might relieve him of his millstone. I imagined him enjoying the gentle aqueous circumstances of his death. My gloomy disposition wouldn't allow for the fierce personal pain of this family calamity. My mind was in the habit of taking flight from that which was truly disturbing, and yet no sooner had I convinced myself of his unlucky but agreeable demise than I began to grieve with a vengeance. I grew angry. I blamed the banker for pushing him over the edge. I blamed my mother for the ridicule that rendered him helpless. I blamed my brothers for being monsters. How I longed to shriek and shed tears and pull my hair out, and might have done so if it weren't for my steely mother, whose cruel response robbed me of my thunder.

She sat at the kitchen table and consumed our dead father's basement collection of marine curio. I watched her crack and swallow his shellfish and then toss the empty husks over her shoulder. One beloved after another, shamelessly desecrated. Despite my earlier rage, I said nothing, my own grief cut short by her ruthless bereavement. I listened intently as she mocked him between mouthfuls. She told stories about his disastrous failings and denied him all manner of noble achievement. I suppose she was bitter about something, but once again I didn't dare ask. I tiptoed gingerly out of reach, watching her all the while as she grew enormous and ready to blow. There came a taunting in her laughter that sounded more perilous than usual. From that fountain of knowledge that was her obsession she drew story after story of seafaring disaster. She told of how wealthy passengers on the sinking *Titanic* hoped for salvation and threw their jewels in the sea as a sacrifice. She told of how greedy seamen drowned, after jumping from scuttled ships, because of the bags of sovereigns securely tied around their necks. She knew the name of every ship lost on the shoals off Sable Island, whether it was Basque, Portuguese, French, or English.

I noticed that every one of her stories indicted those who sought wealth and prosperity. "Bunch of shipwrecked souls at the end of it all," she would say, looking menacingly in my direction. I don't know whether she intended to scare me, or whether she was just scaring herself, but she succeeded in spoiling the sea for both me and my brothers. The family fabric, now thoroughly rotten with salt and seaspray, finally began to crumble. My father's disappearance spurred me on to imagine my own possible escape, although it was often no more than a similar sea-bottom grave. In an attempt to make sense of it all, I read through my father's illustrated collection of Greek tragedies. The bindings cracked when I opened them; the books had obviously not been previously consulted. I tried to relate our own tragedy to these simple stories of revenge. I tried to find a way to forgive my mother for her deplorable behaviour. I saw her face in both the whimsical gods and their mortal victims and playthings. Her grief was peppered with a perverse laughter that suited her husband's untimely descent into the sea, but she looked at me askance when I proposed reading "those silly, brutal stories," that had become a source of comfort and understanding to me.

Sarah came to console me three weeks later. She came only briefly, and with the usual advice. "You still need something else," she said, after seeing my father's books. "Instead of a burial," she added, and flung her much longer hair behind one shoulder.

"Like what?" I asked.

"Something like the shank. A monument."

The shank was a sore spot, and I had no desire to double its effect.

"I don't think he would like that," I replied.

"Then how about setting his marine world free?" she suggested, not knowing that my mother had already ravaged the tanks.

"No. We can't do that."

A long pensive silence followed as Sarah considered our options. I waited obediently for her next suggestion.

"A sea mural!" she cried. "We'll paint him a sea mural!"

I preferred this to accounting for the empty aquariums and found myself immensely relieved by the notion of a memorial. I began to relish the idea of painting a testament to my father's strange life. That the sea would wash it away only added to its celebration. Preparations and planning went on for days. We went from door to door, collecting house-paint remainders. The colours were garish on the fog-enfolded coast where the locals had brightly hued homes. We took whatever they had to spare, even their hardened brushes and sponges. After hauling our supplies to Chebucto Head, we chose a suitably smooth rock face with a gentle incline. A low-cloud ceiling hung heavily above us. The gulls squawked as they flew by. We pried open the crusty paint cans and began painting giant lobsters and squids and bottom crawlers of all kinds, sloshing pinks and purples onto the rough surface, the colours bleeding into crevices and into channels of compacted time. We tempered the speckled granite with colossal yellow chickens, crickets and crabs, and green squiggly plankton. Inspired by my Greek stories, I painted monstrous mixed species, mermaids, and, of course, the always angry Poseidon. The hours passed, the rocks mulled over, and there was not a word between us, until Sarah broke the silence.

"Do you think he went to heaven?" she asked.

"Absolutely not," I answered, convinced that heaven sent angels and shanks and other things, but never retrieved them.

The sea broke at the rock's foundation while I pondered the claw of a creature, the beard of Poseidon, the dripping blue mane of a horse. My sad thoughts were with my father, his underwater destiny and imposed silence. I pictured him on the sea bottom, still holding his breath, green algae growing snug and soft across his face, various invertebrates fastened to his limbs.

A paper airplane wobbled on the hot eddies of afternoon air. It climbed to the ceiling, seesawing upward until tipping its nose ballistic and gliding down toward my desk. The word *ugly* was printed in bold black ink on both of its wings. I flinched, heard the chuckles behind me and flicked the unwanted thing onto the floor.

A death in the family is meant to bestow a certain wisdom beyond what the years entitle you to. But wisdom is one of those bootless sensibilities that never service the will. It comes loaded with prohibitive warnings about its misuse, grants only a detached and passive understanding, and never seems relevant to everyday choices. If I was wise beyond my years, for there was no denying my aptitude in many grey matters, that wisdom had failed to confer any strength of character. I remained as bovine as always. The one year since my father's death had done nothing to bring me any closer to Bay Street. And in the meantime my father's death had made me so unpopular that even Marly steered clear. Offensive paper airplanes were par for the course. They flew over the widening chasm between me and the boys at the back — the boys who suspected me of patricide or worse. The boys who found health class disturbing because it was such pansy stuff, so personal and provocative. Subjects like diet and related skin problems were just plain embarrassing, as were the teacher's comfortable shoes, dowdy dresses, weak mouth, and sensitive, watery eyes. And although I agreed that some private matters were better left in the dark, and I shared their resentment of the scatterbrained teacher and her womanly concerns, I never thought of joining them to shout down her feeble instructions or send her handouts sailing across the room. I always knew that I was the alternative target, and my turn would soon come. I waited patiently as she begged for silence, for cooperation, her frail self ensconced behind the desk, her timid threats ignored. The ease with which the boys overpowered her increased their anxiety. They didn't want to dominate her, but they couldn't resist. I believe it was precisely her emotional instability that struck a desperate fear into their hearts. They spat spitballs at each other and laughed nervously, their backs against the wall, their blood boiling. When she broke, as she always did, they sought other game. Unfathered undesirables like myself were a safe bet. My shape alone invited their jeering. And I was already accustomed to baneful boys. I accepted the humiliation, the insults, the dumb jokes. Oh, how I grew weary of it, weary of being their undefeated prey, weary of waiting for the return of the health teacher, who was always out of sorts in the bathroom. I can only guess why I suffered their pranks. Survival tactics are varied, but mine were likely to be hackneyed avenging angels with a grand sense of justice. I was patient.

Another paper plane sloped and listed across the room, colliding with the cinder-block wall. The class was now in commotion. The boys at the back scraped their chairs across the floor and kicked affectionately at each other's sprawling legs. They slouched over their desks, their bodies never quite contained by the ordered rows. I watched their languid postures and unwieldy limbs. I watched with the well-trained eye of a spy and the paranoid mind of an unpopular girl. This mass of ticking testosterone, counting down the years, the days, the minutes before the inevitable. This wall of avoidance and hedging glances, as if in training for their worldwide deceit; their burgeoning sex, their manhood, all part of a clay mask slowly hardening around their eyes. Some local quack had donated his nineteenth-century psychology books to the library, and I read them religiously and applied tribal theories to all the groups that denied me entry. Boys were only one such group, but were the most uncivilized, capable of anything, and forever reluctant to forsake their fraternal bond. I had watched them wrench each other's nipples in playful communion and whip their twisted wet t-shirts to sting one another's backsides. I studied the few who betrayed their beloved friends and entered into make-believe marriages, exchanging the mandatory kisses and necklaces of teen engagements. It seemed to me that they did so without much joy, their outstretched limpid arms resting on the shoulders of the well-liked girls. The girls to whom I was invisible. The girls whose urgent priority was tempting one of these loaded guns out of its holster.

Two such girls stood at the window teasing the drop-outs who gathered daily in the parking lot. It was late in the day. The sun made silhouettes of their figures, the soft horizontal shafts of light clemently bending through the window, the noise around me dulled by the warm yellow glow of the room's suspended dust. We had been promised a lesson on sex education, but there was no sign of the health teacher. Suddenly, the staid and stocky gym teacher arrived wearing white shorts, bleached knee-high socks, a tight t-shirt, and a whistle. He wheeled in the antiquated film projector, pressing the arc of his belly against the machine. His odd step suggested that something uncomfortable hung between his legs. "Mrs. Dratt can't make it today," he said sedately, patting the pasty black slab of hair on his head. A few cheers were heard from the back row. "She's not feeling well," he added, causing triumphant desk-thumping and hooting all round. A short boy in the corner shouted, "Silly old bitch!" and another cried, "We'll send her to the grave!" The gym teacher casually stuck the whistle into his mouth and blew. The sound pierced and rattled my ears and silenced the class. He shunted to the blackboard and yanked down the white cloth screen. The boys at the back were impressed by his calm, ruthless supervision. They liked to be disciplined in a cold sharp manner, without any sticky-sweet tenderness. They liked his sportive attitude and drummed their desks with their pencils as a sign of approval.

He returned to wrestle with the projector, which stood in the aisle beside me. I watched his blundering fat fingers and heard his heavy baffled breath. He pressed the ragged slits of the film onto the cogged wheel and turned the motor lever. My dread for machinery hadn't diminished since the days of the make-and-break engine, but there was no denying the beauty of the apparatus beside me. I liked its metallic smell and rhythmic sound, and the way it doddered when overheated. The white sound of the fan worked like a sedative upon us all. I looked around to ensure that I was still in the same panic-stricken health class. The faces were the same, but the mood had altered radically. Dust rose up off the window sills as the sun-stained drapes swung slowly like pendulums to and fro. Someone sneezed and the room was suddenly dark and surprisingly peaceful. "It's show time folks," said the gym teacher, his breath reeking of salami and cheese.

The film was an old tattered nature documentary, not at all suited for the subject of sex. Veering in and out of focus were faded images of the volcanic Galapagos Islands. A robust male voice narrated over the images. These were Darwin's islands, cast away in the Pacific Ocean and populated by alienated creatures. Isolation had altered the path of their evolution. The animals had adapted to their exiled existence with odd developments. Misshapen birds performing comic mating dances flooded the sheltered shores. On the volcano's caldera floor around the smoking crater, in warm pools of muddy water, slept the giant tortoises, the islands' namesakes. Their days passed by serenely, save when the volcano rumbled, and the earth trembled, and a sense of impending disaster drove them to mate. Females quietly retreated into their brown-plated prehistoric domes, while males climbed onto their backs and pumped from behind with a plodding two-hundred-year-old pace. The poor creatures moaned with each sluggish thrust, a prolonged almost painful moan caused by no other activity, for only during sex was the male compelled to make a sound.

"That's fucking ugly!" shouted a boy at the back of the class. I blushed, irrevocably bound to these outlandish creatures, linked forever through the nasty name-calling of teenage boys. I felt as if I belonged on that isolated island of misfits and strange developments. Ugly, ill-proportioned, and increasingly ostracized, my only refuge an island of freaks. I hankered for the hard embrace of a high-domed shell. I yearned to touch the tick-ridden scales of those grotesque but endearing earthlings. I sat in the dark, safe from projectiles, convinced that Galapagos was a lesson on affectionate relations, that the subject of sex was exhausted in the mating habits of men and misshapen birds and the one experience strong enough to invoke a cry from a tortoise.

The subject, however, was not closed. Sex was also the reason why Sarah abandoned me. She had developed breasts and various curves of all kinds and was instantly desirable. She wore accordion-like tube tops with red and white candy-cane stripes stretched across her chest. She curled her hair back so that it fell like the feathered wings of a bird. And she ignored me, her country cousin, choosing beautiful affluent friends from the downtown high school to which she had transferred. She went to their cautiously raucous parties, their antique-riddled mansions, and the bonfires that they bonded around at the end of their long, meandering waterfront properties. One night I quietly rowed across the Arm under a moonless sky and spied on the necking couples surrounding the roaring fire. The air was cool, my seat was wet. They wore woollen sweaters lovingly knit by faithful grannies. Their cheeks were flushed by the hot flames and the lemon gin, their hair glistening in the dancing light. Two boys stood speechless poking sticks into the fire, their soft inert expressions frozen on their faces. I rested the two oars across my thighs and listened to the damp driftwood crackle beneath the logs they had dragged down from the house. Pairs of pinned bodies were strewn about, near enough to be lit by the warm yellow light. Sarah lay as if unconscious, her body dispensed on the private pebble beach, a boy leaning over her, his hesitant hand undoing her buttons and advancing up her blouse.

I dipped my oars into the pitch-black water and rowed my strange body back to my own shore.

I hated the wealth of her new friends. Their allowances alone might have garnered interest as investments. Money filled their swelling pockets. It packed their pants. It fell from their mouths when they spoke, but clung to their breasts like metal to a magnet. They might never have existed without it, nor it without them. Money flowed through their lives like water. And Sarah, banking on her body, surged into the stream. She sank herself into their capital, and the returns were handsome. Her boyfriends showered her with heavy gold chains, which hung decorously over her moguled chest.

They pushed precious stones over her knuckles, the jewel boxes burning on the nearby bonfires, while I was banished to the hard granite outside the city to play bank robber with my brothers. They were the armed guards, protecting their bank, their precious rock collection, and I was the gangster.

Soon I saw Sarah only at basketball games. She was a high-scorer and played on a team that regularly beat ours. They jogged out of the changing room in freshly laundered uniforms shouting warlike cheers. Their long ponytails swished from side to side. They huddled, their arms entwined, their strategies settled, and trotted out onto the court ready for the kill. There was no hope for our team, for whom I was the water girl. We hunched on our bench, knees knocking, sneakers worn to nothing, and watched the amazons steal the ball from our beleaguered defence, whose poor dribbling skills marked them every time as easy prey. By half-time we were so humiliated we wanted to lose. The sweaty handshake at the end of each game further stung our pride.

"Your team sucks," said Sarah when our palms touched.

"I know," I replied, "I should quit, shouldn't I?"

She shrugged her shoulders, and I wondered whether wisdom or wealth had made her so diffident. "Do you think I could join your team?" I asked, and without thinking I squeezed the water bottle and sent a dribble down my thigh.

"You always want to be like me. You should try and be more like yourself."

I hated that insipid expression and the saccharine smile that came with it. What could it possibly mean to be more or less like myself? Pure propaganda, no doubt, meant to keep me on course and predictable. I had always distrusted the dictum *Know thyself*, as it seemed inherently flawed and open to corruption. People consoled themselves with lies about their true consistent feelings, when any fool could see the chaos beneath the calm façade. I consoled myself in turn with these unspoken ravings, while being rebuffed by the one person whose strength I admired.

"I don't want to be like you," I lied, and my heart filled with distrust, suspecting her of spiteful intentions. I was suddenly certain her victory was sweeter for my being the defeated flop. I imagined her striking me from guest lists and spreading rumours about me. I dreamt of retribution in a world where I was the star player, where the big house belonged to *my* friends, the fire was *my* making, and Sarah sat alone in the cold black water.

When she vanished from the city, I feared my wish had been granted. Her disappearance was so sudden, like the swift swindling of the tide over an unsuspecting rock. Another lost loved one, another dead soul sunk to the bottom. Swimmers were always drowning, especially rich drunk revellers seeking the sort of sobriety only the wintry ocean can offer. But news finally came from her tight-lipped mother that Sarah had not perished at sea. She had left for Toronto, left behind a cocksure boy, his walloping wallet unopened, the medical bill unpaid. She had packed up her clothes and deserted her oppressive mother and her boorish cousin without even a curt farewell. I was wounded, neglected, confused. I imagined Sarah flush in the fair city, her good fortune sealed.

The night I learnt of her escape was charged with an electrical storm, in itself an uncommon occurrence in the Arm. I walked along the water's edge and envisioned Sarah on Bay Street, jumping up and down in her sport jersey, her ponytail rising like a horse's mane. I looked at the froth of a wave cap as it trundled over the sand and thought about unrivalled prosperity. I stared into the dark night and longed to share her glory. The air was dense, suffused with prickly tension. The boats lured lightning out of the sky. I heard static and saw purply-blue jets of light dancing around the mast of our moored *Fortune Smiling*. I had never seen anything like it. Suddenly the flash of fizzing luminous discharge lit the cross at the masthead top. It lasted only a moment and left me feeling desperate.

Mother's was the kind of laughter that brought disaster down upon it. Her cackle was known to crack ceilings and cement foundations. My brothers resented her unsettling sense of humour, which they deemed to be the cause of our father's undoing. They consolidated every last individual desire as though defending themselves against her. The eldest failed grade eleven, the youngest skipped grade ten, and the middle one remained staunchly average. The three sat side by side in the classroom driven by shared fraternal purpose. Stanley, my least favourite, was the model of mediocrity. His general bull-headed demeanour was the very paragon to which the others strove. Any peculiar quirks on the behalf of Mark or Denis were moderated by Stanley.

At Stanley's urging they dropped school altogether and sold their combined skills in construction and demolition to a local unscrupulous development company. With their six feet now firmly on the land, they refused to set sail with our mother ever again. They hoarded cheap bricks and poured wretched concrete, determined to quell her soused and unsound spirit. The land around us was stripped and seeded with steel girders and brick pyramids. The view from our porch was ravaged by bulldozers and cranes and condominium castles with tiny pastel-coloured turrets. The eyesores assaulted us at every turn. "Places to put your loved ones," announced my brothers all at once. "If you have any, that is," added Stanley.

Their employer sought support for a landfill project. He proposed soaking up the gentle water in the Arm, erasing our shoreline and transforming the peninsula into mainland. The Arm was sufficiently shallow to be filled and forgotten. If sealed and properly packed it might even function as the first underwater inlet dump, and the city would soon spread over the salvaged foundation. The suggestion was considered by a panel of professionals, but discarded early on. But the plans were resubmitted, wayward officials were bribed, and the project gradually gained some ground. My brothers relished the thought of land reclamation. They relished the thought of obstructing wind and water, my mother's twin passions. Each scoop of fill sopped up the vengeful wet dreams from which they assuredly awoke each morning.

"You should stop them," I suggested to my mother. We sat in the cockpit, the boat at its mooring. She rubbed the wood helm with linseed oil, the dirty rag wrapped around her swollen fingers. The sound of high-powered drills and reversing engines came to us amplified across the water.

"How?" she asked, gazing in the direction of our house, which sat concealed beneath a leafy disguise. Her only defence so far was to fortify our world with a thick envelope of greenery that flourished around the four walls. Fat bushes lined the perimeter with choking misery. Wiry vines sealed the windows shut, leaves clogged the chimney, and branches bulging with life barred the sun's rays. This, if nothing else, had nipped the bad view in the bud. But tradesmen of all stripes passed by our brambly walkway never daring to venture in. The house appeared not so monumental in the light of these recent developments, and I felt squeezed breathless by my mother's poor pruning. I wished the house restored to its previous shank-riddled glory.

"Isn't there a law against land reclamation?" I asked, and she laughed uncontrollably.

"Criminals. That's it. We'll put all the landlubbers in prison."

She drummed the helm with her oily rag and screeched delightedly. She pointed at the old prison on Melville Island, originally used for prisoners of war. The locals now stored sails, tools, and motors inside the cells. The walls were made of thick slabs that made my brothers' crumbling stones seem small-fry. "Cram them in there without bread and water," she shouted across the inlet at the bright yellow hard hats.

And she meant every word. Her mood was cheery and violent all at once. I truly believe she would have preferred a draconian world in which all freedom was curtailed. A world where people were prisoners of mind and body, every action and thought shackled to itself. I stared at the pillaged landscape, at the strangled patch of land still belonging to us, at my mother cursing, and I realized in a sudden flash of clarity that she was no longer with us. Her mind had leapt overboard, her thoughts utterly at large. Her profile seemed altered into unfamiliar terrain, and in her absence the awakening of opportunity. I felt my head swell, my fingers tremble. Dare I set her further adrift and seize the moment? It was a moment ripe for plucking, as though a small crack in the family seal. Would the boat sink if she weren't at the helm? Would the ocean drain itself dry after such a debacle? Suddenly I was aware of the exact length of my arm, the span from my shoulder to the helm, and an overwhelming desire to upset the order of things.

I leaned forward, stretching my arm out slowly, tentatively, and reaching through the thick damp air to grasp the wheel. The moment crept down my arm as if the passage of time were tangible, more tangible then the slippery feel of the polished wood upon landing. My fingers flitted and stuttered at the point of contact, hovering there above the precious wheel. My eyes darted back and forth between it and my mother. My skin tingled cold then hot, the nerves no longer sensible. The air was leaden for one big-bottomed fraction of a second, before she spun around and caught me red-handed. The sweat gushed forth from the tiny pores in my palm, and my forearm bristled with cramped muscles. The stern captain with the steely gaze, she fixed her bloodshot eyes upon me, then whipped my delinquent hand with her rag and snapped, "Don't touch!"

My feeble attempt at mutiny was all too easily thwarted. My mother had no intention of surrendering the wheel, despite her lack of self-control. She pressed her hips against the spokes and stared up at the clouds. She seemed tongue-tied by my sudden seditious act, my own tongue also tied like a prisoner in my mouth, while the air tasted sour and defiant.

~~~

The landfill project continued to threaten the Arm. My brothers erected edifices of all kinds. They built a log cabin on Hangman's Island and hosted nightly hellbenders. The sound of their revelry filled the diminishing woods. They chugged beer like carbonated fountains and then flattened the cans under steel-toed boots. They staggered out arm in arm, unzipped their pants and piss-sprinkled the earth. Their bodies had grown brawny, their eyes glazed and vacant. Stanley was the most muscle-bound, his arm an instrument with machine precision. He was the party pacesetter, the strong arm of indulgence. The other two synchronized their excess accordingly. Together they dragged drunken trashy girls back to their party den and undressed them. From behind a fat maple I once spied on the proceedings and watched the girls in their drunken stupor, faces falling off and lower lips dangling during long slurred sentences. They
~~~

stumbled out at regular intervals and vomited. This added to my fascination, since I assumed they were there of their own free will. They crawled back inside after each upchuck, their words of recovery lost to the tinny sound of a cheap tapedeck. They sat and sang along with the ballads, swaying back and forth and off-beat. I winced when they paired off with my brothers, grappled each other's thighs and exchanged sloppy french kisses. I winced again when the boys pulled away, swigging and burping.

At the peak of repulsion, on the verge of leaving, I heard footsteps approaching the cabin and saw a dark hulking figure between the trees. It disappeared into shadow and then re-emerged. I pushed myself up against the bark of the tree so as not to be discovered and glimpsed the hard cheek of my mother, stomping through the woods with a bottle under her arm. The party queen herself had come to join in her sons' debauchery. I felt the shame like pins and needles in seeing her selling out for the sake of a late-night bash. I tried to wish her away, but closer she came. An empty can thrown out the open door dinged the doorframe, and suddenly her silhouette was there blocking the entryway. An ugly silence, and the gormless swilling stopped. The three boys pushed their wenches off their laps and rose to bar the way. Stanley stood in the middle, flanked by the other two. "Go home, old lady," they said in unison. My eyes were fixed on her next move. She shifted her whiskey bottle from under one arm to the other and remained in the doorway. "Go home," came the chorus again. My God, I thought, surely she would lash out at any moment and kick them off the land. I waited for the fit of anger, for the storm of accusation, for the outburst to end all building. But I waited in vain.

She shrugged her shoulders and guzzled whiskey.

"No skin off my ass," she said before turning.

I loathed her then for leaving and yielding to the brawn of bitter sons. Her being there to begin with was a betrayal of her boating vocation, but seeing her submit to their clumsy command was even more disturbing, and I wished there was some way to right the wrong. The brats deserved to be severely punished, but by whom? Never before had I imagined myself as an arbiter of justice, but my mother's sense of fairplay was far gone. I relished the thought of prevailing over their sex games and dissolving their privileges.

Not long after her departure, my brothers left the cabin and escorted the almost-unconscious girls home. The dead autumn grass crackled beneath their step, above them the sky a down-under blue before sunrise. I collapsed on a pile of brittle twigs and pulled out a box of wooden matches from my jacket pocket. I pushed the drawer of sleeping stick matches out from the box. I selected one and began scraping the sulphur off with the sharp edge of a stone. The stuff easily shed from the stick. The red combustible head crumbled and left a brown stain on the wood. I picked another and did the same. I beheaded one short fuse after another. I scraped each match until a small heap of inflammable dust and bald wicks lay at my feet. It was a mindless compulsive exercise. The early morning sun crept into the sky as I held the last match between thumb and forefinger. This one I scratched against the box, dropping its gruff burst of fire onto the pile. With a gentle puff the dust ignited and instantly lit the twigs, which then writhed and smoked for all they were worth. Reeling flaps of burning white light lashed out at the surrounding grass. The flames tripped their way across the fallen dead leaves, and the powdery bulrushes burned like torches, but the damned cabin remained intact, as though protected by a wet ring of excreted party fluids. I watched in awe as the moat of spewed puke and drizzled urine kept the fire from the building. The blaze skirted my brothers' den, which I later learnt was bordered with crushed stone, and petered out at the water's edge.

"You might have killed someone!" cried my mother the next morning. My intention had been to end the binging and, indirectly, save the seashore, but I suspected party-poopers were as much frowned upon as murderers. And regardless of the risk taken, I was thrilled to have made the attempt.

"I didn't mean any harm," I lied.

She stood on the deck unravelling a short rope as thick as her wrist.

"Come here," she said, her voice all discipline. My mind was immediately punished with images of public hangings. I shuffled over reluctantly, my eyes on the rope dangling from her fist. "Go sit on that burnt hill," she said, wrapping the rope around her hand. "And repent!" she bellowed.

It was a soggy ashen day of drizzling rain. Our neighbours came to witness my penance. I heard them mutter disparaging comments. "Seventeen years old and behaving like a child!" Mrs. Cray whispered loudly, and the others nodded and knit their brow with disapproval. I blushed with mordant shame and fever from the cold rain, my humility forever bound to that impulsive fire. Stanley ridiculed my failed match job and said arson was cheap. I knew then that I belonged on burnt-out Bay Street in the city known as the Big Smoke. Its image possessed me. I longed to see its towers and tycoons, and Sarah's flight dared me to follow.

Mother was surprisingly gracious when I told her in the spring that I was leaving. She said everyone eventually leaves the Maritimes.

"You can take JoeHow," she offered.

JoeHow was the old tan-coloured horse that now belonged to her. He was still kept in the neighbouring barn, but she had recently acquired him in exchange for some salvaged goods. I had spent the occasional evening climbing on the back of the tolerant JoeHow and walking him along the shore.

"You might as well get some mileage out of him," said my seafaring mother, who then smiled at some private joke. "You'll stay with Sarah?" she asked.

"Yeah," I answered, although I had no invitation, only an address. "But I'll need some money."

She gave me none that day, but the following week she sold the anchor shank to the marine museum and gave me a small sum sufficient for the journey. I could hardly believe she had sacrificed the shank on my account. It was like she was selling the skeleton key and leaving unlocked the doors of her lunacy. She seemed to have relinquished her hold altogether. It appeared at first to be a sort of suicide, but I soon realized that the gift actually strengthened her sphere of influence. The money she gave me was soiled by disaster, every tainted penny a reminder of my destiny. There was no denying this was deliberate. She wanted me in irons, chained to her forever, bridled like a horse to his master.

"They loved it," she said beside the big black hole in the garden, "They promised a plaque saying Granny was the target."

part two

The tack room smelled of well-oiled leather. On the wall beside halters and bridles hung a beautifully quilted saddle. Its cotton stitches were stained brown with age, and a pattern of wave crests arched over the seat and down each fender. It was a masterpiece made by a local saddler long since dead. I felt unworthy of its workmanship, but it was the only one that fit the big-barrelled JoeHow. I placed one hand on the well-worn saddle horn and lifted the thick girth strap to my lips. It felt seamless and smooth and smelled of horse. I looked across at a pair of matching quilted chaps hanging on another hook, beneath them a pair of mudcaked boots.

I was glad to have a horse and not some dizzying spoked machine that could go either way. Speed had always seemed to me a disproportion of space to time. My eyesight was unsuited to the blur that streaked across car windows. Horses moved at a slow meditative pace with which I felt more at ease. In truth, neither species of vehicle was anymore reliable than the other. Both animals and engines were cranky and vicious in unexpected ways, as Pipsqueak and the boat engine had proved. But at least in the case of complete breakdown, the one might be made a meal of, while the other only rusted. JoeHow, in this regard, was an exceptionally sedate middle-aged meaty horse.

I pulled on the chaps and boots and walked into the bay with the saddle under my arm. JoeHow stood obediently as I retied him and folded a blanket on his back. He whinnied and pawed the ground when I cinched the girth straps. I packed the saddlebags with alfalfa cubes, salt, brushes, hoof picks, liniment, wire cutters, and a compass and then hung them over his withers. In my own knapsack I put bags of grain and apples and then tied my sleeping bag to the saddle.

JoeHow was both long in the hindquarters and heavy in the rump, making a comfortable seat for my equally large behind. I mounted and waved good-bye to my mother, who stood framed in the stable doorway clutching a jib winch to her breast.

The freedom of JoeHow's buck-kneed gait felt promising between my legs. I rocked in the saddle with his wide hip-swinging and shoved my feet deep into the stirrups. With a bobby pin from my own hair I pinned back his overgrown forelock. We zigzagged up the slopes until we reached an oceanview hilltop. There we paused and turned and I looked out at the expanse of sea water stretching out across the horizon. White caps splattered the surface and gulls dove hungrily into the waves. A few small white sails moved back and forth across the mouth of the harbour. The crown of an oil-rig tower hovered over the tip of the peninsula, and down below in the Arm rested *Fortune Smiling*.

JoeHow was a grasscropper and slowed our progress for even the most coarse tufts of grass. He chomped on the resilient huckleberry bushes whose roots spurned all other growth. He was accustomed to grazing on a barren land stripped of almost all topsoil by the last grinding ice age. He weaved his way between the stray chunks of granite, his hooves denting the spongy moss. His nostrils flared at the pungent fragrance of seaspray salty puddles and sweet growing things. Green and pink lichen carpeted the path and the occasional wild iris was seen hugging the side of a rock.

We moved along the shallow stony soil past crooked houses slouching inland from years of offshore wind. Their once brightly painted shingles had chipped to grey and now blended with the desolate land. An old boat rested on its cradle, an ominous crater in the hull, but the name *Deloris* still carefully outlined on the stern. Empty lobster traps sat frail and unused beside unmended nets bungled and draped over rotting dinghies. The land could bear nothing but coal, gypsum, and salt, none of which suited the fine mesh of these nets. I knew the textbook story, how frequent inundations by an ancient sea had destroyed forests that then fossilized as coal, how stranded marine organisms had turned to gypsum, and how puddles of trapped water had evaporated and left salt deposits. Coal, gypsum, and salt. Hardly the gifts from three wise men. These were reluctant resources requiring dynamite explosions, by no means the task for a fisherman accustomed to depths all too easily plumbed. Painting driftwood lawn ornaments was their only remaining option and, true enough, the polka-dot petticoats of wooden lady gardeners were a common sight along the road, although an increase in sea deaths suggested many fishermen preferred suicide.

Taking one's own life in the face of a dying industry seemed absurd to me, but witnesses always said it was done in the name of duty. Fishing was only one example of an industry that could not survive its own diligence and was obliged to sacrifice its own. Salvaging, on the other hand, my family's profession, was safely derivative of other industries, although my brothers' construction permits were not. Those beastly beer-guzzling boys were considered economic indicators, as though noisy activity alone was proof of prosperity. The automated shrill of their chainsaws seemed to trumpet local profits, and their buildings spread like some contagious disease. Their shared dream of a paved planet sent me in search of a higher road, and I hoped to leave them far behind me, buried up to the neck by their own landfill. I rode away from the barren terrain, never having been skilled at anything, coddling dreams of sudden fortunes found on the floor of a money exchange.

Both soil and industry improved as we moved inland. We crossed potato fields and rolling hills of apple blossoms. JoeHow snacked on flowers and drank from the streams made noisy by the spring rains. I ate almost nothing and was always hungry. The land was sectioned off into farm strips where fields were furrowed and dumb domestic animals stood chewing their cud. I often had to cut the wire fences between fields and left a trail of stray cows behind me.

We rode hard and long each day. The leather of my chaps and saddle creaked in each morning's cold beginning. We always started with a walk but changed gaits often, taking advantage of the level stretches to push into a canter. On hilltops we rested and JoeHow caught his breath. I loosened the girth straps and massaged his legs with liniment. In the evening when he was hot and lathered, and our shadow stretched behind us like a fallen tree, we sought out shelter in abandoned buildings or in the barns of friendly strangers. If cattle were spied huddling over bushels of hay, we rode over and bullied our way in. The wives of farmers often appeared on distant doorsteps, their big white aprons a burst of light. They sometimes fed us and sometimes shooed us from the land. They never seemed very curious about my journey, as though they had seen many make the same trip by even stranger means.

We followed rutted tracks and gravel roads or walked in the muddy ditches alongside the highway. JoeHow was at ease with traffic. He never skittered or danced in the glare of headlights, and the roar of eighteen wheelers left him so completely undisturbed I worried that perhaps he was partially deaf and blind.

Deaf even to the massive car accident which occurred on a hazardous Nova Scotia highway just a few days after our departure. I jolted in the saddle at the sight of the carnage, the hair on my head suddenly pricklish and sensitive. It was a thumping grinding collision rife with the smell of burnt rubber and the sound of shattered glass. I watched from a hilltop overlooking the highway as shiny beetle-like cars toppled onto their backs, their wheels and hood ornaments launched into the ditch. Struck by the strange beauty of torn metal and crumpled steel, I dismounted, hobbled the horse, and listened to the eerie silence that followed. Engine coolant leaked onto the road, but no blood and no bleeding bodies. It was difficult at first to discern how this was a human drama and not merely a mechanical failure. Two cars in the centre of the radiating wreckage had plunged into each other, and suddenly I was reminded that my parents first encounter had been a car crash much like the one before me. Both being bad drivers, they drove only occasionally and only in borrowed cars, but one day, on a straight and well-tended road and under perfect weather conditions, they managed to drive directly into each other. Passengers in each car were seriously wounded, but my mother and father walked away unscathed. The question as to who was responsible went unresolved, and in lieu of insurance claims they exchanged vows and began producing babies. I suppose their having escaped unharmed from such a sealed fate spurred them on to other forms of fatalism. From the initial crash of that first date, like a big bang from which the universe unfolds, their marriage was fixed and final.

For years my mother had joked about how their engagement was an accident without mentioning this highway encounter. And for years I had believed that my conception was the accident in question. The kids at school spread rumours to that effect, saying I was the object of unplanned parenthood. My mother told me the real story when I began menstruating, as if understanding that original car crash was my admission into the fair and gentle world of women. It seemed that her intention was to scare me into being female and to prepare me for collisions that demanded consummation.

I recalled her words as I watched the survivors crawling out from under their wrecks. They dragged themselves and their loved ones away from the crash. I imagined my mother and father bonding in the midst of crisis and wondered why tragedy alone seemed the seal of romance. The highway was jammed in both directions for as far as the eye could see, and in the distance a siren wailed. Unharmed drivers ran toward the crash to lend a hand. I mounted JoeHow, slapped him on the rump and walked him through a pungently fertilized field.

When we crossed into New Brunswick, I was surprised to see a landscape of slippery red mud moulded into large lumps and semi-spherical mounds. A smooth seductive red clay bearded with seaweed. The bumpy bottom exposed, embarrassed, blushing, waiting for the sea to roar in shamelessly over its curves. Finally seeing the seascape that had haunted me in early adolescence was like receiving a gentle remedy for all my fears. The Bay of Fundy had always been that tumultuous body of water separating Nova Scotia from the rest of Canada, but it left tracks deep into New Brunswick as well, and its strange beauty was like a tonic to me. It looked like the territory of another planet, maybe the Moon, but wetter. Fishing boats, like alien spacecraft awkwardly stranded on the slick mud, waited patiently for the rush of salt water and plankton to carry them back to the fishing banks. The entire area was waiting for the sea, waiting within a silence broken only by the squeals of air bubbles bursting through the muddy surface. The earth was quietly giving up its breath, bubble by bubble, until the water's heavy return.

My mother had always feared the mighty Fundy tide. During her honeymoon at Cape Blomidon, she had strolled about on the infinite stretch of red sand, tracing the strands of green-cord seaweed and Mermaid's Hair. She said she enjoyed the slick red mud between her toes, but suffered what she called a "sudden panic" when she tried to survey the slippery horizon. The mist fractured the sun into a thousand sources of light, causing her to squint in all directions. "I couldn't see where the sand ended and where the water began," she explained, as if that distinction alone determined her presence of mind. The words of a local fisherman came into her head, something about how quick the tide came in and how it took you unawares. She heard the surging water and felt her feet sinking into the thick mud. Then she turned from the expanse of wet sand back to the red rocky walls of Blomidon Point and ran for her life.

I wondered if her honeymoon fear of the Fundy tide concealed some other tidal anxiety. Perhaps she dreaded her own fertile outflow — the four regrettable infants who would transform her, the bride, into a demented matriarch. She may have foreseen what her womb would bring forth and then ran from the truth. I found the red slippery terrain all too intimate under these reflections. What had seemed at first to be a tonic now turned into a stale reminder of my past. The sea bottom was too shapely and deferential, a breeding ground for sullen offspring. I loathed its sloppy wet curves and open spread. I longed for the sea to come and cover up its rolling surface. The unseemly sight of boats balancing on their keels made me nervous. I rode JoeHow onto more level ground. I rode him hard. A saddle sore slowed us down and forced us to rest for a few days in an empty barn. The farmer applied bagbalm to his wound, and it quickly healed.

People were glad to help us, offering grain and mineral supplements for JoeHow and hearty breakfasts for myself. They volunteered advice about short cuts and badly flooded areas to be avoided. We rode down the slopes into the St. John river valley and walked alongside the delicate but vigorous river, a charming underling of more industrious rivers. Its lower banks were lined with trees that overhung both the river and the Trans-Canada Highway. We frequently had to clamber up onto the side of the road when the ground got too swampy. No boats came up or down the good river once used for fur trading and logging. Trade had taken to rail and road and the water had long become simply a border between two countries.

We stopped at dusk and I sat on the bank above the weedy shore. The setting sun brought a gentle warmth to the slender river. Willows, lit from behind, wept onto the silken surface as the eloquent current brought back another century. The heavenly still air turned golden with the last long rays of sunshine. A sparrow flew with the current, its beak an inch above the water; I followed it with my eyes until it disappeared. The evening stretched into a soft silence, the water into seamless glass. I felt lulled into a serene sleepiness, but suddenly the surface was alive with thousands of shad-flies born that instant on the river's bottom. They ascended in dense swarms, wispy insects flapping their transparent wings, frantic to be fertilized in flight before their short lives ended. I pictured their nymph carcasses cracked open and abandoned on the river bed where their fresh eggs would soon be laid. The sky was thick with them; they flew into my eyes and my ears. I covered my face, rose and turned away from the river, feeling their fragile bodies buffet my back as I walked JoeHow toward the road.

Further upstream a dam changed the water's destiny and sapped its energy. We rested on a high bluff and watched the generator tap the water's movement. The land had been shaved of trees as if to make the cement wall all the more visible. The river's confused current spun around and twisted back on itself. The dam had created a massive headpond, drowning islands, cemeteries, and settlements. The people had moved but the spawning salmon didn't know any better. They still swam furiously upriver and threw themselves hopelessly against the cement wall. I had been told that some of them were transported to tributaries for the sake of sports fishermen. Those that avoided the nets were unable to resist their calling and lost their lives in a meaningless struggle. My mother had always said salmon were admirably stupid fish, and here was proof. I swore I would never eat one again. I rested my hands on the pommel of my saddle and sat amazed by their fury. I decided that creatures were creative to a fault, and that spring was a desperate time, driven by reckless instinct alone. The reproductive impulse cheated the bearer of all recourse. I decided instincts were swindlers one and all, deceiving their hosts into thinking only the moment was at stake. My eyes followed the misplaced currents of energy streaming over the hills via electrical wires. I felt a great thirst, grabbed the canteen hanging from the pommel and took a swig. JoeHow sniffed and nickered, wanting to move on.

We averaged a good distance each day in the flat river valley amongst the evergreens and Irving Oil stations. JoeHow munched happily on the thick wild grass and spat out the bitter cedar leaves. I ate take-out whenever I could. One day we came to a high ledge of slate and limestone where savage water exploded at the base. The falling water roared into the gorge and bullied the contours of the rock, forever chasing the glacier that had carved out the deep walls. The river was so plenished with oxygen that its surface showed hissing white veins. Two boys in baseball caps dropped twigs and other buoyant objects into the tumult and watched them disappear. They wore their bright white windbreakers tied low around their hips. They leaned over the bridge dangling pendulous spitballs, then jabbed each other's pudgy guts, dropped their bombs and kid-laughed. A parent further down the path called for them to follow, but they pretended not to hear. I watched as one grabbed the other's elbow and pointed in my direction. He was very excited, rising and puffing with anticipation like a prankster having found fair game. He covered his mouth as if struggling to keep secret some smutty suggestion. Then both choked on laughter in an obvious attempt to save it for after. Without thinking I reached into my saddlebag and pulled out the sharp wire cutters, but neither of them noticed the glint of the blades. I wasn't sure what they were planning. The one untied his windbreaker and punched a fist into each arm. His accomplice followed suit.

"Hey lady!" he shouted over the roar of the water, his face now slung in shadow beneath the cap. Lady? The name sounded more rude than respectful. They pronounced it *laydee*, an almost indecent word evoking lower life forms. I searched my mind for the single most decisive response, whether to ignore or acknowledge them, whether to brandish my weapon or keep it concealed, charge the bridge or await the ambush. Option after option delayed my reaction. I sat second-guessing until the wrongness of everything ended in stalemate. I then noticed that the dilemma was all mine. The boys turned and stood with their backs to me, their chins on their chests, their hands fumbling with their belts. Each thrust his right arm down, unzipped his fly, and dropped his jeans. Then each hooked his underwear, pulled it down to his knees, and chucked a fair-sized glowing moon. Shining celestial spheres now the summit and not the seat. Their eyes and ass inverted, they peeped from between their knees to see the upshot of their action. My recovery from the insult was immediate, as I had never seen such radiant shapely bottoms exposed only for my scrutiny. That they intended a wisecrack and not an honourable gesture was clear to me, but the roundness, the rosy-cheeked, the unfledged beauty brought a feeling of elation. It dawned on me then that the land around me was nowhere near as beautiful. I wanted to thank them for uncovering the smooth sunlit surface of their half-moons, for being so bare-assed about making me the brunt, but they vanished over the bridge and joined their family before I could express my gratitude.

Maybe big buttocks weren't such a bad thing. Maybe the overfamiliar face paled in comparison to the rarely seen fanny. It seemed to me that the immaculate symmetry of those bald and beefy twin cheeks paid homage to my own oversized bottom. I wanted to disclose the precious posterior end of all other subjects. I rode JoeHow through the wall of shale slates and climbed up to a crown of birch trees. We walked along the high rocky path, my eyes wide open in search of other naked truths. The river carried on gently through a forest that had been brutally logged throughout the centuries. The earth had been stripped bare of its big white pines to make masts for the needy European navies. What remained was junk wood used in the pulp-and-paper mills dotting the countryside like the back doors of devoted industry. Junk wood was no good for construction, but when pulped and pulverized and pressed through giant rollers, it turned to paper. A mercurial transformation attended by a suitable smell. The smell from another exposed hole, from the commerce of bottom-feeders, from a moon chucked long ago.

We spent that night on a stud farm. JoeHow was a gelding and behaved badly amongst the large sheaths and high testosterone levels. I tried to calm him, chatting with him all night and grooming him with a dandy brush. I told him stories about the wild horses on Sable Island, how they walked freely over the dunes, their coats thick with sand, their manes knotted and long but they themselves bored to death by their freedom. I assured him that a gelding was worth at least three stallions. He fell asleep with his ears cocked at odd angles. I put my bedroll down in the tack room, thinking of Sarah, the stud-magnet, a stallion's dream girl, sensitive to the even gaze of male horses. Her address was still in my pocket, her discouraging words in my ears. She had said that I didn't belong on Bay Street, but I hoped she was wrong.

I slept soundly until late morning, dreaming of cracks in the earth's crust, myself looking up from the core at deep jagged crannies through which the light burst. I found JoeHow finishing up his hay and slobbering over some grain supplied by the stablehand. The rows of studs whinnied as I walked him into the yard. We saddled up and went on our way, but he punished me for my choice of shelter and stubbornly insisted that we jump irrigation ditches and low wooden fences. His pride had been wounded. Each time he raced toward the obstacle, I thought we were doomed. His head was too low and I was an inexperienced jumper. I pulled hard on the reins to balance myself, my knees tight against the saddle, afraid I would be thrown. But every time he sprung gainfully off his haunches and landed gracefully, our two big rumps coming down together.

We were lost. A warm suspicious wind came from what seemed to be the south, but the clouds moved chaotically in all directions. The farmland we had been travelling across had suddenly turned to forest. The path we were following through the forest had first narrowed and then petered out. My compass behaved erratically and my commitment failed me. My image of Bay Street, the portal of the nation, that orifice through which I planned to see so much, grew dim and frayed as the wave of doubt swept over me. The fierce density of the trees and their ruthless growth stripped me of my determination.

I rode cautiously, even reluctantly. My mother had warned me about forests. She said they were dense with escaped convicts, crazies and other queers banished from the towns and cities of the nation. For who, she wondered, would possibly choose of her own volition to live in cramped quarters with such branched and leafy creatures? Gibberish-speaking gypsies populated the short-shrubbed forests of the eastern shore, and presumably, she argued, things got worse as one went inland. "Trees are the work of the devil," she often said, and yet the greenery around our home was flourishing, and it was she who had planted the entrapping pines.

I wondered what she would make of my present predicament, surrounded by mottled grey bark and twisting roots all too eager to choke a weaker vessel. I began to hate the trees for having nothing within but layers of time. I felt threatened by that simple series of concentric circles exposed in any cross-section. It seemed a mean joke that a life form so vibrant and persistent was composed only of these rings. My frequent childhood visits into the woods as captain of the Living Fire, where I subjected my brothers to their weekly dose of torture — some minor spanking and prodding — had done nothing to prepare me for this thick layering of tree trunks and spindly budding branches.

The sky was beginning to close over like the lid on a box. An old farm house appeared sliced between trunks and gradually became whole as I approached through the lines of young maples. Twigs cracked and popped and no birds sang as the storm set in and we approached the house. JoeHow stepped over the remnants of an old rotten fence, relaxing his gait to a sloppy meander and swinging his tired hips across a small overgrown yard. Low branches had scraped his shoulders and whipped his hindquarters, leaving thin white welts. I spoke calming words to him and tied him carefully to a tree. He quaked and shivered with the journey's motion still in his body.

Bowlegged from all the riding, I walked through the wild grass to the front door. In every window hung dirty sheer curtains, a warning that life lurked within. I crouched beneath a sill and spied a bleak but furnished room. Two torn chairs bloated with mildew sat in opposite corners. Dusty Canadian landscapes hung on the papered walls, and a large spiralled rope rug centred the room and lured the eye. I knocked at least six times before the door opened slowly. An old man poked his head out defensively, as if he were expecting the Wicked Witch of the East. His frightened ragged face caused me to stutter.

"I'm lost. Could you help me?"

He stared and said nothing, still no more than his head poking out from behind the door.

"There's a storm coming. I'll need shelter," I appealed to him a second time, surprised to hear the urgency in my voice. My fear of bush fever had made me desperate. I was incapable of imagining that the trees themselves offered shelter. Their destiny was pulp and mine was beneath a man-made roof, or so I hoped. I stood needy and vulnerable before the old skull floating in the shadow behind the door. But finally, as if all his energies had been called upon to move his tongue, he grunted a reply.

"I don't have no barn. Not any more."

I hadn't expected this obstacle, although I had been prepared for a refusal. But no barn? What could I say? We were deep in the forest where there were no barns. Everyone knew that. The old man stood unstirred, expecting something from me, but I was at a loss to further my request.

"That's a shame," I said, pushing my hair behind my ears and wondering what strange habits kept him alive. My off-handed sympathy drew him partially out from his protective shell. A goose neck showed itself attached to his head.

"If you keep on west you'll find my brother's house. He has one." He threw his chin out in a general that-a-way gesture and closed the door. I stood on the stoop waiting to hear his footsteps disappear down the corridor. The silence on the other side meant he stood waiting to hear my own departing steps. We remained there with the door between us for quite some time. The wind whipped through the trees, causing branches to dance and freshly born leaves to clap and shiver above my head. The darkness of the woods rushed toward me as I stood cowering and wondering what next. I looked down at the faded welcome mat beneath my feet. The door opened a second time and again the old man peered out.

"Cuppa tea?" he asked. I accepted, following him gingerly into his dreary house. What little light there was in the sky was diluted and smudged by the ancient filthy curtains in the windows of the sitting room. A hanging bare lightbulb lit the swarthy linoleum hallway. It illumined the water-stained walls and swung from side to side, its chain having just been pulled. The hollows beneath the old man's cheekbones turned black when he stood beneath it. He wore a brown housecoat over stained and faded pyjamas. I smiled nervously. He turned and shuffled away. I followed his small figure into the kitchen where he plugged the kettle in and dropped two tea bags into two cups. He pointed to a chair. I sat down. He asked me where I was from and seemed annoyed when I responded.

"Halifax? Not much going on there these days, is there?" Exactly what he was referring to was unclear, but I presumed he meant the slowdown in harbour traffic.

"You mean the harbour?"

"Yes, sir." He leaned against the counter and crossed his bony arms. "Used to be one busy harbour. Boats coming in and out. And the city was alive — a real port town, full of sailors and girls." He nodded assuredly and then went silent as he watched the kettle.

"Course that big explosion really emptied it out. Biggest man-made explosion ever. Until them Japanese bombs, that is. Always trying to outdo us, those Japanese." He caught something with his tongue in his lower left cheek and began chewing it. I feared that the world would offer me one disaster fanatic after another until my mother's sense of crisis was satisfied. I watched the old man and wondered whether he had ever been a sailor.

"Not much going on there these days," he repeated, as he picked up the kettle, not yet boiling, and poured the lukewarm water into the two cups. The tea bags puffed up and bobbed about like life jackets. He took a spoon and pushed each of them down.

"Milk or sugar?" he asked. I chose milk. He peeled the foil paper from the rim and poured the canned milk into my cup. Then he slowly shuffled back and forth from the counter to the table, having to make separate trips to carry each cup. The tea swished, threatening to splash over the rim and onto his shaking hands. He settled into a chair, breathing heavily from the exertion.

"Halifax during the war. That was its heyday, let me tell you." But instead of telling me, he remained disturbingly quiet, his head shaking as if rattled by the wind at the windows. Then suddenly his face cracked into a smile, and he began chuckling. It was a small dry chuckle, the scraping kind that sounds like it hurts.

"That's one ugly horse you got!" he screeched between chuckles, his body twitching like a string puppet, his vascular arms wriggling in his lap, and his head shilly-shallying as if it were not wholly attached. The quick spasmodic movements gradually slowed to one last quiver, and he was able to compose himself. He leaned forward and carefully sipped his tea with beet-red paper-thin lips. Then he lowered the cup and wiped his chin with the crusty sleeve of his housecoat. I felt nauseous and noticed a few brown particles floating in my cup. He leaned over and squeezed my knee, his smile a row of corn kernels.

"It sure ain't gonna win any beauty contests. Got a rump the size of the Moon!" he added and chuckled again. I held my breath against his own sour smell and waited for his hand to be removed. As a guest I felt obliged to be tolerant. So JoeHow had a big ass, so did I, so what? I stared at the crumbling plaster and water stains on the ceiling above the television.

"Got a leaky pipe?" I asked coldly. His eyes lit up anxiously. Had I said the wrong thing? He removed his hand from my knee, raised himself and shuffled to the television. Two newscasters appeared instantly in colours utterly at odds with the dim surroundings. Their sculpted hair and shoulder pads mocked the bald head and crooked body of my host.

"This is the news station," he said, shuffling back to his seat. I had never properly appreciated television because I couldn't quite convince myself that my every move wasn't seen and recorded by those who peered out from the box. And I had never heard of twenty-four-hour non-stop news, which promised at the outset to be a blending of local heroic acts with global crises of war and pollution. The old man pulled a pair of dice from his housecoat pocket and began rubbing them together between his palms. The tinny, nicking sound of gambling cubes filled the room as story after story splashed onto the screen. In the beginning there was a hostage-taking, then a famine, an election, a new law, a tribute, a murder, an earthquake, an oil spill, a hole in the atmosphere, and, finally, a case of arson. The loop began again and I assumed it was meant to establish a sense of history, but connections between the events remained obscure outside the sequence. We sat obediently watching the reported horrors of a world that seemed bored with its roundness.

The old guy was mesmerized, handcuffed by the gallant announcer's passive reporting. He never once threw the dice but kept them moving at all times, like worry beads. Eventually he seemed to lose all sense of the room and my presence in it, so hypnotized was he by life's small loop. I tiptoed out of the kitchen into the sitting room and lay down on the twisted spiral rope rug, which proved to be the most uncomfortable bed I had ever slept on. My skin felt stretched over the hard braided waves. I tried first lying on my back, staring up at the wood-framed landscapes, cheap monochrome green copies of the world outside. The sounds of the newscast carried down the hallway and into the room where I lay, unhappily. The two upholstered chairs in opposite corners appeared churned by toothy-nosed rodents. I rolled over and inhaled the floordust. Sleep came in dizzy teasing waves rippling over my sore muscles and weary head.

I dreamt of nothing, and in the morning I woke with rope patterns pressed into my face. Close to my ear was someone else's heavy breathing. I turned my head abruptly. The old man's rotten breath greeted me. His ashen flesh hanging off his cheek bones, a drool forming at that instant in the corner of his mouth. He was still in pyjamas and housecoat. His knees were curled up at his chest and his arm rested across my back. I panicked for a moment, worrying that sleep had betrayed my body. But the old corpse beside me was an unlikely culprit. I doubt he had the strength to even unbuckle my chaps. I lifted his frail limp arm off my back and placed it at his side. He puckered his dry thin lips and groaned, as if he were in the midst of a voluptuous dream. A dream in which I feared figments of myself were subject to his fancy. A lucid dream like a private disaster flick, the news-loop having set the stage for his amorous pursuits. Scene after scene utterly of his own making. Doubtless he dreamt himself the hero and watched his heroic rescue of feeble maidens from smoking wrecks. Doubtless he carried the flopping rag dolls in his arms. I resented being doctored into a damsel drawn in delicate feminine lines. I wanted to withdraw myself from his fantasy. I wanted to reach into his gaping mouth, pilfer his sleeping conscience and remove all trace of my being there. He had no right to take me and transform me into beautiful injured prey. He had no right to dream so far from the truth.

No one had stolen JoeHow during the night. He was damp with dew and seemed cranky. I led him back into the enfolding bush, which seemed even thicker than the day before. We headed west, the "that-a-way" direction indicated by the old man. We walked for hours and hours, deeper and deeper into the crowded forest. I worried we would find ourselves at an impasse where JoeHow's berth would prove too wide to pass between trunks. With each step, the bush grew more intense. I saw watchful eyes in the deep green canopy above. Suppose we were to be sacrificed? Suppose the forest furies were waiting for us to become wedged between two pines? Beavers or black flies might eat us alive, although it was the trees I most distrusted. Trees appeared unconscious and passive, but in reality they were conspiring to trap us. They hid behind one another and joined branches, like the constricting bars of a cage.

I began to hear voices. Chiding wordless voices from all directions, like the universal schoolyard shaming taunt. The woods echoed with the chastising. I wondered if the trees knew of my forest fire on Hangman's Island. Perhaps their kind had sworn to take revenge. "It was an accident," I muttered, but my words had no effect. The taunting continued. I imagined vengeance crouched beneath every hanging branch. I lay forward on JoeHow's neck, the saddle horn in my gut, my face in his fur, and pressed my heels against his belly. We raced through the woods, my body battered and scraped by branches. The same adrenaline pumped through both myself and the horse. Against my cheek I felt the tightened muscles of JoeHow's neck and heard his short excited breath. He leapt over fallen trees and spongy moss, dodging trunks and brittle branches. I buried my face further into his hair and held on for dear life.

A sudden coolness and steady pace marked a clearing in the woods. I opened my eyes, sat up and reined in JoeHow. My hands were bloody. I wiped them on my chaps and then sucked at the deep cut across my knuckles. On my cheek I felt blisters where branches had flailed against my skin. I licked a finger and stung the cuts with my salty saliva. I poured the remains of the canteen water over my face. JoeHow's breathing slowed. We climbed a gentle incline and from the summit spied an old house, similar to the old man's I had left that morning. For a moment I feared we were going in circles, like those cursed lifelines in a tree cross-section, as if there were no way out of the forest, no way through to the Big Smoke. I studied the house and the surrounding area and noticed that a small barn, absent the previous night, sat distinctly and agreeably near the edge of the clearing. I knew then that I had found the old man's that-a-way brother.

He answered the door in the same reluctant manner. And like his brother, he wore dirty pyjamas and a faded housecoat. He stared suspiciously at the scratches on my face and then looked over my shoulder at the horse.

"Looks like a donkey," he said.

"Yeah, well we've had a rough time."

"I can see that."

A well-travelled JoeHow stood grazing on the spring grass.

"Your brother said that you had a barn."

"You know my brother?"

"I stayed with him last night."

"That where you got the scratches?"

"What?" I asked, confused by what he was suggesting, "No, no, the trees. The branches scratched me." I raised my hand to my tender cheek.

"Can't trust that crazy bastard," he said, shaking his head and ignoring my answer. The menace of the previous night was doubled.

He gestured for me to move out of his way. He slithered out of the house in pink velour slippers and was tediously careful in closing the door behind him. He checked the knob twice to ensure it was locked. Then he flapped his hand at JoeHow and began trudging toward the back of the house. I hastily untied my horse and followed him, thinking only of JoeHow's hunger. The yard behind the house was littered with mechanical odds and ends. Rusting engine pieces, stray wheels, and torn wire floated in a sea of unrecognizable gadgets. Rising up from the disarray was an old leather chair, ripped and stained but still intact. A curled-up dog slept soundly in the throne, oblivious to our arrival.

The old man walked like a turtle, with a steady, easy pace. My stride was so long I had to pause mid-step, foot hovering unnaturally above the ground so as to keep beside him. He must have connected this strange pixilation with my curious glances at the junk pile. He slowed to a stop, pulling the drab housecoat closer around him.

"Like my junk?" he asked. I nodded my head, sincerely impressed. He pulled his pale hand out from the protection of the housecoat and began pointing at objects and explaining their origins. His words became eloquent and enthusiastic. He grew straighter and stronger as he spoke, like a conductor before his orchestra.

"That's old Ginger's chair. Used to belong to a dentist fellow over the hill. He didn't practice professionally or anything, but everybody round here used to go and see him if they had a problem. Then something happened with one of them Zwicker girls, and bam, the son of a bitch disappeared. He left everything. Looked like he left in the middle of breakfast, a plate of eggs right there on the table. Just like that, in the middle of breakfast." Mystified by the abandonment of a meal, he slowly rolled his head from side to side, his neck apparently too frail for anything more vehement.

"I always liked his fancy chair. So I just went right over there and took it for my own."

He paused and we stood in silence and appreciation. I felt a drop of rain on my nose and looked up at the black cloud above us. It drooped down in heavy pockets near enough to touch. I felt another drop and glanced with longing at the dry barn. The old man pointed at another object and launched into another story. As I scanned the junkpile again, I began to notice the strewn body parts of dolls. The longer I looked, the more there were. Their pink phoney flesh specked the mass of oily black instrument parts, and their hard little hands poked out here and there. Most arms and legs had found their way onto pieces of furniture. Pink puckered lips and a mess of blond hair belonged to the detached head of a doll staring into a mirror. A torso, presumably hers, rested on the rusted shell of an old lawnmower parked at the base of a bureau. A two-seater chesterfield in a bright paisley pattern made soggy by the spring rains lay with its legs removed. On it rested the three broken parts of a small porcelain figure.

Most of these pieces of furniture had similar stories attached to them, quite often involving one of the numerous Zwicker girls who lived in the area. The old man proudly recounted his tales of acquisition, but it was the dismembered dolls that most disturbed me. I had coddled the hard plastic of these creatures and had seen my own mutilated on many occasions, courtesy of my brothers. Sarah, whose Barbies were always spanking-new and spotless, insisted that a prince would someday come to the rescue of mine. But he never did.

"The dolls are a different story," said the old man, wrapping his housecoat tightly around his sunken chest. He looked up at the dark persistent storm cloud and crossed his heart. He moved his dry lips as if in silent prayer. The storm seemed suddenly prepared to shred the meanly woven blanket that had weighed so heavily upon us for days. The only sound was of air being sucked out of the clearing as the confrontation between high and low reached explosive proportions. A flash of lightning struck, the thunderclap instantly next. The barn turned neon blue, as did the old man's face. The earth shuddered and JoeHow hissed like a cat. The glowing junk-pile seemed plugged into a long-awaited electric source. The chrome glittered and the steel gleamed. The dog sat up in his dentist's chair and howled. The air felt weightless and free of oxygen. And boom! the sparked barn exploded. The roof flew off, combusting into thin air, and the walls crumbled without a single flame. The powerful jolt instantly galvanized the building. The bushels of hay, the dry wood-beams, the bags of grain, all startled into nothing by that fickle voltaic finger.

A torrential rain fell too late to kill the destruction. It hammered down on my swimming head and stung the cuts on my cheek. The old man stood and stared at the smouldering ashes turning rapidly to mush in the rain. His wet pyjamas were pasted to his spindly legs, his housecoat wet and heavy on his shoulders. The loud sound of the downpour drowned out all other noises. It was a relentless pounding. The world was saturated with the small thuds of raindrops splattering, so pervasive that time itself was made slow and wet. Drenched and stunned, I watched the dog drop from the dentist's chair and take sluggard steps to a hideout beneath the bureau. The old man stood frozen, his blinking deliberately slowed, as if hoping that the barn might rematerialize.

Then he turned and began shuffling back toward me, staring right through me all the while. His short, measured steps seemed protracted in the downpour's time warp. He was soaked through and decrepit. He stopped in front of me and took my wrists. His cold, bony hands felt like shrinking manacles. He moved his face toward mine, but I could barely see it through the rain in my eyes. Only his pockmarked volcanic nose came nearer and clearer. He leaned further into my face, tightened his hold, and wheezed the word *jezebel.*

I have invented excuses to account for my behaviour, but none is adequate. The only plausible explanation is that I was possessed by the violent storm. Lightning bolts are said to reverse personal magnetic poles and alter dispositions. Perhaps the sudden blue flash that afternoon obliterated my own disposition and left me reeling in some unattended realm. I remember an unfamiliar wolfish feeling and a strange metallic taste in my mouth. I remember that my sole objective had been to break free from the old man's grasp, which I did with a quick and easy thrust. I should have then gathered my wits and parted company. I should have pointed to the sky and absolved myself, but my hands acted of their own accord. I watched as they slammed into his ribs and sent him flying onto his backside, where he lay like a bag of bones in the downpour. I listened for his wheezing, but heard only the pounding of the rain and feared that his heart had stopped altogether. Had he suffered the fatal shove into a world beyond? My hands hung like dirty rags. I shook them out with loose wrists as if to sever the culprits. The old man raised himself on his elbow and puddles spilled from his hollowed face. He could barely hold his head up against the pull of his mud-slicked housecoat. His struggle seemed the sort bequeathed to those returning from the dead. I feared the demon justice that would have me manacled once more. But his hands and slippers were sunk deep into the sludge, and from there he spoke in a calm unruffled voice, "Get the hell away from here, before I get my rifle."

I turned without a word, jumped JoeHow and hightailed out of the clearing and back into the woods. We squeezed between the swarthy trunks, the bark swollen and wimpled as if ready to be shed. JoeHow stumbled over the slippery tree roots. My bones ached after the hard rain, and my heart pumped at engine speed. My mind raced through the incident again and again, but there was no making sense of it. I couldn't forgive myself for that one aggressive act, despite all mention of rifles and menacing old men. Wet slumping leaves and bending branches slapped my face as though it were well deserved. At dusk I dismounted and walked JoeHow through the white irises that carpeted the forest floor. They stood quenched and deathly pale in zigzag patterns traced into the distance, no wind to flutter their petals. They glowed with an eerie purpose that put my own into question. When I crossed my eyes, I saw through the trunks on to vast tracts of white linen flowers leading me westward, I hoped.

We walked a great length through the ghostly bed of smiling irises. The trampled undergrowth sprung back with unearthly resilience. The woods were quiet and subdued, filled with the scent of berries and flowers, a scent that worked upon me like a sleeping potion after the panic of my escape. We passed shallow ponds thick with algae and by nightfall reached drier ground. The slow incline of a drumlin finally led to a summit and a small bare patch of land. A few scantily clad trees hugged the ground. We rested beneath a night sky dark with cloud. I lay my head down for just a moment and woke sometime later, shivery and weak. I rubbed my hands together hoping to bring warmth, but it came only briefly before rising into the cool night air. I heard the haunting sound of nighthawks singing as they flew over. Leaves rustled fitfully around me and beyond in the distance was a strange constant hum.

JoeHow stood grazing, wrapped cozily in his thick coat. I watched his muzzle as he chewed a mouthful of grass. He raised his head and glanced at me, his long uncurled eyelashes shading enormous brown eyes. He was doubtless considering more than the mere mush in his mouth. His look was scornful. I saw my beastly incompetence reflected. I saw myself, his miserable master, his wet and weary mistress. The perpetrator of a shameless act, I was unworthy of his services. He knew that my pushing the old man had been more than self-defence. He knew it was both savage and willful, that my sudden strength and driving thrust sprung from experience, that slams and pushes were familiar family encounters for me. JoeHow was the witness to the crime and blamed me for the barn and the wasted hay, despite all my storm disclaimers.

I tried to ignore him and began searching for kindling. Dry twigs littered the edge of the summit where the woods thickened, and a large tree, felled by lightning, lay splintered into long, thin segments. Using my boot as leverage, I cracked large dead branches into smaller pieces and carried them to where my bedroll and bags were. I placed seven rocks in a circle surrounding a clump of grass and there leaned the forked and knotted sticks against each other. From my bag I retrieved the replenished box of waterproof matches that I had emptied on Hangman's Island. The box itself was damp but the match lit easily off my pant zipper. The dry grass at the centre caught instantly, created a mushroom of smoke and then promptly went out. I stuffed more grass between the branches and tried again, and again, until finally the reluctant kindling caught. The flames flicked hues of green, orange, yellow, and blue. They rippled and heaved, were stunted and suddenly sparked again. Their curl and twist and warmth mesmerized me. I lit a tiny twisted torch and then extinguished it in the ash. At least I controlled my little fire, if not my horse. At least I could feed the fire, harness the flames, and keep them within the circle of seven stones. I sat sovereign over what had been so recently wild and destructive.

JoeHow unlocked his knees and shifted position. The bright flames caused dark jolting shadows to jump from tree to tree. Spectres soared through branches and rattled leaves. Nature herself was conspiring against me. The night suddenly transformed into a wall of grey trunks encroaching on my camp. The pure white light of my fire drew me in closer, and yet its tame service was what stirred the forest. The shadows begun at the moment of combustion had ignited their imagined partners. Just a short distance from me a world of predators lay in wait. I turned my back on the beasts I knew to be lurking in the dark and sat bolt upright, alert and close to the fire, casting brief curious glances at my horse.

He had slimmed down during our journey, and a pair of pendulous jowls now hung from his nose. The musculature of his sinewy legs held tightly to the bone. His massive ribcage rippled his skin. I imagined entering him through an invisible trap door, curling up tightly and hiding inside his huge ribcage. I imagined fitting snugly into his sunken trunk, travelling for days in his belly, the slow steady heartbeat of a walking horse resounding in my ears. Carried like a human cannon ball, my knees against my chest, kept safe and sound in a cavern lit with a warm, comforting light. What simple joy to be hidden and carried like a parasite, without the pain of conflict and mastery. To curl up like a fetus inside a womb. How easy life would be if it were lived off the energies of a hapless host, taking only enough to survive, never too much. How time would stretch out forever after the moment of attachment, that one fateful moment of signing up as a silent partner. And if that host was erased by a hunter or a god or an earthquake, then another could be found. Opportunities must be made at such moments, I assured myself and imagined arriving at the Big Smoke, leaping out from the horse's belly and startling all those who foolishly thought a horse had come without a rider.

In the morning I awoke to the sounds of JoeHow's wind-sucking. He was swallowing air and burping. He puckered his muzzle, let his long tongue hang down and released the swallowed air. Then he threw his head back and swallowed more. The sky was orange, still heavy with storm. We moved on in search of grain. The source of the mysterious hum from the previous night turned out to be a busy road not far from our camp. At the side of the road was an all-purpose gas station. Two white gas pumps stood with their nozzles in their sides. One monstrous truck was parked in front of the restaurant, where the windows were decorated with garish photographs of the kitchen's daily specials. The attendant, who also worked the store, sold me a small bag of grain. I tied JoeHow to the legs of the neon sign at the side of the parking lot and then fed and watered him.

When I opened the glass door, a chime jingled and the cardboard *Open-For-Business* sign knocked against the handle. The air inside was deep fried and onerous with bacon fat and grease. The moss green and coral pink speckled linoleum floor stretched out in both directions along a line of red vinyl booths. I walked directly to the counter and sat on a swivel stool. I ordered soup from the waitress. Indignant, she threw down her magazine and ladled a bowl full of boiling beef broth. Glutinous and inedible, the soup sat steaming on the counter in front of me. I drew figure-eights with my spoon in the oily surface.

A few stools away sat a bleary-eyed truck driver, slurping his coffee and inhaling from his cigarette as if it were the most profound moment of his day. He stared at the counter, rearranging the cup, saucer, and ashtray in what seemed to be a game of highway driving. He lined them up one behind the other, decidedly slid the saucer out of line and reviewed the new arrangement. I dropped my spoon in my soup, and someone instantly began weeping in a corner booth behind me. Deep sighs, muffled wails, and then a loud honking as the nose was cleaned out in a hanky. Both the trucker and the waitress calmly ignored the abject booth, but I couldn't help but listen to the sobbing. I felt drawn to the sounds of anguish, blurted out like the breathless bawling of a drowning victim. It was as if my ears were particularly sensitive to that particular pitch of wailing, but not because of sympathy, for sympathy was a luxury I couldn't afford. Only the blessed and the fortunate had the freedom to commiserate with the wretched. Good will was an indulgence in my world, a world of pushed and fallen men. I was drawn to the corner booth like the blind are drawn to light. Vaguely sensitive to the source of misery, I wanted to press my impervious skin against the hot element and revel. I wanted to palpate the broken heart, to probe its crevices and canyons. Or, if nothing else, applaud the gumption of those who weep in public places.

I pushed my soup bowl away and walked slowly over to the table. I slid into the booth along the opposite red vinyl seat. Across from me was a heap of utter unhappiness, neither male nor female. Strands of blond, brittle hair shot out in all directions from a head buried in despair. The heap heaved, but beyond this there was nothing.

"Want some coffee?" I asked.

Two bloodshot eyes and a red, swollen nose emerged from the darkness of coat, collar, and tangled hair. "Sure," she said, gazing like a shock victim in my approximate direction. I slid out of the booth with her empty cup in hand, returned to the counter and asked the waitress for a refill in the same quiet respectful tone that had earlier annoyed her. She looked up from her magazine and rolled her eyes. The beer sign above her blinked on-off in a golden hue. I wondered if she was wretched as well. I wondered if the entire world was wretched. Perhaps ours was a planet rife with muffled cries, our geography a study of despair. Perhaps wretchedness was born into the world at every instant, like a constant interruption. With time the making of a cold, hard species, the kind who inherit the earth, the kind who fear the earth itself will then rise up in revolt. The article the waitress was reading was entitled "Hollywood Horror," and true to her kind, myself included, she revelled in the black and white photographs of star victims, burnt mansions, and highways cleft in two.

The nose was honked clear again in the corner behind me. I carried the coffee cup back to the booth. The heap volunteered a tiny smile on lips that were a mess from trembling and biting. She thanked me, again with a slow hurtful voice. She poured two packets of sugar into her coffee, one in each hand. Then she stirred, the spoon swinging from a limp wrist.

"You from around here?" I asked.

"This fucking hole? Are you joking? Do I really look that bad? Like the town slut? Hanging out at the local diner, all teary-eyed?" She shook her head. "No, I'm not from here. Thank God. I've got a bigger and better nowhere behind me."

I glanced out the window at JoeHow's big rump. Cars slowed as they passed, fingers pointing in his direction. A mangy cat sat in the middle of the parking lot as if meditating on JoeHow's bondage. The woman across from me pulled out a cigarette from her pack. She seemed suddenly aware that she was speaking aloud, suddenly conscious of someone else sharing the booth. "I'm from a long line of lousy romances. Can't you tell?" She reached into an inside pocket and pulled out a handful of junk. The cigarette lighter was picked out from amongst the confusion of dried berries, crumpled rose petals, and various coloured pills. She lit her cigarette and tossed everything back into the pocket to be retrieved, presumably, for the next lighting. "And I need another one like I need a hole in the head," she added in an ambiguous tone that made it unclear what it was she did need. She pushed the spoon handle along the coffee-cup rim and made just the tiniest scraping noise.

"Beware men. They're all assholes, without exception." She looked up at the ceiling, as if they were all there, hovering above her. She puffed dramatically on her cigarette and blew smoke hard toward the phantoms.

"Every single one of them?" I asked, incredulous.

She tilted her head.

"In a manner of speaking, yes." She sighed. She had a delicious way of talking with her lower jaw jutting out and expressive lips pursed and puckered to emphasize certain words. Her drama seemed entirely different than any I had considered. Perhaps I had led a sheltered life, untouched by real tragedy. I felt foolish for believing that bloodbaths and sudden deaths were the usual tragic fare. Her failings didn't fall from the sky, they arose from her own misadventures, her doomed alliances. Perhaps plummeting anchors were the least of my worries.

She plucked a rose petal from her pocket and began burning cigarette holes into the soft red tissue. The wrinkled flesh was easily gutted by the red-hot tobacco. She dropped its remains into the ashtray. The pine smell of floor cleanser wafted toward us from the kitchen. We said nothing to each other. The truck driver who had been at the counter appeared at our booth as though heralded by the silence. He was tall and rickety, with sunken cheeks that shivered slightly when he spoke. He towered over the table, his back bent, his body permanently listing.

"I'm going now. If you still want a ride." He shoved his hands deep into his pockets, his eyes focused on an imagined median between himself and the booth. My companion blew her nose, patted down her hair and then gathered up her belongings. She reached for my hand and squeezed it goodbye, that small hurtful smile back on her lips. I watched their reflection in the mirror on the wall opposite me as they marched out of the restaurant. She followed him out the door and across the pavement to the white truck. She climbed into the passenger seat and slammed the door behind her. He started the engine and cleared the smoke stack. The truck twitched into first gear and rolled onto the highway.

The restaurant was suddenly unbearably foggy. The windows turned misty, as did the mirror on the wall behind the booth. My image was a blur, nothing distinct, not even my satellite ears. Every line and feature was bent into unfamiliar profile, and yet the same someone was sitting in a booth with one arm resting on the table. The same someone was haunting herself from the outside. I sat looking at my reflection and saw instead the man I might have been. The man whose life was a mere shadow cast by my conception. For one fleeting moment I imagined the alternate mitotic path my genes might have followed. Just a split-second glimpse of him, the smudged chin a smidgen bigger, the splotched cheeks smeared ruddy, and the deep set eyes sunk deeper. That potent quality of premeditation pasted there to my forehead before a blink cast off the imposter, or the asshole, as the woman had dubbed him, and he vanished altogether. I searched the mirror in vain, and found only an empty hole where I had just made room for him, as though some part of my anatomy had been confiscated. In his stead I felt the first tentative scratches of an inclination. I sat meditating on the wretched romance between the sexes, the two persuasions paired for life in what seemed a painful commerce. One moment of controversy and I had hesitantly entered the business of desire. My heart crept out at that moment, the air moist with starved pheromones, and I began to imagine a man.

We galloped madly toward the St. Lawrence River. The storm remained behind us suspended above the forest, the wood a magnet for its own destruction. We moved briskly along the banks of the river, the water tumbling beside us in the opposite direction. JoeHow's general health had improved, although he had taken to weaving from side to side. Jumping was out of favour and time was lost in search of gates and free pasture. My chaps were wearing thin on the inner thighs but were still comfortable. My big apple ass and JoeHow's moon-rump fit together like horse and rider should. We had survived the insanity of the woods, that nowhere terrain of outcasts who had neither sea nor city. We had reached the brackish frontier where the salt water of a massive estuary became gradually more fresh. It occurred to me that only water could transform itself so gently, only a river could be both sea and lake. On the other edge thrust the granite shield, a vault of stone locking the river in. Strip farms like fingers touched the river's eastern edge. I dismissed all my doubts about JoeHow's loyalty and sang aloud a free floating serenade to the deep river. The lyrics, when there were some, sprung unchallenged from the scenery around me. The colours of the sky, the sunlight tickling the budding branches, the fresh leaves on the maples and oaks, and the always rippling water — all of these entered the song of their own accord. Road signs announcing turnoffs, the amenities to be found in this or that direction, and the hazards of deer crossing, even these entered the song. My voice never tired.

It crooned of senseless signposts like a singing automaton, evoked by the dancing light and given rhythm by the horse's clonking hooves, his breathing, his hip and head swinging, his being there beneath me. It was how I imagined the magic of a lullaby.

In certain places the rapid melting of ice had caused flooding and the trees stood awkwardly, their roots beneath water. The river widened and low mud banks and broad reedy marshes appeared. Beneath them lay the shale ledges that were once the beaches of an ancient sea. My song was suddenly suspended by thoughts of these buried worlds. I felt as if the muddy sediments formed a false floor ready to collapse at the slightest suggestion. The entire shield might shift and grind in a moment of boredom or anger. The crack at the bottom of the river might widen and an avenging ocean rush in reclaiming its beaches. Catastrophes explained how the world was created, and more were expected if the world were to change. It wasn't a biblical flood that I had in mind. That book held no patent on such theories. My father's science also alleged random mutations and sudden chaotic movement. High-powered microscopes had revealed an accidental nature at the most minute of levels.

I stripped the land of geologic time and saw the seven volcanic blisters that had formed the island of Montreal, long after the time of mountain-making. The city sat in a tactical mid-river position selected by the finest French explorers. I might have stayed if it weren't for the founders' clever choice of strategic location. The many sensible reasons for settling on the St. Lawrence made me wary of doing so. Dominion was all too easy from such a prudent vantage point. I preferred cities that seemed to rise up for no reason whatsoever, like the Big Smoke, which was said to have profited from its lack of good motive.

We rode along the river's eastern shore, forgoing the pedestrian grated bridges because of JoeHow's innate inability to cross them. Like other hoofed animals, he distrusted that odd sensation of walking on a perforated floor. Graffiti decorated the embankment and discarded needles and condoms were strewn along the river's edge. People always had a good time near water. I felt a pang for the arm of the ocean which had nurtured me as much or more than my mother had. Her sea-wreck stories had faded altogether from my memory, and I felt only affection for the Atlantic after such a long journey by land. I had lost track of the days, but I had seen one full moon wax and wane since leaving the coast. I missed the buoyancy of salt water and the weightlessness of swimming. I wanted to feel my body rise and fall with a swell, no mention of a whitecap, no bottom near enough to turn the wave over on itself.

JoeHow stumbled, his knees swollen from the cement terrain. There had been almost nothing to graze on for quite some time, save the diligent dandelions that sprouted up through the cracks. He sucked the flowers off the stems and spat them out. Gulls, pigeons, and black birds swooped down in turn to check our trail of yellow slobbered dandelions for edibility. My head ached, so blinding was the light reflected off the water and the high-speed chrome that passed us. We found a fenced-in field further upstream in a less trafficked area. Once again the wire cutters came in handy. I slept fitfully beneath the sun, feeling the shadows of clouds racing across my face. I sat up and watched JoeHow grazing in the white clover meadow just beneath the dam diverting all but a trickle of the river. Against my single horsepower the hydro plants measured five million more. That much power was mind-boggling. The image of my horse peacefully grazing beside the massive power generator was disturbing, the disparity between horse and hydro astounding. I was accustomed to feeling small and insignificant under the threat of natural disasters, but not at the foot of insurmountable cement walls and divine pieces of construction. My defences were down. A warm fuzzy feeling that seemed far too furtive entered my head. If I had known then the truth about power, I might have surrendered and enjoyed myself. But fuzzy ecstatic feelings were not my strong point. They reeked like scented pin cushions, like puffed-up pregnant bellies. An unsavoury excess of emotion, and just the sort of fluid sensation I both wanted and feared. I quickly retrieved JoeHow, mounted him, and we walked away from the dam.

Upstream was a boat preparing to leave dock. A flat-bottomed river boat dangerously low in the water. Ripped car tires as fenders were tied to its deck. The rough river water slapped the hull broadside and the tires bulged between dock and boat. From the black transom hung a black tattered flag announcing its lack of allegiance. Since my own sense of belonging was so meagre as to be missing altogether, the flag seemed a friendly invitation. I approached without trepidation and asked the captain to take us across. His ample mustache lay stretched across his cheeks, pasted there with hair gel like the unswerving hands of a broken compass. Mottled bad skin ranged north and south of it, and resting on his nose was a pair of teardrop mirrored sun glasses. He leaned his small hips against the wheel.

"Lady Luck and her stallion?" he asked, his voice a flat baritone.

"Maybe," I replied.

With thumb and forefinger he trundled his mustache and then repasted it to his cheek. The two crew members appeared at his side, their wrists wrapped with red bandannas. JoeHow suddenly farted and began fanning his tail back and forth across his rump. All three men laughed uproariously as if they had never before been so amused. JoeHow let loose a second time, the noxious air whistling out like a rocket. Fart jokes were the standard fare of my brothers' humour. They had often created quite sonorous stinks through their combined efforts and claimed their farts would go down in the "Anals of History." Despite my own commodious seat, I did my best to produce only *silent but deadlies*, as we liked to call them. Men, I realized, were different. JoeHow's sustained wind convinced the boat crew that we were worthy cargo — they ushered us on board.

We tied JoeHow with a number of halters to a series of upright posts near the engine room. He stood squeezed between crates, trembling, his brown eyes slick with terror. The scraping stuttering start, the grinding clutch, the chug-chug of sluggish diesel stole what little composure he had retained. Every inch of his hair bristled as the hull shuddered, every muscle taut against the boat's vibration. I gave him a nosebag of jostling grain pellets and went to sit alone near the bow while the men huddled around the helm, and the boat plodded through the water like a barge. The crossing seemed narrow at the outset and wider the further we went. The strips of land I mistook for the opposite shore turned to small uninhabited islands.

I leaned over the edge of the paint-chipped hull and watched the layers of water peel away in the boat's wake. The throbbing engine went through the boards and into my bones. My body felt numb from the constant convulsion. I lost myself in the lines of water sheared by the bow, lost myself in wistful memories of other boats and other waters. I remembered being in our small dinghy in the Arm. The sound of my father gently dipping the oars, my three brothers over one gunwale, myself over the other. We peered down through the water at the rocky bottom. I leaned all the way over, my ass up in the air, my face under water with eyes still open, surprised that my vision remained so clear in that other world. A world of rocks and grass very much like the one we lived in, and yet so inhospitable, so unkind and intolerant to oxygen buffs. My lungs were entirely unsuited to its weedy reclusive milieu, my nose too automatic with inhalation, and my limbs a sad substitute for unfolding fins. But still I imagined the quiet and remote bliss of being submerged in a world from which we had all evolved.

The St. Lawrence, however, was musty and opaque, and my vision was thwarted by the heavy slick surface. Just as I decided that the bottom was, in all likelihood, not so attractive, I heard voices behind me, and turned. Two men near the wheel were arguing while the other opened a crate and examined its contents. It suddenly dawned on me that I might be amongst terrorists smuggling guns and explosives. I worried that I had come this far only to be in a boat blown to smithereens. The wind changed direction and I was forced to inhale the black diesel smoke that poured from the engine room, my cough completely unheard as every rotten plank of wood gave out a desperate rasping sound. The man who had opened the crate screamed and reached in to grab something. Our time had come. I crouched, my hands over my elephant ears, my jaw clamped shut. I tried to concentrate on keeping my limbs attached, my body whole. I kept seeing that dirty river bottom coming toward me. What a waste, I thought, to end headfirst in the sludge.

But there was no bang. Whatever explosives they were carrying were set to go elsewhere. The engine continued throbbing, the boat beams grating, and the small wake we caused carried on across the water. The three men stood amiably eating chocolate bars and smiling at the tamaracks on the approaching shore.

"Jersey Milk?" shouted the smallest when he realized I was watching.

I walked across the deck, my knees still knocking, my pulse still throbbing at my temple. I ripped the wrapper from the candy as if the bomb were in it, balled the crinkled foil and voraciously devoured the bar, pressing the chocolate chunks against the roof of my mouth and swallowing every soft, sweet morsel. The captain picked up the wrapper and tossed it overboard. He seemed about to offer another bar from the box when the opposite shore came suddenly upon us in the shape of an unattended private dock. He swerved the boat to meet the dock broadside. The engine sped up as we turned and then it sputtered and choked, deprived of fuel as we glided in. The crew had hotfeet, carrying the crates onto the dock and setting up the ramp for JoeHow to disembark. A truck, appearing out of nowhere, drove down onto the dock and picked up the cargo and the men. They threw chocolate bars at me and waved good-bye. I led JoeHow down to the water where he drank and blew his nose clean of grain powder. We spent the night there, surrounded by candy wrappers. In the morning I awoke with fagged bones and granite-like muscles. JoeHow was beside me, standing as always, like an upright Buddha, perpetually waiting for me to mount.

The St. Lawrence is still a youthful river. The flow of water hasn't yet smoothed the river bed. The many rapids along its course are the angry and ungoverned exhibitions of its restless adolescence. I envied the river its youth, for it was younger and wilder than I had ever been. My much more recent beginning and fledgling life in geologic terms had been cramped and aged by fear from the outset. Granted, the river had also been commandeered by a heavy hand. The seaway had tamed the troublesome parts and allowed for ships to travel deep into the continent. Canals and locks raised these floating giants over two hundred feet, so as to introduce them, gentleman-like, into Lake Ontario.

When we arrived the lake sat solemnly on the shore, as if too grave to budge. I had never seen so much water entirely possessed by its shoreline. It lay trapped like a giant puddle. I couldn't help but imagine that beneath its placid appearance lurked a crankiness from being so thoroughly shut in. I felt anxious for the coveted water and wondered whether someone or something compelled it to stay. How long before the rain residing at the bottom was drawn into a river or evaporated under the sun? How dreadful to be kept down forever. I assured myself that time means nothing to water, which is probably true, and that the shoreline embraced and subdued the lake. But I wasn't convinced. The shore's embrace seemed too eager, too suffocating, like that imposed on a timid child.

My St. Lawrence melody degenerated into warbled uncertain whistling. My body began to ache, and my mood swung, but I had no explanation for this change of heart, save the lake and its dubious calm. I imagined my mother beside me, sturdy, frowning, seeking out a ripple, a tear, some indication that the water was not completely shackled. I heard the ice cubes knock against her tin mug, the sound tittering out across the landlocked lake. I felt within me the same funk that had beset her at the sight of insufferably dull seas. The lake was one big suspicious calm which might erupt violently with the hard slaps of a sudden storm. Here was my mother's worst nightmare. I felt a queer pride as I rode on, heedless of her haunting, and wondered whether my crossing the country was meant to dredge the depths of her despair. I hoped that I had been cured of my sea-floor affliction and that my reasons for persevering were above all that.

We rode on through marshland and were watched by wary red-winged blackbirds perched on the tops of dead reeds. The river crossing had permanently affected JoeHow. He shied away from the smallest puddles and kept twisting his neck inland. The sticky grass and slippery footing in the marsh added to his fretful state. It was as if he did not trust the ground he stepped on; every foot forward was a chance event.

Once out of the marshes, I cleaned and oiled the ornate saddle. The pattern of waves came to life in the moistened leather. I passed my rough palm over the smooth leather wavelets and then gripped the saddle horn. The strong smell of horse and leather blended with the odour of rich rural Ontario. I saddled and mounted JoeHow, and we marched onward. Toronto kept itself out of reach like a precious jewel. Two days of anticipation, of Great Lake water going nowhere. What I first mistook for the metropolis emerged instead as the Darlington nuclear power plant; its impressive towers, barbicans and massive floodlights fooled my unaccustomed eyes. I confess to having expected a city of medieval castles.

My understanding of cities was more feudal than modern, evoked by the coastal peninsular city over which our anchor shank had once flown. I imagined markets, public hangings, and bell-tolling hunchbacks. I assumed that crowds always strove for such things. I looked at the power plant and saw a cathedral. Then I heard the hydro corridor, humming over the hills and away from the lake.

A documentary distributed to schools and shown in science class had featured a happy hydro woman who touted the potential for bird-watching in the clean environs of nuclear plants. She sat with binoculars on her rooftop, framed by an immaculate blue sky, the perfectly tame image of healthy curiosity. Yet her peaceful observations didn't quite suit the breaking down of atoms. I held my breath and kicked JoeHow to speed up our passage. The fear of a nuclear disaster was deep in the marrow of my bones, although no deeper than any other. I expected disasters of all kinds, and most were on a much more grand scale, although none concerned such a common public utility. The arduous task of imagining this once destructive force turned beneficial was beyond my powers. I awaited the avenging atoms, splitting my shadow from my body. I awaited the sirens, already too late, announcing the pernicious leak spreading sickness across the nation.

I might have reassured myself if it weren't for the albino deer that crossed our path and spooked the usually unflinching JoeHow. One of my mother's gloomier baroque tunes filled my head as we steered inland. We left the lakeshore behind and reached the highway. We bedded down in the ditch and in the morning we rode alongside the highway, past hotel signs and isolated mammoth office buildings, until finally reaching the main attraction — my peerless city.

I was surprised to discover a series of swollen arteries pumping through suburb after suburb and postponing our arrival. I had forgotten all about the suburbs. I expected a swift and sudden shift from country to city and imagined a stone wall or a moat dividing the two worlds. I blame these misconceptions on my mother's misinformation and my skewed understanding of development. I didn't believe in natural growth. My personal theory of chaos didn't allow for gradual predictable developments. Both expanding suburbs and individual maturity fell under this title. I can't defend the theory here. It was a sword in my side, and I hoped to find the prince who would pry it out. I hoped to make sense of cause and consequence and found the constant engine hum around me reassuring in this regard. The highway seemed the sole incentive for decisive movement. Rows of houses turned their backs to it as if denying their dependence on it. Drivers stared suspiciously at us and then disappeared off ramps into the silence of these ordered residential interruptions. With all the excitement, JoeHow tended to gallop. I had to rein him in time and time again. At last we descended into the humble crack of greenery known as the Don River Valley and followed the dirty trickle of water while the stupendous expressway thundered above us.

We rested near the ruins of an old brick company whose deep quarries were once a measure of the city's success. The pit had widened with the rise of those first tentative two-storey buildings. Heaps of broken brick and sandstone and shale slates littered the old quarry. I sat down and examined a small stone, its face etched with trenches and crescent lines. On its reverse side were flawless bivalve fossils, the ridges of their husks having left soft depressions in the stone. The cross section revealed that the stone itself was comprised of untold layers of compacted shells. I picked up another and rolled my thumb over the remains of marine animals shaped like flowers and wheat, their lime exteriors built from the ancient salt water that once covered the land. I looked around at the many other rocks that showed similar marks. I was surrounded by marine fossils. I sat in a Devonian graveyard. The reef colonies that had cemented themselves together and had then drowned beneath the sediments of the ancestral sea now sat exposed in an old Toronto brickyard. The needs of high-rises had reached the old ocean's bottom. The Don Valley was a big hole that had once been a silt deposit.

Many harbours might meet similar ends if their bottoms weren't frequently dredged. My father often went down to the Arm in front of our house and collected samples of sludge worms covered in decaying organic ooze. The sink was his scum holding tank. The specimens were transferred onto glass plates and scrutinized under his microscope. He ogled the overworked bacteria, enlarged one-hundred-fold, and let out long deep sighs as he watched them gorge on our worldly waste. Beyond adding to his distaste for seafood, his findings seriously disturbed him; he looked utterly defeated by the bottom's prolific bloom. I wondered if he prophesied a marine graveyard much like the one I then stood in, but had kept his mouth shut because disastrous ends were my mother's domain.

I walked JoeHow past an old brick hut labelled *Explosives* and prayed against the random rekindling of any remaining dynamite sticks. I heard my heart sputter as caution slowed the pulse, my mind struck by the sense that I didn't belong here, that I was ill-prepared, that I was dead wrong to have risked everything, and, worst of all, that my mother's impressions of the city should never have been trusted.

part three

When JoeHow and I clambered out of the valley, we found ourselves deep in the city. I looked up and saw the famous Atlantean tower. Its shape was familiar, like an anchor's shank, the longest shank I had ever seen. Some gigantic alien ship had exploded in our galaxy, and its anchor split in two, the flukes buried in the Milky Way and the giant shank here in Toronto. Hulking buildings stood like disciples surrounding it and reflected its image in their mirror windows.

The air was warm and dirty. Dust, or ash, rested like a veil over every building. I searched faces for signs of the great fire, for a vestigial fearful glance or look of awe, a flame flickering in a pupil, or even smoke-blackened faces, but found instead a glazed wintry look, clean and waxen, as if just out from hibernation. It should have come as no surprise, for the fire had been out for ages. Cool level-headed prosperity reigned, or so it seemed. Bloodless blue faces turned toward me and my horse. "How much for the beast?" asked one nonchalantly. "What are you promoting?" asked another.

Bay Street was near at hand. It sat cradled in the nest of skyscrapers. I could feel its powerful aura, a deep throbbing vibration emanating from the city's core and resonating through me. A giddiness percolated through my bones, but I tried to keep myself in check, slow down, savour everything, keep high in the saddle lest I fall off my horse. JoeHow's neck was wet with grimy sweat. He skirted the sidewalk vents and stopped for a mouthful of spring tulips from a planter. The sheer quantity of motion, of sprinting bodies and whizzing vehicles, heightened the temperature in the cold metropolis. Cars honked at us, their windows down and opened for the angry fists that were shook, as if a common greeting. Fire engine-red trams rumbled by, their mesh of electrified wires hanging over the streets. I glanced at the gloomy shop attendants who stood behind their storefront windows, saddened, so it seemed, by their own unpurchased merchandise. We pushed through droves of shoppers, lugging purses and purring as if with pleasure. A teenage girl dressed entirely in black stood stock-still amongst the commotion. The rest were far too driven to be distracted.

"Are you for real?" she asked.

Beside us on a portable grill sizzled a row of enormous hot dogs, the charred, blackened skin ripped, the pink uncooked meat bulging forth.

"Yeah. I'm looking for the stock exchange," I answered, trying to sound imperious. JoeHow chewed at his bit and flicked his tail across his ass. I asked the girl if she knew where the building was.

"Beats me." She shrugged her shoulders, then turned and walked away. She was lying, of course, lying outright. I was convinced that everyone was lying. I began to suspect a city-wide conspiracy. Each busy body refused to cooperate, each reply meant to discourage me. That despondent shrug of the shoulders was a sly attempt to check my advance. I saw how they safeguarded their investments through feigned ignorance, afraid that the strange woman on the horse might disrupt the market. I saw the cautious miserly glint in their eyes, worried that I would steal their profits. Even mild-mannered matrons who called me *dear* said they couldn't tell me.

I wasn't dissuaded. I gathered up my courage and rode deeper into the city, past flocks of hurried people and dark stairways dipping underground, past isolated and humbled trees, their roots trapped beneath concrete, past hordes of children screaming and struggling within their caged play areas. I was going for gold in a city of liars. From several corners came the soul-stripping sound of jackhammers cracking open the sidewalk. The broken asphalt struck fear into JoeHow, who had never been too trusting of foundations. He knocked over a cart of oranges and shat in front of the old city hall, which was clad in rough-hewn ashlar and stood lording over the financial district. A large woman, whose clothes were pasted with numbers, warned me of the approaching Judgment Day. It seemed a good omen.

Bay Street was brimming with swinging briefcases and billowing suit jackets. It was shiny and immaculate without a trace of the fire that had once demolished it. Multi-storied monsters hoisted themselves up into clouds and carved the sky into blue slivers. Black marble and steel and glaring gold amalgamated glass stretched from one block to the next. The buildings leaned over the sidewalk, each window a watchful eye. The old decorative stone showed rain-stained Roman gods and fierce dragons. The more modern sky-boxes were schizoid marriages of monstrous shape and reflective glass. Across the street a tan-white flash caught my eye — JoeHow's warped reflection, split between windows. Our slow pace pixelated amidst the surrounding speed. His shoes were loose, his tattered tail full of knotty burrs. I threw my head back, my eyes climbing up the glass walls. Crowned with company names on their roofs, the buildings were otherwise unencumbered, but the death-defying heights seemed distended at the top. The higher levels broadened and made as if to topple. For a moment the vertical stretch lost itself to the black and white image of destruction that I had carried in my heart for so long. I closed my eyes and swayed in my saddle, thinking of ruins. I felt calm with the lasting warmth of that originating fire, the fire that had ensured my future.

"Move your big ass!" said a bike courier, who left me little room to manoeuvre. On either side of me men marched down the slope toward the sewer lake. They carried newspapers tucked under their arms, their shirt sleeves rolled up, their ties swinging, their eyes hidden behind sunglasses. A strong wind bounced off the high-rises and blew secretaries from street corner to street corner. JoeHow nudged through a crowd of shoulder pads and aerosol-sculpted hair. People covered their mouths as if embarrassed on our behalf. Someone joked: "Are you the new bank teller?" and everyone laughed. Things weren't going well. People were heartless and hostile and succeeded in embarrassing me. JoeHow snorted at the grey mottled pigeons that cocked their heads and hopped on their gnarled claws from under his hooves. We stopped beside an arched entrance where the scent of cologne overwhelmed the sensitive JoeHow. He sneezed repeatedly on the shoes of the doorman, whose pallid face turned truly wretched before retreating behind a coiled wrought-iron door. I raised a hand and caressed the smooth stone of the building. Classy, I thought to myself, very classy.

When I glanced across the street and saw the word EXCHANGE carved in stone, I congratulated myself. At last, and without the help of anyone, I had found the stock exchange. It sat surrounded and surmounted by lean black towers. A parade of striding industrial workers had been carved and drilled into its limestone exterior. They forged across the building, smelting and shucking and digging, their pure geometry a measure of the century's progress. They stepped in profile, one streamlined figure connected to the next. Their faces free of expression, their brawny builds in standard overalls, their fisted hands around impaling tools.

I spied the lone figure in the parade who wore top hat and tails, the banker or broker, the man who worshipped money. He shoved his hand in a labourer's pocket to feel his butt or steal his wallet, I wasn't sure which. But I knew he was the one I wanted.

I tied JoeHow to a parking meter, opened the heavy steel doors, ran up the spiralled staircase in my chafing chaps and mud-crusted boots and burst into the trade room. No one greeted me. The floor was devoid of bankers and brokers and traders. Not one colour-coded coat cruised the room. No paper slips, no gold watches. The lacquered maple trading posts sat empty. The old analogue clock ticked with a slow thud. I spun around, searching for the source of my celebrated street, searching for the money-makers. I grew dizzy tracing the frosted opalescent glass ribbons that stretched up the walls and across the ceiling like giant conveyor belts. I felt dwarfed by the murals of robust industrial workers and bottomless resources that rose to the high ceiling. I wondered where everyone was hiding. I assumed they were hiding from me, and I hated myself for being so despised. My resolve crumbled. My hopes were dashed. No money, no gold, no noise. Only the gentle swish of someone sweeping nearby.

"They moved house," said the old janitor, his arthritic fingers coiled around a broom.

"Where to?"

"Where else? The new Exchange. Right around the corner. You can't miss it." He hugged the broom against his chest and lowered his voice. "You got a tip for me?"

He meant a stock tip, a piece of inside information, but I was so upset and confused, I could hardly understand him. I heard only the spoken shell of his words, while their meaning dragged behind. I felt only the rough exterior of a request that I couldn't comprehend. He must have been partially blind to have expected something from me. He waited in silence for his tip. My head ached with my efforts. I offered nothing, and he roared.

"No tip eh? Not one little tip! You're all the same, you goddamn penny-pinchers. I've been working here for seventeen years. Seventeen years! And I've never been given the smallest tip." He shook his head and tucked the broom under his arm, "Goddamn penny-pinchers. Don't know why I keep asking."

The morning's rancour pitched low and hard in my stomach. I watched as a rainbow of colours pursued the bad temper across his face. He clutched at the broom, his weapon, as if planning to swat me. I tucked my hair behind my ears. I smiled. I just wanted things to go smoothly. I had no pennies to pinch, no tip to give, but I promised him a handsome one after making my fortune.

"That's what they all say," he growled and shambled off awkwardly in an unhinged gait, his hips shifting as if in and out of gear. He stopped abruptly before leaving the room, turned his cheek to me, and in a tired and true voice he added, "First Canadian Place. You can't miss it."

~~~

The new Exchange was reached by a series of escalators. I stepped onto the moving stairs and was conveyed from floor to floor. My enthusiasm had been checked by the many unfriendly encounters of the day. The rubber belt hummed beneath my feet but brought me little comfort. I saw my stretched image in the buffed banister and my shrunken image in the trench of each moving step. I rose starward, past bull and bear constellations that twinkled on the wall. Toward a market that was all bull. Toward a market that was
~~~

pumped up and ready to blow. I scraped my muddy boots on the grooved steps of the escalator, glanced at my rising reflection in the mirrored wall and knew only one thing — fear. My nerves were a wreck and I feared being denied access at any moment. The security guards eyed me suspiciously, as if they suspected doom and destruction followed at my heels.

And yet no one stopped me, and finally, from a glass booth, I peered nervously out at the sea of money-traders. They swam across the room, through liquid greed and gurgling profit. They waded through the floor of crumpled paper slips, swinging their turbine arms and churning up the already overheated market. Madly talking hands blabbered back and forth and were waved like fins fanning water. Blue-breasted jackets flapped beneath their beating arms. Pin-striped pork bellies floated about computer screens and white-shirted piranhas darted in and out. I watched them squint their twitching eyes at the digital indicators, straddle their overpriced stocks and press their palms against their ulcers. It was all too sly and crafty. Nothing along the lines sketched in the prehistoric encyclopaedia I had consulted before leaving. My idea had been of elderly noblemen respectfully guiding the nation into sound investments, selling stocks of public-minded companies with real and reliable material output and sagely recommending safely moored retirement savings. Obviously I had been misinformed. But even the daily paper, which I admit to reading only infrequently, had done nothing to amend my opinion. I expected an upright cooperative atmosphere where honourable traders struggled to ensure a secure future. I didn't expect the air to be thick with speculation. Nor did I expect the massive stations wired into trunks of electronic ganglia that speedily performed transactions of money, commodity, and promise. And I was startled, to say the least, by the predators on whom our future depended.

One man stood out in the squirming mass of fortune-seekers. His hands were deep in his pockets. His hair was a fuzzy orange as if on fire. The heave and toss subsided only around him, like the eye of a storm, a dead calm amidst the hysteria. He stood grinning and looking up at me in the visiting gallery. Bodies bolted to and fro but left him undisturbed. Paper airplanes glided by him, and still he stared. My first-ever admirer, so I thought, and blushed.

To have been so mistaken reveals how wretched and vulnerable I was. In one measly moment my mind betrayed itself wholesale. I stood there like a dumb devotee, deaf to the obvious. I watched his arm reach out into the bedlam and stop short a passing shoulder. He pulled the man toward him and whispered in his ear. They stood shoulder to shoulder, the only two fixed to the fluid floor. Another trader quit the chaos and joined the pair. The secret was shared. Their torsos bent forward in a purchasing posture, their feet planted firmly beneath them. The three looked up at me, of that I was certain. But they weren't admiring. No, admiring wasn't the word. Something else was going on. The fuzzy redhead reeled in other traders from the surging pool. Their bids would wait for this moment of camaraderie. He shared his tip with all his buddies, each the chosen confidential. Each slowed to have the tidings retold and diluted. Soon the entire floor was glancing in my direction. A sea of snickering men, their faces beet-red with rising blood pressure, their chests sunken and tummies swollen. The scornful muted sound of tittering and hooting seeped through the glass seams and chased me out of the gallery.

I was mortified. The Exchange was no better than an adolescent boys' club. No better than the hooting gym class whenever I appeared in shorts. I had come all that way to find boys as mean and juvenile as my brothers. Tears of utter frustration streaked my cheeks as I untied JoeHow. I regretted my devotion to a Bay Street that had openly shunned me. I cursed it and wished back the flames that had once devoured it. Some might say that my ultimate achievements were driven by the revenge that I fostered on that day. I don't know whether that's true. I do know that I wept as I rode away, clinging to my one last hope — Sarah, my beloved cousin. It had been one year since she had left Halifax so abruptly. I assumed she was by now firmly established, and I pinned my ravished hopes on her.

JoeHow was on his last legs. I sat slumped over in my crested saddle. We wobbled westward, away from Bay Street. The ugly dismissal from the Exchange had burst my inmost aspirations. That Sarah would somehow be my saving grace was a sluggish but comforting thought on an otherwise disastrous day. A day that had only reached mid-morning when we rode through the grandiose gates of Exhibition Place. Straddling the poured concrete columns of the overhead arch was a rather placid angel of victory, a figurehead on the prow of progress, a tribute to labour and industry. She seemed a cruel joke after my all too recent failure. Neighing unbridled horses swam at her stern, her boat riding through fitful cemented waves. She was busty but not bare-breasted, which meant she wouldn't quell any storms. But as we passed under and around to the backside of this emblem of courage and pride, I couldn't resist wishing she were *my* angel of victory. I glanced up at the cheap concrete and imagined my strong-armed cousin there above the gate, a dove on her wrist and a laurel wreath in her hand, ushering me into the empty fairgrounds. Sarah, my last-ditch angel of victory, lording over the bleak asphalt, which then seemed dedicated, in my own dismal opinion, to the end of the noble labourer.

JoeHow moved like a broken wheelbarrow over the paved expanse and toward the Horse Palace, one of the few remaining buildings on the fairgrounds. It was an equine mansion to which all others paled in comparison, the swankiest stables ever. Horse motifs pranced across its limestone façade, their dusty manes and tails drilled into the stone, their whittled hindquarters above the restroom doors. Bushels of shit-steaming hay lay in piles outside the entrance. JoeHow's nose twitched. He pulled hard at the bridle. The local police cavalry advanced through the doors in tight formation. I fixed my eyes on the riders' white helmets and tinted masks, their shiny boots pressed against the well-groomed rippling coats, their bludgeons at their hips. It seemed entirely plausible on that frightful day, to a mind lacking all manner of peace, that my arrival had summoned the riot squad. It even seemed likely that my appearance at the Exchange was the main offense. I shrunk in my saddle and saw once again the sea of snickering money-changers. I felt like some reluctant horsewoman of the apocalypse, all too prepared to denounce myself. And might have done so, if JoeHow hadn't lurched aside to let them pass, as if he hoped to secure my freedom. I swallowed my confession, pulled myself together and rode my own scraggly mount into the stables.

Inside seemed like a sanctuary to me. The sunlight poured through the glass roof and swamped the ring where ponytailed girls exercised their young geldings. Everywhere the sound of thumping hooves on the sandy soil and the fluttering wings of sparrows nesting in the rafters. I glanced at the corner where the steel fingers of a forklift were dripping with hay-strewn dung. It was moist and still warm, the humid vapour rising, the sodden yellow hay lit by a beam of filtered sunlight. The spirited rank of horse manure stirred my dulled senses. The police quarters were vacant, but other bays showed flapping tails and blue-blooded snouts pushing through the ironwork of the elm stalls. A girl in golden jodhpurs lugged buckets of water from horse to horse. The animals dipped their noses and sloshed their rope-like tongues. A man wearing a bushy mustache greeted us disdainfully. He curled his lips around a soggy unlit cigar and sneered at my bedraggled horse. JoeHow was led to a whitewashed corner and sponged clean. He rolled his world-weary eyes as they plied off his time-worn shoes, filed and buffed his hooves, and gave him scant shelter in a cramped cell.

"You got his papers?" asked the same man.

"No," I said, quite certain that JoeHow had never had any papers.

"No? Listen lady, I'm not about to hide a stolen horse."

"He's not stolen. Honest." The only proof was in our matching chaps and saddle. The manager stared wolfishly at the stunningly beautiful workmanship, but he wasn't persuaded.

"There's no hiding from the law here. You saw the police."

"You can have the saddle," I offered, "the saddle and the horse, free of charge. How could you turn that down?" JoeHow glowered from behind his stall door and smote my conscience.

I won't deny that I betrayed him. I asked for nothing in return, as if he were worthless — though unremittent guilt depicted his future exploits. I saw his bones in bubbling vats at the glue factory, his hide stretched, cured and cut into wallets, his hair sown into suit jackets. I watched his big-barrelled body broken down into parts and devoured by the all-consuming market. Better him than me, I thought, and cushioned my remorse with lies and excuses too shameless to recount here. Disposing of JoeHow was necessary, I decided, if my reckoning was to be more than mere public nuisance.

Just then a sparrow dove down and flew between his cocked ears. He shifted his weight on enormous immaculate flanks. The manager chewed loudly on his cigar, and again the wolfish look as if struck by some ingenious idea. "Okay lady, I'll keep your horse. Where can I reach you?"

I showed the manager a crumpled piece of paper on which was written Sarah's address. He asked for my signature on a contract. I signed without reading it. I wanted to flee immediately from the sham haven and the loyal but reproachful JoeHow. My mind was littered with muddled images: the rawboned JoeHow bucking the red-headed trader, then sold to the circus, and finally his head mounted on my mother's bowsprit. I deny ever devising these vengeful thoughts. They arrived like visitations sent to spoil my prospects. I swallowed their foretaste and cleared my head and promptly forgot them. I asked the manager for directions to Sarah's address. He pointed through the palace doors. "Go to Parkdale," he dared me, his ragged lips clamping down on the cigar. "Just follow the cops."

I walked away, slow and swerving, my gait forever changed. Gone was the horse once snug between my legs, gone was my yoke, my link to the land. I was stunned to discover such bereaved sentiments. I felt divided from my better half, as if in his absence I hovered sixteen-hand up off the ground. I felt disabled, having only two legs instead of four. I loitered at the Parkdale Library, browsing through books about the neighbourhood. It was heartening to learn that rich industrialists had once retreated to the gentle lakeshore where Sarah now lived. Pictures in a book showed city founders at the close of their daily trade, leaving behind the dirt of downtown business to join long-skirted wives on pastoral lawns. The muck however had gradually made its way west and Parkdale sank into decrepitude. The building of an insane asylum sent the God-fearing folk further out into safer suburbs. A wave of poor and sometimes demented people rolled in, a slow rising of the born-to-be-blacklisted and, with them, their entrapments. Parkdale became the edge of the city, a last-stop chance before the deep ravine, the lake, the highways, and the untouchable prosperity that lay beyond. I wondered why Sarah lived in such neglected surroundings. Rumour had always been that Sarah was born with a horseshoe up her ass. Surely she deserved a penthouse suite in a more prosperous part of town? I hoped there had been some sort of mistake, but I was reluctant to know whether it was mine or hers. And suddenly I was in no hurry to find her.

Outside on the street, strays approached me with chatty street-corner invitations, lewd suggestions, and coin requests. Parkdale was awash with chatterers, whether they had companions or not. I sat on a bench and glanced up at the arched windows and florid masonry of the second storeys that teetered like top hats on the dollar stores at ground level. Displayed for sidewalk sales were plastic substitutes of all kinds. I followed the example of others and rummaged through bins of weakly woven cloth stamped with patterns of leopard, alligator, sun and moon. Everywhere the scraping sound of grinding gearshifts as guilty trucks carried the junk in and out of the district. Everywhere street stooges and homeless weekend releases. I watched shadows shrink beneath listing bodies, the mad sun directly above, and sensed the unanswered in sedated fish-eyes. A woman reached out for change and caught the sun in her palm. Noon seemed to be a time of grace in Parkdale. The precious hour when the day divided in two: the wakeful rise of morning, the recline of afternoon. Even the gaunt prostitutes looked radiant, their faces full of light, their asses lit as they leaned into car windows. I passed a tattooed man resting his wasted arms on his meagre hips. Of the seven blue scrawled names on his shrivelled biceps, I could make out only mine. Mary.

The Lucky Donut Shop was empty save three elderly men squished into swivel seats and spaced two tables apart. They sat smoking peacefully and studying the street antics. The smell of sticky doughnuts and bland coffee saturated the air. I ordered a double chocolate from the rows of segregated doughnuts. My first bite broke the ring, right through to the empty centre. Powdery crumbs fell from my lips. The spongy cake dissolved easily in my mouth. A doughnut, I decided, was a perfect thing. A circular, single surface, a mystery, a hole that was neither a way in nor a way out. I imagined the doughnuts bubbling in hot vats of oil, a kind of origin to the universe. The sea of doughnuts from which we had all evolved. I feared that mine was the kind of quaint theory adhered to by the dispossessed. I looked up at the waitress, a sugary white doughnut hovering above her head like a halo. I looked at the three pudgy sedentary men in their swivel seats, forgotten, stale, jelly-filled.

A woman, who I presumed was a recently released psychiatric patient, pressed her face against the coffee-shop window, singling me out as if she knew what I was thinking. Red, unctuous lipstick circled her eyes like war paint. The same oily stuff was smeared around her lips. She flattened her nose against the glass, as a grey dusty tongue licked at the corners of her mouth. I winced and prayed that I might be saved from such a horror. Only a thin sheet of glass separated our two faces. I patted my thin greasy hair much like her own few strands she wore coiled around pink curlers. "Go away," I heard myself say and watched as she pushed herself off the glass with two cracked palms pressed up beside her face. She pitched back on her heels and left me the smudged imprint of her life. Traces of the tiny cracks and pores of her skin remained as seams and trenches in the oily smear, an unbearable reminder of how easily one could fall from grace. I rose abruptly, unable to stand the sight any longer and rushed out of the coffee shop and onto the street.

Dusk came all purple and bruised. The day's residue rays curled over the westward streets and surrendered to the city's electric glow. Shiny surfaces of all kinds doubled the effect and advanced what seemed to be a second dawn. I was suspicious of the neon blush, as if it were a disguise, as if the night had been stolen by the thief of nights and the sky was simply paper painted black. At any moment the scene might collapse and the world would fall into ruin. Thoughts of Sarah offered so little solace I began to suspect that it was she who caused my consternation. I asked the occasional stranger where her street lay, but I didn't listen, I didn't go, I didn't want her to see me weak-willed and destitute. I didn't want to remind her of my frequent failings as her misshapen cousin and unlucky kin. I didn't want to arrive on her doorstep the same loser she had left behind a year earlier.

I followed my nose to the lake where thirteen lanes of demon-speed secured the shoreline. I took the foot bridge which arched over the expressway. A few other fragile pedestrians hurriedly did the same. I rushed to the other side where a paltry beach ran parallel to the loud angry lanes. The sand was as hard as cement. I crouched down and drilled my thumb into it. There were no broken shells, no crab legs, no rotting jellyfish. The sluggish lake sat useless beside the coursing traffic. I felt endangered, like a small infected fish in a dying lake, gradually adapting to my environment of doom. The city lights and chains of headlights overshadowed the lake and blotted out the shoreline. I had to rely on faith and the peevish sound of hesitant waves, in believing I walked beside a lake and not on the precipice of an ominous black hole between two nations.

Hungry, I returned to Queen Street and entered the Honest Variety Store. The proprietor watched me with unfaltering fear and circumspection. I peeled two sticks of licorice from the conglomeration on the counter and threw my last pennies near the cash register. A group of boys in red berets, candy-red bomber jackets and watermelon military pants surrounded a woman in front of the store window. She swayed from side to side in high heels and fluorescent lycra leggings. She scratched her crotch with blade-like nails and pushed her other scissor-hand through the bog of black roots on her blond head. With each venomous word that was spat, her white vinyl purse swung from her hip and knocked against her studded belt.

"You don't know a fuckin' thing! You're just a fuckin' fuck! You don't even live around here! I do! And I work here too! And if business is bad, I'm gonna move my ass over to your fuckin' neighbourhood!"

One of the red berets crouched and tightened the laces in his army boots. He chewed his bubble gum like JoeHow chomped grain. His jaw was wide like a shovel. Sweat collected on his upper lip beneath a large oval mole where sprouted a single wiry hair. His eyes were full of suspicion and shifted up and down the sidewalk, his lids heavy with surveillance. A shaft of fluorescent light floodlit his crimped white hair, which glowed like the seared feathers of a bird too near the sun. He rose and readjusted his beret, then nervously tore and repressed the velcro straps of his fingerless vinyl gloves. A battle between doing and undoing that exposed the silver Medic-Alert bracelet around his wrist. When he doled out a custodial smile, I impulsively repaid the gesture and couldn't help but warm to him. He was handsome. His big flat forehead shone like polished leather. I wanted to reach over and imprint my finger onto the lustrous surface. I wanted to squeeze the tight vinyl gloves, to slip my fingers under that velcro strap and feel his hyperactive pulse knocking against his medical bracelet. I hoped, through contact, to seize his sense of purpose. I hoped to tap his strength. Here was my first cordial encounter.

"Lost?" he asked, pushing his gob of gum aside to allow for greater freedom of speech. I showed him the piece of paper with Sarah's address. He examined it carefully, flattening the folds and creases, holding it up to the light, and turning it over and over in his palm. He bit his lip, the mole stretched, the wiry hair twisted. I followed his darting eyes as he assessed the situation. A man walked by with three whippet dogs attached to a tripartite leash. Their bony pinheads popped up and down like parts of an automatic sewing machine. The sound of shuffling flip-flops came from across the street where another shop owner watched the proceedings.

"Follow us," my red beret commanded.

The traffic light turned green and a songbird chirped to guide the blind.

"Follow you?" I asked, utterly surprised.

"Yeah. We're going that way."

A spiral of dust swirled in the gutter at my side, whipping and whirling pop cans, paper, and dirt. A grackle swooped down to inspect the rising swirl for edible insects. Finding none, he flew away and landed on a swollen transformer strapped to the top of a telephone pole. I was pining for male affection, but was woefully stunted in all sexual matters. Mating was for two-hundred-year-old tortoises and beach bums, and love was an exchange of obsessions for tulips. I watched the spinning wind rise up the trunk of a stately chestnut tree, rustle the drooping fan leaves and knock together the small green fruit that hung in pairs. Men, like the wind, seemed a primary cause of all movement, a source of action and reaction, an invisible force to be reckoned with. And like my father, they could either blow you over or retreat defensively at a moment's notice. I eyed the grackle and felt an itchiness crawl into every pore. I stared at the handsome boy's face and was soothed by the sight of the well-greased white wavelets lapping at his ear. His shovel-jaw jerked up and down as he chewed his compassion, a rubbery white speck appearing and disappearing between his lips. Could this be the wind I needed? The grackle screeched, the woman swore to high heaven, and the oily boy stood staunchly in his puffed-up inflammable jacket.

"Nice part of town, eh?"

"Yeah." I nodded and smiled shyly.

"I'm joking of course."

The patrol leader threw his head back and drained a can of pop, wiping away the stray driblets with the back of his glove. His cheeks were bloated, as if struggling to digest an excessively large meal consumed minutes earlier. He belched and the patrol marched on. I followed at the end of the two-by-two formation. "Basically a buddy system," said the boy beside me, spitting his gum onto the nearby sewer grates. He bounced up and down, his eyes skirted the sidewalk, and he nodded a greeting to all the single women. Without the compulsion of chewing, his jaw hung open, and a spade-like tongue rested on his lower lip. Glances from the people of Parkdale were less than encouraging. Amblers rolled their eyes at the ripples of concern sent forth from the vigilant gang. An older woman stopped in her tracks and glared, as if even the presence of slapdash soldiers put her in mind of a homeland raped and pillaged. A horde of kids hung out on a corner, posing like stick-legged cormorants on the one dry rock protruding from the sea. They stared menacingly at what the tide brought in — a mock military sent to monitor their behaviour, a youth gang to which I unwittingly belonged.

We halted in front of a darkened doorway where an unconscious drunk lay vulnerably splayed, his inflated limbs barbed at oblique angles. The caked blood on his forehead, the jetsam from a neglected wound, kept his hair pasted in an oddly respectable way.

"Hey, buddy, need some help?" shouted the patrol leader. The drunk promptly withdrew his body deeper into the protective darkness of the doorway and opened his jaundiced eyes a sliver. He gurgled and flapped his arms against the stone like a beached whale.

"You gotta home?" asked the wall of steel toes.

"Fauwk Awff!" he spat back.

I looked away and saw a leathery hand grope the enormous ass of a woman. Her dirty white skirt ballooned beneath the pawing. Her arms were straight at her side, each hand holding a beer bottle. Her head nodded uncontrollably as she shook with laughter. She pressed herself into her grappling crony, his case-hardened hands now tugging at her hem. The brick wall behind them cockled with the weight of their leaning bodies. Each zigzag crumbling cement seam rippled as the wall heaved, the old brick tired of witnessing such sleazy love. The building long since condemned. The man buried his haggard face in the woman's hanging bosom. She heeled from the hips and drank from one of her half-empty bottles.

The soles of my boots were sticky from sugary puddles. I looked around at the red berets, their discipline much like my brothers. "Here's Sorauren Avenue," said my marching companion, his shaved and prickly neck like a thorny spindly rose stem. "Thanks," I mumbled, and promptly snubbed him. I should never have trusted a soldier whose gallant sport was chasing vagrants, even though I felt like an indigent on the rebound from lawless Bay Street. But the boy easily shrugged me off and forged ahead with the rest of the foot patrol.

The old drunk tried to hide himself under his seedy raincoat. The smell of urine added another protective spread. His vivid stink set my memory aflame. An almost blinding recollection revealed a science lesson by my father: that smell was the most privileged sense in the dark subaqueous world. With his own shoes so cheesy they caused others to choke, my father explained how water transported chemical messages like no other medium. I pictured his sea-bottom grave, his unclipped toenails and high-arched feet. I watched his crooked legs sweep back and forth with each gentle wave, alongside swaying sponges, corals, and weeds. I found myself wondering if his nuptial disputes nourished dreams of an odorous intercourse, dreams of a world where emotions were diffused. I wondered if Parkdale would have suited him. The streets were inundated with smells, some spicy and others gritty and sour, and all commingled and shared the street. My arms swung loosely as I swam through the aromas until finally the lake's fragrance dominated all others. A polluted lake, not yet completely dead, it emitted a pharmaceutical rank, a clean toxicity on top of approaching death, like an old lady, too weak to bathe, who swabs perfume on her ancient flesh.

Sarah answered the door wearing a blood-red kimono tied tightly around her small waist. The silk had such rich depth, but seemed without texture, without end, as if a hollow space and not a surface. The red folded into waves of light and dark, and when I timidly touched it, the cool slippery absence made my fingers tremble. She stepped back, out of the lamplight, and a shadow collected above her delicate collarbone, a murky shallow at the base of her neck. A shallow that prompted a memory of waves coursing up a beach channel and filling the moat of a sand castle, while two bikini-clad children jumped up and down with delight. The warmth of summer pulsed through my memory and I grinned like a baby.

She knit her brow and narrowed her dark eyes, as if she didn't recognize me. I assured myself she was half-asleep and forgave her for the long disarming silence. Finally she responded in a slow dopey drawl.

"Holy shit. What are you doing here?"

I heard the reproach in her lumpish words and swallowed my remaining pride. What was I doing there on her doorstep? What did I want from her? If I hoped to reminisce, then I was badly out of luck. That one goading question lay waste to my nostalgia and brought back the branding of those difficult years when a cold shoulder and a sweaty handshake were all that she would offer me. I stammered at nothing. Why hadn't I prepared some pat answer? Some quick and easy way to justify my visit? I racked my brain for something she might applaud.

"I'm here to make my fortune." It sounded good to me.

"Then you've come to the wrong place, sweetheart," she said grinning, her lips crooked, their corners chewed.

She had never called me sweetheart before, and never sounded so sluggish and stupid. Was this an imposter? I looked over my shoulder in search of JoeHow. If only I could see his big apple ass, his stolid countenance, his beautiful weak knees, if only then I might be comforted.

"How've you been?" I asked shyly, but she didn't answer.

"You look great," I lied. She looked lousy. She had aged a hundred years. Her skin was permanently plum-wrinkled as if from prolonged periods in water. She shifted her weight from one pale white foot to the other. Then relented and opened wide the door.

"It's been a long time," she said, her head nodding, as if counting seconds. Time had obviously sped up for Sarah.

"Do I look different?" she asked.

"No. Not really. Well, maybe a little," I waffled.

That night she drove me to the oyster bar where she worked, left me at a small, round table, and disappeared into the kitchen. I sat sipping my complimentary ginger ale and watched, incredulous, when she reappeared minutes later. The kitchen staff carried her out and perched her on the glass wall of a large aquarium. She was naked above the waist and sheathed in a glittery scaley fish tail below the waist. Two bubblers oxygenated the enormous tank, which had been draped in black cloth, but now glowed an eerie sea green in the inky black bar. The water was smokey with algae and fish debris. Snails slithered across the glass; their oily trails streaked the tank. Live crabs scuffled and lobsters lumbered amongst the foreign coins strewn on the glass floor.

No amount of knowing in advance could have adequately prepared me for Sarah the topless mermaid in her life-sized sinkhole. She had always been an aquatic wonder, always the first to dive if dared, but such a grievous misuse of her talents was beyond comprehension. What made it worse was the awful violation of my father's innocent science, those once familiar marine tubs made tawdry. The oyster bar was an offense against his basement brand of reason. He would have cursed the world and buried his head in his sludge grave at the sight of a skin-trade aquarium. I could hardly make sense of it myself. I sat with my jaw slack, a mouthful of fizzy ginger ale at the back of my throat. The ticklish carbonic fizz increased my sense of dismay. I sorely regretted impounding JoeHow, the only companion who had served me well. I imagined him cropping heavenly paddocks in an after-life. "Told you so," I thought I heard him say in a sleepy voice, but it was the voice of the bartender, who then announced the sea starlet Sarah, "Our own sultry mermaid direct from the East Coast."

She cambered back, balancing on the aquarium rim. The breasts that had become her future glistened, large and alluring beneath the spotlight. Her thick brown hair now curly and slick on her shoulders, her nose pinched shut with a clamp, her legs encased in a rubbery tail of electric glittery green. She flapped her forked flipper and sent waves slapping against the sides of the aquarium. Then she shoved off the edge and slipped in, caudal fin first.

A few attentive fans applauded as she tumbled and gyrated, bending and arching with each kick, her iridescent tail fluttering, her hair undulating in the green light. She swam in circles, weaving between the plastic fronds and sinking lily pads, over the glass bottom and through the giant conch shell. She pressed her bewitching white bosom against the glass and stroked her laminated lower half. One of her plastic eyelashes unfastened and floated away. A small fish bolted toward the eyelash, gulped as if to swallow it, but spat it out instead. Sarah ignored the minor setback, wagged her tail, paddled the soupy water. I couldn't help but admire her show-girl grit. She let loose a ball of air from her lungs, and sculled down toward the bubbler. She puckered her lips, wrapped her mouth around a thick pipe and sucked in the oxygen mix. Beside me, an excited customer slurped from a purplish shell and swallowed his last oyster. I surveyed the room, amazed. Trays piled up everywhere with oyster carapaces showing rough elongated exteriors like wizened ears. Short flickering candles scattered on tables about the room lit drawn faces in ghastly shadow. Men mouthing the plump coppery Olympia or the briny Buctouche, swallowing the raw meat swaddled in its own liquor, their cocktails rising to their thin lips, their thoughts made randy by the brackish siphon, and everywhere the sound of slurping and the clinking noise of tossed shells.

The bar was a haven of craven Bay Street boys, each pretending that he alone lived a depraved and double life. Someone more savvy than myself would have seized the opportunity. Someone more shrewd would have ingratiated herself. If nothing else, I might have stolen a few business cards, but I was still reeling from my experience at the Exchange and had invested all my hope in Sarah. I sat waiting for a sign from her. I don't know precisely why, perhaps mere momentum kept me devoted. I examined her every gesture for hidden meaning. I watched as she floundered in the tank, first horizontal, then slanted with her heavy tail scuttled on the glass floor. She placed fish food shavings between her stupendous mounds and enormous gold fish darted about her nipples and snapped up the grub from her breasts. Glassy-eyed, unblinking, and unappreciative, the fish leered at her cleavage, their membraneous scales scraping her belly. The pointed snout of a dogfish butt in and bit one of the pretty fishes in half. A chorus of "Aahh" came from the crowd, myself included, at this impressive show of aggression. Sarah casually pushed aside the rubble and placed a snapping crab on her right breast. It swung its claws like cleavers, grazing the tender skin and nipping at her nipple, but never once catching flesh. Bubbles of air streamed out of her mouth and clung to the edge of her painted lip. The crowd clapped and hooted.

I bemoaned the day she had been so beautifully built in such classic proportions. When she joined me after the show, I could hardly look her in the eye.

"Before you say a word, answer me this: have you ever gambled?"

"No," I muttered into my lap.

"Do you think risk is a four-letter word?"

I didn't know what to say. She lit a cigarette and raised her eyebrows, astounded at the poverty of my life.

"Yes," I replied, thinking the obvious might be true in this case.

"Wrong. Risk isn't a word. It's a way of living. I'll give you an example. Me and this guy just got back from Las Vegas. A real saucy guy. He kept spilling drinks in my lap because he liked my wet mermaid thighs."

I only nodded.

"He was a creep, I should have known better," she groaned, her smoke-laden syllables deepening the drama, her sad swooning eyes roaming the room. For a moment, I wondered why she hadn't known better, but the question quickly passed into oblivion, unanswered. I would sooner leave than admit that her brain had been damaged from too little oxygen. My mind sought solace in more abstract questions: did the plane coast on the wind, or was it pure rocket, its wings a mere romantic gesture? Did it fly high in the cloud-quilted sky, above sun-scorched plains and infallibly straight roads, or dangerously low? Dumb questions, but just the evasive sort I relished when faced with the floundering truth. Especially then, with buxom Sarah still dripping before me, offering her list of lurid details: the airline devilled eggs and plastic pitchforks, the cinnamon-flavoured sweet mints, the stale cabin air, and the impatience of her companion, who grabbed her and the carry-on baggage upon landing, bolted off the plane and pushed through the gambling hordes to the car rental desk.

"He insisted we see the desert first, the desert first before the casinos."

The desert conjured images of the ocean's opposite, an arid landscape, a sweltering vista of wind-blown contours without bedrock or bottom. The creaking sound of soil baking in the sun, and the retentive, resilient flowers that braved the ruinous climate. I had always regarded the staunched and sterile desert sand as an emblem of the end, as if time's remote intention was to sap the planet dry. I pictured the sooty blur swelling up behind the car as Sarah and her guy raced past bleached stones, parched shrubbery, and nondescript carcasses, toward a few gallant cliffs that stood up against the stressful expanse. It was without question a mermaid's nightmare. "I was really thirsty," she said, and for her sake I tried to will my imaginary clouds into cumulous proportions, filling them with fluffy down until busty and creviced and full of water. I strained to make the desert more merciful. I filled a shimmering mirage with clean water and sent Sarah, like a vanquished Eve, to step into its cool undressing.

"God, it was hot! We were both covered in dust. I followed him up a hill. He kept palming the soil, examining handfuls of small rocks, searching for what, I didn't know. And I didn't care. I just sucked on the saliva in my cheeks and watched for snakes. And then finally he found his chunk of pyrite, his little piece of fool's gold, and placed it very ceremoniously on my palm." She tapped at her water-wrinkled palm with a painted nail. She tapped at her lifeline where the chunk of phoney gold had sat like a blockade upon her future. I saw it flare and flicker under the blazing desert sun and wondered whether a similar token had squashed my own fortune. The flying anchor shank came to mind, for there was no denying that the shank had stacked the odds against me. I listened to her story and decided that life was cruelly determined by inanimate objects, with no one to blame, not even the men who threw them. I pictured her man hot and bothered, his soggy chest-mat seen through his sweat-soaked shirt. I watched as the drops of salt-roiled smut tumbled off his cheek and onto hers.

"It was a mistake," she confessed.

"What? The desert?"

"No. No. The guy. He was the wrong guy."

Sarah saw culprits where I imagined invisible forces. She saw creeps where I saw destiny.

"Later, at the casinos, we played the wheel and raked in the chits. But at the first sign of losing, the asshole excused himself from the table and was never seen again. I vaguely remember dropping the pyrite into my martini glass and stumbling away with my bucket of coins. I must have shoved them all into one of those fruity slot machines. I remember lemons. Always lemons."

She told her story in abject tones, and I couldn't help but think that this mawkish desert romance was her finest triumph, and that the telling of the tragic tale was her vocation. She went on to tell other heart-wrenching tales. In only one short year she had squirrelled away quite a handsome collection. She thought her stories proof of her intrepid nature. The perils of her algae pool, the desert fraught with danger, the many risks she had taken in only one year. Our original golden friendship was deeply buried. Far below the refuse crouched the little girl I had once known like the first shell on which a coral reef is built. Layers upon layers of needy lives had since clamped to her wet and well-endowed body. Every crack and cranny claimed by some hungry soul. Every one of her movements and gestures mapped out passages already taken, devotions already bought and sold. How foolish of me to expect open arms, an apology for my betrayal, and a promise to always include me. My fierce adolescent envy returned with a vengeance. I hated her for once again denying me. I hated her fate so suddenly determined at the side of a Halifax bonfire.

"Sarah, you're a wreck." I had to say it.

"Maybe. But at least I'm taking chances."

I spent the night in a spare bed in her dark, damp basement. My makeshift independence scrambled between the sheets. I was exhausted. The smell suggested a recent flooding, or just an abiding basement miasma. From above my head came the sound of bath water released and rippling through the building's pipes. Sarah was draining her bath. She had been soaking herself in strong solvents to kill whatever fungus had anchored to her. I imagined her removing barnacles, snails, and unknown slimes from her puckered skin. The dank air around me was filled with the hissing and cranking as her soapy water strained the metal joints. The sounds brought back reluctant images of the bar where she worked. I should never have gone, I said to myself, my eyes following the twisting pipes, my ears the gurgling water. I should never have listened to her late-night confession. I lay on that mouldy mattress, my hands cupped over my ears, unable to stop the sound of water flowing from the basement out into larger pipes and sewers beneath the sidewalk. I heard it purling down the breathless stinky siphons, pressure pumped to treatment plants and ultimately poured back into the lake.

Sleep suddenly circulated through me like a poison. I dreamt that I was stark naked. My wrinkly toes at the edge of a springboard. A black oily liquid below, the night dark, cold, and foreboding. The stars spun spirals above me, confused and chaotic, their paths unpredictable. An unearthly silence sprawled over the flat lake. I shivered. My body lit by the unruly stars and made luminous white like a beacon. No way to cover my shame save diving in. The pitch black my secret salvation, as the sound of tittering voices approached at my rear. The deep moan of a foghorn travelled across the water. No way to treat the circumstance with reason. My mind alert and yet absent, my mind like a machine, alive only to the gas lake. "Don't drop a match," whispered a voice behind me, but I didn't dare turn. The springboard began to bounce without my doing. Up and down, each bounce higher than the last. I swung my arms hard and lifted off. The air brushed roughly against my bare skin. Thrust high into the starry night, and still higher, until wary of the height, and the crash to come, I pressed my hands in prayer, my arms outstretched, and prepared for the deadly plummet. Heavy with gravity, I fell, faster and faster, the slick oil racing toward me. At any moment I would slice the opaque surface and enter that black smothering viscous world. At any moment plunging into that dreadful lake. But always postponing the final submerging instant, like only a dream can do. Not quite yet, and again once more denied. My mind repeatedly censoring the worst moment, keeping at bay the inevitable, until the moment itself abruptly overpowered me, and finally I felt the cool transforming *swoosh!* The sudden crawl of liquid from my fingertips up over every inch of me, tickling the tiny hairs and the goose-pimpled skin, like a huge unwanted embrace. Deeper and deeper. The inertia of my plunge pulling me down through the slithery water. Just a little further and I would reach the bottom. But the bottom never came. Every blood vessel screamed out for oxygen. Every muscle like soft butter. My lungs ached under the crushing pressure. And finally when my fingers touched the sandy floor, to my horror, it felt slippery and unsound. My heart sank into the sludge. I paddled feebly against my dragging weight, having nothing buoyant within me, and the surface fathoms away. I panicked, trying with such despairing effort to rewrite the dream, that suddenly a surge of energy and air opened me, and I awoke.

My reason was restored, at least for the moment, and yet I cannot remember what passed through my mind upon waking. I know I did not want to interpret the dream, which felt like the swaddling of death. I quickly freed myself, opened my eyes and saw a tattered poster of Venus. She held the ends of her long golden hair between her pearl-white buxom hips and stood squarely on a giant seashell. The grooves of the arched shell fanned out from umbo to edge. Her freshly born bosom was entirely erect. Her neck was tilted as if wrenched, and the slope of her shoulder was too steep to be properly hinged. She looked double-jointed, I thought with envy. She looked like someone wise to her own charms. She floated on choppy waves and delicate foam, the lapping sea turquoise against the brown snaking shore. Her flying companions blew hot air in her direction as if to set free her tendrils and completely disrobe her. I envied the lustful wind at her back that would bring her ashore, where another beauty waited to receive her. The pomp of her arrival mocked my own dreary one. Here was someone who was offered a hearty reception.

My own surroundings were meagre. Three small windows offered limited ventilation in the small room. An anaemic dash of natural light reached through and lit a small patch of grey cement. The bed rested on four uneven legs. The small pads of felt, used for balance, had shifted during the night. My mouth was dry, my lips chapped, a residue wetness between my legs. The dream was still riding my beating heart when I climbed the stairs and entered the bathroom.

Shower water soon drummed at my crown with a loud lulling noise. I stood studying the ring around the tub, the stain from Sarah's soiled existence. I worked the olive oil soap bar into a thick lather that cloaked my body like fleece. I smeared it onto my cheeks and forehead and let the warm spray wash it away. The thick plastic shower curtain showed a map of the world. The continents were bright primary colours and the sea transparent. I stood beside China, the dilated underside of the flattened sphere. Meandering droplets streaked the curtain. Steam rose and misted the plastic. The Galapagos Islands, where I had once imagined myself belonging, were pink unlikely specks surrounded by sea. Soap lather and the dirt from my journey collected between my toes and at my heels. I scooped up a handful and noticed a white spider hunched in a dry corner, his web long since sucked into the drain. He moved abruptly behind the curtain and hid there on the backside of the South Pole. I watched him slide and scramble with all eight gangly legs. The water pounded at my head, poured over my face and pooled in my ears. The roar and gentle pummel slackened my muscles and eased my mind. It felt like rain, a soft warm rain. The stream pelted my chest and sounded a hollow space within my ribs. I opened my mouth and let the water fill my cheeks, pressed my gapped teeth against my lip and squirted spray at the Galapagos Islands.

I forgot Sarah's story in the pounding stream. My thoughts turned to an earlier day when the world was still round. A foggy, pensive day, so foggy the ground on the south shore had turned to mist. The mist cooled and thickened the air and licked the hard surfaces slick. Sarah and I pushed through it, feeling each water drop condense and cling to our skin. My bleak house floating on the creeping smoke, its chimney swaying, its porch silent. We snuck down the cement stairs to the forbidden basement and squatted on the last step, keeping close to a quick exit. From the laboratory came the usual sound of motors gently pumping and water bubbling up, but something was different. Sarah elbowed my ribs and pointed. I glanced over, through the mesh of wire, and saw my father sitting cross-legged and naked on the cold concrete floor. He stared into a tank, transfixed by a few slow-moving snails and nothing else. Grey light from the basement window came refracted through the tank water and lit his sad face.

The shower water pounded at my chest, the sound so hollow I feared nothing was within. My heroine floundering in her sinkhole, my father drowned off the salt-and-pepper granite of Chebucto Head. When I saw him naked in the basement, his frail frame hunched over, his hungry eyes sopping up that other beloved world of bottom-dwellers, I wished I could set him free. I wished him away and into that murky green water, under into soundlessness, where his painful slurs would be muffled and perfect bubbles would double for his speech. Underwater, where he would finally feel the embrace of a calm quiet solitude.

Sarah knocked on the bathroom door.

"Are you coming?" she asked.

"Where?" I shouted over the drumming water.

"To find your vocation. You can't stay here forever."

Her words hung dampened in the steamy bathroom. Solemn, wet words. *Your vocation*. Yes, my vocation, my timid future, thickly saturated and hanging dearly onto the bacterial air. Allowed only one night under her roof and already my own nascent underwater career was to be pursued. I felt weak and vulnerable, my lungs too feeble for the depths that I feared Sarah had in mind. Another mermaid at the oyster bar. Another maritime misfit. I dreaded that. If nothing else, my bulk would flood that damn aquarium and send a gagging spray over all the customers. Surely that would be bad for business. I turned off the water, scrambled out of the slippery tub and patted myself dry with her wet stinky towel.

The day was severely sunny. We walked quietly together and stopped in front of a Queen Street store window. Above our heads hung a swinging sign that read *CASH FOR GOLD* in resolute block letters. The wind buffeted the thin board and rasped at the hinges. We cupped our eyes against the glass to eliminate the glare. I drew shallow nervous breath, as if already submerged and short on oxygen and sucking on the bubbler pipe. I leaned my forehead into the glass and looked down at my dark indefinite shadow, no more than a smudge wedged between wall and sidewalk. Sarah shifted her weight from one high heel to the other. She kept her face against the glass, her painted nails like a red steeple closing over her brow. Sarah, my bosom-buddy, my love. Where was the Sarah of the underwater tea parties? Where was Sarah the expert spy? She swayed on her high heels and worshipped the purple velvet beyond the glass, where the finest of relinquished belongings lay. Chunky engagement rings, platinum cigarette cases, china dolls, all pawned at some precipitous moment when their sentiment was revoked and their pledge forgotten. "Every promise has a price," said Sarah, studying the precious objects that sat naked in the window, all the more inviting for having once been intimate and intended forever.

"Remember how we used to spy on people?" I asked.

"Yeah," she replied, distracted.

"Remember when we saw my father naked?"

She was silent.

"You don't remember?"

"No."

But she was there, I was sure of it. She had watched him, greedily, her big brown eyes wide with fascination. She had put her hand over her mouth to keep from laughing. How could she forget? Crouched on the stairway watching the old geezer meditate. How could she ever forget that? I remembered every unfortunate detail, including afterward, when we ran from the house and along the shore, and she screeched, "What a crazy bastard," her voice deriding me, her laughter stabbing sharp, and my tears tight in the corner of my eyes for fear that she might notice them.

"Oh yeah, I remember now. In the basement, right? God, what a crazy bastard he was! You're lucky you survived. We spied on your brothers as well. We spied on a lot of guys, if I'm not mistaken." She moved away from the window and smiled with a tired coyness. "But I don't think you're the private-dick type. Too conspicuous."

I looked at my reflection. Conspicuous meant ugly. Wisps of fine hair were blown and twisted into knots about my small head. The flash of passing cars behind me, like an automated heartbeat. Each blip brought a deep hollow sound as cars drove over the sewer grate, each hollow sound felt in the very marrow of my bones. Sarah stood beside me, her shape top-heavy and teetering like a downtown office tower, her curls cascading over her shoulder and plummeting over her breasts. What did she know? A mermaid with a shattered heart. Did our maritime blood predispose us to oyster bars and fish markets and boat shows? Was there no way of casting off the sea? Sarah was a failure, I said to myself, reassuringly. I had principles that would keep me afloat, principles driving me to seek mettle and pluck. I would never get into an aquarium, I swore.

We entered the pawnshop. The walls were heavy with portraits and painted plates and gilded mirrors. A door chime clattered and called forth a large box-like figure behind the counter. It was a middle-aged woman, her face long and ungiving, her blouse buttoned up and tucked under her chin. Her eyes spoke permanent reproach, her look of appraisal disarming, as if too accustomed to the usual tale of broken promises and bad luck. Was she playing a guessing game? A kind of mental assessment of our debts? She patted her cotton-candy hair, which swirled up and off her head in a dry brittle cocoon. Then she leaned on her fat elbows and dared us to come closer. Curvaceous Sarah met the challenge, arched her back, pitched forth her chest and walked directly over, grabbing my hand and dragging me behind her. My principles had already pussyfoot their way into denial, my volition all but gone, my resolve no more than a faint murmur. That brief glimpse of mettle was already an elusive memory. I let Sarah pull me along, and, to be utterly frank, it felt better that way.

The woman withdrew her elbows from the counter and offered a pert smile on matted peach lips. Behind her a rear door opened onto a private living room, as equally cluttered as the showroom. Her husband sat at a desk squarely positioned so as to keep the cash register in sight. His doughy hands were mending various dispossessed valuables. He said something to his wife, placed his brush beside a chipped doll and spooned soup from a bowl to his lips. Beside him rested a thick book, a dealer's guide presumably, a mercantile bible in which, I imagined, were tables and tables of market prices. I was still ignorant at that point of the truly odd ways in which objects were valued. In my innocence I still believed that markets were simply places where commodities were exchanged.

"Do you like that one?" asked Sarah, impatient and surly, pointing at a grotesque necklace hanging around the headless torso of a display model. I tasted in the air the harmful vapour of sprays and time-resisting ointments. No, I hated necklaces. They were instruments of death, worn to tease the beloved with a strangler's dream, an invitation to choke, to sever head from body. I had borrowed my mother's on occasion, and found them imminently dangerous. From an early age Sarah had always been draped with the amorous gifts and had won numerous medallions for most valuable player. Perhaps it was only envy. I had to admit that the murderous necklaces were also emblems of faith, memory, and achievement, like leashes proving loyalty and obedience. And feeling particularly unloved, and especially useless, I told Sarah that I liked the one she had pointed to. I imagined the cold metal hanging above my heart, a brand of compassion, snug between my breasts. If there was death in devotion, then so be it. I prayed that Sarah would buy it for me as a measure of retribution, as a symbol of her love, or, if nothing else, to show me that she could and that her life was not as powerless as it seemed.

But instead she pushed her hand deep into her jeans pocket and produced a tangled mess of gold jewellery. Glittery chains, some with thick links, others slinky like snakeskin, twisted and coiled around stone-studded pendants, brassy horns, and flagging jewels. She opened a picture locket, removed a photograph, folded the thumb-sized face in two and shoved the tiny teen image into her tight pocket. I felt my heart sink, seeing the keepsake so easily overthrown. She had no intention of buying anything. I felt like a fool for having wanted what she now hoped to exchange for cold, hard currency. She set to work unravelling a charm bracelet of miniature American monuments and then unscrambled the other prizes of her youth. A pocket full of dating trophies, the tarnished collateral from lapsed affections, the handsels given in the hopes of high returns. She was pawning the entire collection.

The woman wedged an eyeglass into her eye, placed a square felt pad on the counter and stretched each chain, one by one, across the pad. She examined the clasps and the detail of the charms and pendants, tested the frailty of the links and weighed the gold in her hand. She blinked behind the lens, her eye magnified to glaucomic proportions. "Well?" asked Sarah. "What's it worth?" The woman heaved a heavy sigh, frowned and finally made her offer. Sarah rolled her eyes and responded with a much higher number. Estimates darted back and forth until my cousin shrugged her shoulders and reluctantly accepted the deal. "Robbed blind," she muttered, as she opened her palm to receive the countdown of dog-eared bills.

Outside in the harsh sun, she gave me the money. She took my limp wrist, turned my hand palm-up and closed my fingers over the bills. I was speechless. She had sold her trinkets, sacrificed her bounty, all on my account. Sarah my bosom-buddy, my long-lost pal, hawking her petting prizes for my sake only.

"It's not a gift!" She scoffed at my innocence. "It's an investment."

She had melted her memory banks hoping her revenue might double. My personal well-being was not at stake, my affections immaterial. "I'm gambling on your future," she said, her voice rich with venture. Our friendship was no more intimate than this game of Jeopardy. I was the slot machine, the roulette wheel, the betting board. I looked down at the fairly fat wad of dough.

"Now go on, go find yourself some man who will offer you the world," she said, grinning.

Sarah's investment dredged up the memory of my mother's shank money. An old wound was opened, and my sense of disaster rekindled. I was driven down beneath the city in search of hidden landscapes and found myself on a hushed subway platform. My spirit was plagued with morbid thoughts of scrambled suicide bodies tossed onto the tracks. I pictured the blood squirting out on cinder-block walls, the dressed limbs severed, the sad twisted heads ruptured, their necklaces thrown. Above the tracks hovered a footless angel in a white robe. The figure dove and swivelled and gyrated, just as Sarah did in the oyster bar. I rubbed my eyes in the hopes of obliterat-ing this new phantom. But the stagnant tunnel wind fed my ghoulish thoughts. I swallowed the stale breeze that came without brazen sea smells or saline taste. I glanced cautiously at the underground pageant of lone travellers, fearful that some freak might rush forward and push me onto the fatal tracks.

"Wanna be a movie star?" cracked a husky voice from somewhere near my knee. In a miniature blue swindler's suit, upright and less than half my size, stood a middle-aged dwarf. His oversized head was ponderously angled, his curly brown beard branched and skewed on his rotated chin. He stared up from big eyes sunk deep beneath his brow and bald crown, which was creased and wrinkled like tanned hide and which reached no higher than my thigh. But his size seemed to afford him an aggressive vantage. He raised his one ropy eyebrow and urged me to answer. "Want what?" I asked nervously. His thick hairy fingers grappled a clipboard the size of his torso, which he then shoved into my crotch. The string-tied pen swung like a pendulum and knocked against my knees. Clamped firmly to the board was a list of names and numbers. "Sign up," he said, "it's easy money."

I wondered if this was the man of whom Sarah spoke. In size and proportion he was my perfect match, our deviant body parts were exactly in reverse. We would make a dashingly odd couple, our differences perfectly resolved.

"What's easy money?" I asked.

"Wearing sequin gowns, partying in palatial suites, eating the finest gourmet foods. Just being a movie star, that's all."

I signed. How could I not? He was offering so much.

"Mary? Now, that's a pretty name. I can see it big and bold on the screen — Mary Seeburth, the hot new bombshell, starring in all the season's remakes."

I liked his vision. Of course he was only scouting for extras, for no-names to paper the scenes, but I didn't know that until later. And I was impatient to fulfil my calling. Determination had entered me as stealthily as a disease.

"Casa Loma, the big castle on the hill. Be there bright and early. The day after tomorrow." He spoke like a secret agent, his voice confiding and urgent.

He winked and sent a ripple across his crown. Big castles on hills sounded promising. Perhaps Sarah's ghost had risen in order to trumpet the little man's proposal. Her sacrifice justified in light of my coming success as a bombshell. "Be there, or be square," he added, guffawing as the train burst into the station. We both turned to watch the moving wall of sullen compacted faces plastered to the passing car windows. The doors slid open and out poured streams of discarded passengers. They flooded the platform, collided with other streams, cascaded down escalators and carried the dwarf away. I watched him jostled and jarred and spun round in the gushing swirl. Both of us ingested by the mob in different mouths and directions, his the outrushing turnstiles, mine the pinching push to catch the train. The mass urgency swarmed and seized my slow, tired soul. The crowd nudged and shoved and drew me in to the crowded car. Two warning bells chimed, the doors abruptly closed, and the train jerked forward. I grabbed the warm steel bar made sticky and slightly adhesive by the previous moist palm.

I fell in comfortably with the listless riders. The dwarf's invitation had bestowed a sense of belonging. I stood amongst commuters commuting and could sense that this was a peaceful time of postponement and anticipation. We had all graduated from the frenzied rush to the calm apathy of abiding distance. Everyone lingered, without choice, hypnotized by the clack of the rails and glad for the close uninhibited appraisal of others that was then allowed them.

A group of three private-school girls sat lovingly on each others' laps, their slender thighs ensnared, their socks down around their ankles. They lolled about in the space confined, saucy-coloured briefs beneath their tartan skirts and blouses untucked in disarray. They tickled, petted and giggled, arousing the rest with their intimate show. An anti-smoking poster above them said *Be Yourself*. I hovered over a seated passenger who sent them hungry glances. His suit was a thin knit of threads so harmonious their colours cancelled out. His flop of fire-engine red hair burned brightly below me. He sat cautiously upright on the hard seat, holding a folded financial paper and scanning the columns of price/earning ratios. The crease of his ironed pant was pressed flat between his knee and mine; his fine leather shoe touched toe-to-toe my worn shaggy boot. We were one amid the bump and bounce. He tilted his head and dropped the paper, his face suddenly lit in full fluorescence.

The light in the subway train was brutally humbling. It unveiled the scarred and unclean, revealed blemishes and thinning hair and pointed to the old and weary. But the face below me endured the harsh scrutiny. Any original defect or irregularity had slowly fallen in with gravity to furnish the valiant features of an older distinguished man. The imperial lines around his eyes were crossed with crow's-feet and resembled dollar signs. The skin, slackened from years of leisure, or so I thought, hung decorously off his cheekbones. He swallowed, his peaked Adam's apple rising, his august jowls quivering. He smiled at me and let a pink impulsive glow rosy his cheeks. Holy shit, I said to myself, borrowing Sarah's expression. Fate was muscling in on my future. I felt its heavy abiding presence amongst the commuters, their limp limbs jiggling with the rattling vibration. My frazzled nerves triggered déjà vu, and my fatigue fed the foggy sense of recognition. I shuddered to think that the same trader who had stood stock-still on the Exchange floor and had prompted others to spurn me was now sitting with his knee against mine.

"I do diversified investments," he announced without my asking, "and you have an investment to make."

"I do?"

"Yes. You do," he said with utter certainty.

The doors suddenly shuddered as another train passed, the two air currents colliding and tumbling into each other. I braced myself against the heave and toss as the train passed over a bumpy track transition. A woman rose from her seat and pushed through the congregation, warning passengers that the world would soon end. "God will flood the netherworld of electric snakes, and you will all drown!" she bellowed, a blue vein bulging from her thin-skinned temple. She wore two poster boards, front and back, with numbers and names of biblical significance spelled out in furious crayoned markings. The corners were dog-eared and ripped from trudging through unfaithful flocks. Woven into her hairnet were pieces of toilet paper, and around her wrists she wore bands and bands of candy bracelets. I recognized her as the same doomsayer who had hailed my arrival. I felt fate take a tighter hold. She brayed at the schoolgirls who strove to smother their laughter but failed. She shuffled toward me in shabby lace-free shoes, their dirty-white tongues flapping. My heart pumped, fearful that I was her target, that she had seen into my stricken conscience and would betray me to the other riders. Fearful that she would brand me with her prophecy of doom. She was not a good omen; I had learnt that much since my arrival.

I tried to dodge her divination, to hide from her crayoned predictions. I heard her dragging feet and heavy breath beside me. I sought the grey eyes of my broker and noticed his five o'clock shadow, the measure of the day's growth, of accumulated interest and swelling investments. He wore the stubble crop of red hair across his cheeks. It seemed to me that he flaunted this budding beard because it vouched that behind the clean shave of early morning lurked a lion or bear. This subtle civilized sign manifested his animal vitality and seemed to spook the prophetess, who turned her attention to another after laying her eyes upon him.

"What kind of investment?" I asked, as the train slowed.

"Of body and soul, of course," he replied and rose to his feet.

Through the windows seeped insidious station light that turned his shadowed face moss green. I was reminded of the soft fuzzy growth that carpeted seashores. I stared shamelessly at his face and found that my earlier fears had faded altogether. I felt instead a confused desire to follow him, anywhere. He fumbled in his inside pocket, pulled out a card and placed it in my palm. I felt its four sharp corners and the carved embossed hillocks of its message, but I kept my eyes on the redhead as he picked up his briefcase and went in the wake of the Armageddon lady, who was also disembarking. I struggled to do the same, but my passage was blocked. The other two escaped in the nick of time, just as the second bell chimed, and the doors slid shut.

Inscribed on the card in a bottom-heavy scrawl of gold inlay were the words: *Henry P. Gates, 222 Bay Street, Investment Risk Consultant*. I felt a romping rush of blood. Finally, here was an invitation to that miraculous strip, the source, the powerhouse! The summons came just when I least expected it. I could hardly believe my good fortune. I read the calling card again, certain that Sarah would approve of Mr. Gates, the man who had parted the sea of traders. I glanced through the window, trying to catch sight of the risk analyst who had dared solicit my presence at a money market. But the platform was already a blur, the train on its way. Benches blinked on and off between flashes of body parts, digital clocks, and the red flicker of public messages. I felt myself distended along with the platform, like the tiles consolidated into their glue seams and the fluorescent tubelights stretched into one continuous stream. The window turned black when we entered the dark tunnel. I saw my reflection in the glass. Larger than my neighbours, towering and off-balance, I leaned into the motion to steady myself. The needling light from above collected on the roofs of my sizable ears. They glowed like two swarms of fireflies on either side of my face. And although my head appeared even smaller than it was, I couldn't help but feel alive to my potential. I rode the subway back and forth, and back and forth, with Sarah's pawn money burning to be spent.

A spinning glass door churned brokers and bankers onto the sidewalk the following morning. The inward draft pulled me between spokes and spat me into the lobby, a cold marble echo chamber. Passing suits flashed their identity cards or greeted the security guard by name. They gathered before the row of mirrored elevators and watched the countdown of floor indices above the door, their heads nodding with each descent. Sesame openings invited them into carpeted compartments and sent them shooting up the elevator shafts into their cloud abode. Henry later told me how he and the others cherished that yummy feeling of sudden acceleration. He swore that many of his colleagues spent hours going up and down and were thrilled by their weakened knees and butterfly stomachs.

When I reached his executive suite Henry greeted me like an old friend. He squeezed my shoulders and said how very happy he was to see me. Two walls of his office were big chunks of blue sky. Fierce sunlight filled the room. A gold-tinted desk was aflame with reflection, the glare almost blinding. Henry wore dark sunglasses. His body was incandescent against the savage red carpet. My eyes tried to adjust to the radiant room, to what I surmised was the source of the Living Fire. Gradually I identified various odd inventions arranged on pedestals: wave machines, lava lamps, knocking steel balls, and other half-assed attempts at perpetual motion. He offered me black currant tea. We sat on bean-bag cushions filled with glass marbles.

"Business is bad," he admitted, his pin-striped legs spread over the mushrooming pillow. I nodded encouragingly and peeked out of the corner of my eye at his quaint machines. The market, he confessed, was too volatile. The risks were all too high. Currencies floated without anchor, dollars were shorted and discarded. Traders churned pension funds and predators seduced financial innocents. His psychic forecast a crash, a shipwrecked market, bankruptcy and even ruin, and all occasioned by the appearance of a doomful lady.

"You," he said, shifting on his cushion, the rasping sound of scuffed glass in the seat of his pants.

"Why me? Why not that other woman with the crayoned warnings?"

"She was a fake. You're not."

The two steel balls promptly stopped their eternal knocking. Henry explained that my appearance at the automated market had triggered explosive selling. Inflated stocks had popped and wizened and had spiralled down like burst balloons losing air. The men on the floor had been clamoring at the falling stocks indicated on the screen beneath the visiting gallery. What I mistook for outright ridicule had only been their dismay. Most would agree that my timing was bad, but Henry believed that my timing was perfect.

"I'm what they call a merchant of misery," he proudly announced before refilling my teacup. "I manipulate markets at the cost of human lives, I trade in commodities without a thought to their material consumption. And I always bank on economic havoc."

Gold was his rising star. Misanthropic gold, its polish and value varying with the nation's poverty. Paranoid investors coveted the yellow ingot, knowing the prices of precious metals would soar when legal tender crashed. Buying gold was a bid for disorder and economic chaos, a bid against good government. Henry said he owned mining companies currently sounding the continental shelf between Alaska and Siberia, where rich mineral deposits were likely. His consortium had hired an underwater crew and sent it dredging for fist-sized nuggets. Gold and other heavy metals were said to lie on the sea bottom, left behind by the last ice age. Dredging was just one of his many disruptive enterprises. He profited from unpatriotic ventures of all sorts. "Lots of booty in offshore protected trusts," he chuckled, "It's not safe to keep your money in the country, not safe at all."

We stood at the window. The placid lake sleeping on the paved shore. A rooftop jogging track glowed neon green amid the glass skyscrapers. A mere rope functioned as barrier between the elliptical course and the edge — jogging made high-risk to supplement the adrenaline rush. Henry peered through a telescope at the street antics far below. He grew melancholy, his breath heavy with some burden.

"Sometimes I go up on the roof and drop pennies."

"Have you ever hit anyone?" I asked, picturing the dense coin, filled with the weight of gravity, penetrating the skull of some unlucky soul. I promised myself to stay safely in his shadow and save my skull from falling pennies.

"No. I haven't hit anyone. Not yet."

At lunch he plied me with food and drink. We dined at the Cambridge Club on the eleventh floor of the Sheraton Tower, where women were only allowed as guests. The restaurant was carpeted blue, the ironed napkins folded into crowns, and the vases gushing with orange crocuses. Framed in the window were the curved shells of city hall like the ridged valves of a jumbo clam. Henry showed me pictures of his wife, professional pictures with soft yellow lighting and storybook sky-blue backdrops.

"Today's my wedding anniversary. I had entirely forgotten." He sighed, full of remorse, as he recounted his wedding day. He recalled walking past pews packed with the unfamiliar faces of cousins, aunts, and uncles, their eyes full of prodding good wishes. Beside him, beneath her veil, stood his small-boned, timid bride. Henry's voice grew thin and dry as he described her.

"I was very nervous. I hardly recognized her. She had become a strange bird, a heavenly dove, her wings ready to lift off. But worst of all was that look in her eyes, that small measure of pure unselfish love. I couldn't bear it. I looked up and there was Christ the Saviour, crucified on the cross. Christ! I thought, and panicked, and then I heard the priest bellow, *God has called you to each other!* and my composure slipped away completely, and it was all I could do to just drop the ring into her little manicured hand."

Our lunch marked their tenth anniversary, but there was nothing coincidental about it. Henry and I were also called to each other. Our meeting was bid by the fickle finger of fate. The finger that coiled, tip to palm, and then uncoiled, again and again, luring the pawns into the play. The finger that grasped and pointed, like my mother's hard and craggy digits. True, Henry hadn't offered me anything specific. And true again, he had a funny habit of dropping pennies from rooftops. But why dawdle over details? Henry was exactly what Sarah had recommended. He controlled money, markets, and nations, and had it in his power to offer me the world. That his wife had so disappointed him, and that he felt compelled to tell me, made the offer more personal, although not yet explicit.

Two generous plates of seafood were served. Henry sipped his martini and cleared his throat. He spun his gold wedding band and offered a small wounded smile before continuing.

"Our honeymoon was a disaster. I had never felt so cheated. Paris was a joke. The Eiffel tower was overrated, the view disappointing. Even the Mona Lisa was pint-sized and not so inveigling in reality."

He downed his martini and pressed the lip of his spoon into the tablecloth. He remembered plodding through the crowds beneath the richly wrought ceilings of the Louvre, dragging his wife from masterpiece to masterpiece. She liked them all, but tired easily, so he left her on a bench, beside others equally weary.

"I had to see the Venus de Milo. I know, it was self-indulgent. My wife certainly thought so. But there was no stopping me. I left her alone on a bench and went looking for the statue. I remember turning a corner and being blinded by camera bulb flashes. I couldn't see a thing. But when I opened my eyes, there she was. After centuries of being buried in a farmer's field! Crops had been planted and harvested, and animals had grazed and slept, and she lay only inches away. It meant a hell of a lot to me. I wanted to meet the man who had uncovered her. I imagined being there the day her breasts rose up out of the soil. Imagine that. Imagine the farmer cupping those breasts with his thick dirty fingers." He dropped a baby shrimp into his mouth. "I just stood there lusting after that moment. And to be perfectly frank, I had never before felt so vigorous. I'm not afraid to admit it — that lust rubbed out the memory of my wife. I had hoped marriage would anchor me to life. I had even hoped that my bride would answer all my prayers. Very foolish hopes. Wedlock is far from holy."

I knew exactly what he meant. I knew what it was to have one's life disrupted by busty Venuses and momentous uprisings. I knew the abandon felt beside anchor shanks and other monuments to world wreckage. And I knew, from my parents, that wedlock was a kind of pit in which explosions were allowed. I double-crossed my legs beneath the table and looked out at clam-shell city hall. I felt on top of the world.

The restaurant was quiet in the afternoon lull. Henry sucked the juice from the lobster legs. He liked things a little different now. The armless beauty had broadened his mind. "I'm obsessed with oddly proportioned bodies. Take the lopsided lobster, for instance," he said, pointing to his plate where both a massive claw and another only a fraction of its size lay flawlessly cleaved in two. "Nothing quite so compelling as mismeasured body parts," he said, poking at the stringy white flesh, "Except for missing body parts," he added, laughing, and I laughed with him. He cleared his throat and swallowed, and then spoke with the same sort of certainty he had used on the subway. "I'm drawn to women whose physical features and general shape are remarkably disproportionate." On the cramped subway, with its low ceilings and its seats for only medium-sized hips, he was involuntarily drawn to the large in general. He leaned forward over the remains of our lunch and whispered his approval.

"Your body breaks the laws of decency and balance. Your ass is sufficiently grand to question the berth of any plastic fixed or swivel seat. But your crowning glory," he paused, as if searching for the right words, "is an aroma, a fierce almost pungent aroma that reminds me of the sea."

"Do you enjoy nature?" asked Henry in the lavishly green park where we walked after lunch. The grass beneath our feet was tall and thick in fertile clumps, the virile results, so Henry said, of last season's dog shit. Branches above our heads gushed with vernal leaves and were whipped and shaken by the wind. Their frantic shadows flit across the gently sloping public grounds thickly sown with yellow dandelions. My eyes followed the spring seeds that floated and twirled and thickened the air. The sun kissed their wriggling forms and lit their strange motion.

"Enjoy nature? It sounds like you're offering dessert."

"Maybe I am," he teased, as he held an upturned plastic bag and dumped his supply of breadcrumbs.

From all over the park swooped large white gulls, their impudent cries loud and abrasive. They pitched and scudded on the air, squawking their selfish reproach, flapping their clumsy wings. My heart quickened as these stupid birds flocked to feed on breakfast crusts, landing on webbed feet without grace or decorum or precision. They fell from the sky like ugly angels from my past, here to remind me of how unsuited my marine sensibility was, here to expose me as no more than a big awkward seabird in a city park. I flinched, fearing the poke of a stiff feather. I blushed, convinced that the damn demented birds were determined to humiliate me. I hated their seamless feathered breasts, their lack of pride, and how they fished and scavenged without restraint.

I quickly took his arm and directed him away from the heap of white bread, away from the squawking white birds and the frenzy of wings and webbed feet. We walked further into the park, deeper into the rampant dandelions.

"You don't like gulls?" he asked, bemused.

"They're horrid. They don't belong here."

"And you do?"

I gaped down past my cracked leather chaps and riding boots, unwilling to openly admit to my being somewhat marooned in the Big Smoke. Henry stooped to pluck a tall swaying dandelion crowned by an uncommonly broad yellow bloom. He pulled the jagged-toothed leaves away from the flower and snapped the thick stalk. Watery milk flowed from the stalk over his palm. He pushed his finger into the carpeted florets that formed the flat face of the flower. He seemed aroused by the shaggy sensation and pressed the pad of his finger further into the spongy mass of tiny silken petals.

"I only ask because you seem uneasy, like you don't trust me." He spoke quietly and turned his face toward me, his bright red hair a vivid flare against the green surroundings. I looked up and my vision was glutted with the lush-coloured movement of wind-swept branches. He was wrong. I was very much at ease with him. It was the very fear of falling pennies that shackled my heart to him. He stood with his legs apart and his two hands as if on a holster. "And why should you trust me? You of all people, Miss Doom and Destruction."

I smiled.

"Because you like me?" I suggested hesitantly.

He pointed his dandelion at me as if it were a gun. He squeezed the flower stalk between his thumb and forefinger, flicked his thumbnail hard at the base of the flower and launched the yellow sun into my hair. I blinked and felt the petals cleave. "Mary had a baby and its head popped off," he sang in falsetto, as if it were a favourite rhyme from his childhood days.

If we had been in a schoolyard, and he had been a boy spurred on by my hateful brothers, I might have walked away annoyed. But here was a full-grown man, so it seemed; here was a financier. I dragged the flat flower through my fine hair and dropped it delicately at my feet. No, I wasn't heartbroken. I was thrilled and kept my head bowed to hide my blush. In the hallowed patch where I stood, many of the dandelions had already been fertilized, their blooms already gone to seed, their petals shorn off with age, and their organs inverted into impossible spheres of fly-away frailty. I bent over and examined a potent fuzzy ball of hungry seeds, the wind having not yet dispersed them. I plucked it near the root, brought the blowball close to my lips, felt the furry arrows just a breath away and blew the seeds into Henry's face.

There was something beautiful and becoming in the gentle way he received them. He closed his eyes and let the almost intangible wisps play over his mouth, his cheeks, his temples. They rolled lovingly across his face. One parachuted seed snagged on his eyebrow, another in his ear. How I longed to be like those tumbling seeds and snag forever in his wrinkles. Under the charming sway of that moment, I fell for him and all of his foibles. It was as if we were married, our vows exchanged over the spawning and beheading of a common weed. Nothing had ever felt more sacred; our union was beyond mere man and wife. The world seemed subdued by a weird silence, the air feathery-full of twirling seeds searching, searching for their snagging last chance to be sated.

But wafting into our world was the smell of cat piss. It came from a sand-filled pen where a group of men were playing horseshoes. They had gathered at one end to dispute points.

They spoke loudly in disagreement, with tobacco-trilling voices, tongue-tapping vowels and large shoe-swinging gestures. One walked away in exasperation and began raking the sand into a pattern of even wavelets.

"Do you play?" asked Henry. I looked from him to the sand pit, and back again.

"Sure," I replied, although I never had played before and felt it must be horse treason to toss horseshoes about. What would JoeHow think? Would he condemn me for the irreverent misuse of these cobbled iron shoes? Would he rise up from wherever he was to accuse me, once and for all, of betrayal? How I dreaded that and hoped, instead, that my most-recent success sanctioned his disposal.

The other men greeted Henry as if he were a long-lost relation. They then stepped aside and fell silent when he rolled up his sleeves and retrieved a lone horseshoe half-buried in the sand. He was all concentration. He weighed the object in his hand and spied his target — an iron rod planted at the far end. He kicked at the sand and shoved his feet into a ready-made trench. He swung his arm high behind him, forward with spoke-like precision and then hurled the heavy shoe up through a perfect arch, a peerless path, toppling over and over into good luck, bad luck, good luck . . . until it landed with a deep thud on the packed sand and a clang as the buttress arms hooked the iron rod. I applauded.

"Who wants to make a bet?" he asked, but the men declined, as if they knew better.

"Think I can do it again?" he turned to me.

Yes, I was thinking, Henry of all people, against all odds, could do it again. His throw was perfectly engineered, purely divined, controlled until the very last moment of impact, as though he had not only designed the rules of the game, but also determined the very laws of nature. How could I hazard a bet against him? Why risk squandering Sarah's dowry? And yet part of me longed to cast my lots and cross his purposes. Part of me was aching to trip up the inevitable. I wanted to gamble against my own destiny, although moments earlier I had blown seeds of devotion across his face. Why throw a wager at him now? Why, indeed, I don't know. I suppose my wager was simply meant as a kind of warrant or guarantee of our being bound to each other.

"A hundred bucks," I shouted, and a cloud blotted out the sun, suddenly turning the park dark arbory green. A park that now seemed to me, in my wild state of gambling abandon, to be completely contrived and artificial. The trees were studiously arranged, the grass genetically engineered, the entire untouched meadow no more than a cultivated sample.

"Make it two hundred!" I doubled my bet. Why not, I thought, as three men in matching overalls pushed whining lawn mowers over an incline, beheading weeds by the hundreds. I looked at Henry rigging the odds, divesting the game of chance and preparing once again to swing his horseshoe with the same concentration, the same excessive formality, and the same precision. He tossed it toward the target, and I swear it swept the exact same arc, spinning over in exactly the same sequence and thud, once again, hooking the rod in exactly the same way as his first throw. The entire event was flawlessly repeated. Each moment was a faithful replica of its parent in the previous progression. The other men shook their heads in disbelief and disapproval. Henry turned to me and grinned. "You owe me," he crooned.

I forked over the dowry bestowed by Sarah. Sarah, I was certain, would sanction this transaction with a risk analyst. Henry, after all, tamed chance. Losing money to him was like investing in the gods — big pay-offs if they existed and nothing lost if they didn't.

"Chase me," he said suddenly, as he turned and ran. Not the slow and easy pace that postponed the fatal heart stop. No, he ran like the devil, swift and light-footed, his red hair a fiery blur. He ran at speeds I could barely muster, but I did. I chased him into the adjoining cemetery, past leaning headstones and palatial tombs, past house-sized mausoleums and gardening gravediggers. We jumped over the long morning shadows cast by husky pine trees, their roots entwined with the interred. We ran through the rocking sprinklers, leapt over gravestone steeples, crushed cut flowers laid even earlier that day, and tore through throngs of grieving widows. I felt painfully alive on top of the dead, my muscles cramped and strained. I relished the thought of skeletons beneath my step, their flesh devoured by earthworms, their eye sockets empty, and their gumless teeth deranged. The acid soil ripe for hungry moulds, I wondered what fungus grew on their rotten remains. I hoped colonies of bacteria thrived on their meat. I hoped their shrivelled ears heard my heavy breathing and the tapping of my toes. And finally, out of breath, I hoped Henry would stop. And he did.

"I love puffballs and field smut," he panted, "but my favourite is the stinkhorn."

The phallic stinkhorn stood before us. Its cap was covered with slimy spores and exuded a cadaverous smell. Henry crunched underfoot an uprooted trunk laced with lichen and picked the sunless shroom. He wiped the noxious ooze across his fingers. I found myself savouring the dank air and the smell of decay. I found myself admiring the ghostly white stalk and its means of moulding onto dead wood and humus. I was confident Henry could distinguish between poisonous and edible species, the high-risk fungi versus the nibblers. I had heard that the vibrantly spotted parasols were always safe, but saw none amongst the trunks and ancient gravestones.

We walked into a field adjoining the cemetery and reached a small pool of stagnant water. My boots sank into the absorbent black peat surrounding it. Henry crouched and pressed his hand down on the pallid sphagnum that carpeted his secret bog. He told me he cherished the spongy moss, its ticklish feel and earthy smell, its dense low-brow existence.

"I own the lot," he granted. "I encourage decay."

"What would the dead think if they knew?" I asked.

"They'd thank their lucky stars," he said smiling, and once again I wished I was all over him, like the stinkhorn spores he had rubbed into his skin.

He led the way and I followed, back through the graveyard and the park, back toward the downtown core. We walked along King Street, past the empty majestic factories west of Spadina, and arrived at an old decrepit property. I looked with curiosity at the brown broad wooden beams that had curled with age and the crooked brickwork beneath the tarred and likely leaky roofs. I even found a certain grace in the slanted front porches that emptied like slides into each dirt yard. But I wondered why they were allowed to stay, for surely they were a blemish on Bay Street's prestige, an ugly scar from an accident years ago.

"How old are these buildings?"

He shrugged his shoulders.

I wondered if what stood before me was the only existing monument to the Great Toronto Fire, the flames having consumed everything else, save the sleazy ramshackle row, now an awful landmark in memory of that fated fire and its financial ruin. Perhaps they remained a reminder of how suddenly real estate values can plummet. Citizens were to consider their good fortune and pause for a moment in gratitude.

"Bless you," said Henry when I sneezed at the dust clouds spawned by the commotion of day into night. The glum blue light of dusk crept into an alleyway between two buildings. Puddles thick with dirt had collected over cracks and potholes and reflected the scarped brick walls, listing with age on either side. Three boys crouched over caps, dashing rocks onto strips of gun powder. Their figures were drawn in blue silhouette and reminded me of my three brothers. I watched as each held the sharp point high and hammered hard the paper strip, intent on creating his own little explosion. The loudest bangs brought the most joy. I watched as they tossed their weapons and sought replacements, then brushed away the gravel and hunkered down. I should have known that gun-powder games signalled danger and at the very least exploding sea vessels. I should have remembered that simple fact and left Henry then and there. But I was mesmerized by one boy in particular, the one who heaved too large a rock and pulverized his strip without success. He bent over to scrutinize the ragged remains of magic red paint, his profile pure determination.

Henry stood beside me, grappling the coins in his pocket. He seemed anxious.

"You've come this far. You may as well come in." He ushered me through the door of the corner relic building. We climbed rickety stairs to the second-floor office. The focused beam from a desk lamp spotlit a woman's hand tapping pencil-point to pad. A small precise sound was emitted with each strike of the graphite point. The glowing white paper was lit like a stage, and the woman's hand like a stringless puppet. The room was otherwise unlit, and her face, in dark shadow, was hardly visible. The curly black telephone cord was taut to her ear, the receiver rivetted between tilted chin and shoulder, and a muted male voice could be heard pleading across the wires. Beyond the line of light hulked the cheerless dark, in spartan contrast, the rest of the room utterly unseen. The woman's deathly pale hands and deadly precise gestures troubled me. They were not the flourishes of someone taking chances. My initial presence of mind was easily undone, and the day's achievements put into question.

"Don't be afraid," said Henry, as he opened another door and led me down a corridor lit by the wan twinkling of a chandelier. Plastic prisms and cheap coloured beads hung on thread from its arms and snagged in my hair as I passed under. A fake parrot, whose wire legs were wrapped snugly around the main stem, rolled its glass eyes at my blunder. I freed myself and glanced nervously down the narrow passage. The chandelier's dim light cast dolefully out onto a series of hanging paintings, all ornately framed. The first was composed with impressionist motes in muted colours, a painting within a painting, a landscape within a group study. I blushed at the bare bottoms of the ethereal nudes who turned their backs to me and looked upon their own luminous vista that lay beyond the edge of their drawing room. A sample within a sample, I thought to myself, squinting at the thousands of brush impressions that pockmarked both the bodies and the land. Every solid line disintegrated into spots, every rock decomposed, and the horizon itself dissolved. If this were the world Henry offered, then I was hard up. For there was nothing of substance, nothing tried and true, nothing a machine might not have made.

The other landscapes were no better. They hung at eye-level with only an inch of shadow between each frame. The more grand the brush stroke, the more gloomy in the dim light. Some showed peaceful workers of rural industry tilling the land with sluggish determination, their kerchiefs tied around their brow. Beside them brawny women bending over, their billowing skirts upturned to burgeon mushroom-like. Some showed grazing animals, as plump as any lounging god, their fleshy shapes and rippling coats, the fatty bulk of a slower century. Most showed the unkempt wild: the thick virile growth of forest, the impossible steep repose of a mountain, the clear cold blue of water unfrozen, and the impenetrable bush. Henry stopped to examine the swirling sugar maples and contorted jack pines, their branches blown crooked by the unfailing north wind. He pointed at woolly boughs of green needles bundled to one side of the twisted trunks that held fast to outcrops of wrinkled rock.

"Aren't those pine trees perfect?" asked Henry.

They were far from perfect. Too woolly, too much like green fleece drying on branches, too fluffy, soft, and pea-green. I couldn't hold my tongue.

"They look like dead trees wrapped in wool blankets."

Henry scowled and looked back and forth between me and the painting.

"I suppose you think the water's too blue as well?"

I nodded. It was too blue.

"Nature's very difficult to capture," he said. Suddenly, from the other end of the corridor, came scuttling a wheezing wiener dog. Its paws pitched forward and overgrown nails scuffed the floor in a sort of gallop that ended in witless panting at our feet. The eyes were blind with cataracts, the whiskers frayed and droopy. Bad breath wafted upward from its poorly digested dry-food pellets. Henry patted its bristly fur. "This is Dick," he announced, reaching into his suit pocket and tossing down a dogbone. Dick swivelled awkwardly on his stocky legs, his nose delivered up with each sniff and attempt to place the source of food. His ears cocked in anticipation, his kinky tail wagging all the while. Finally, he located the bone, pressed his nose against the powdery finish and inhaled. Then his swollen knees buckled beneath his tubular frame and he fell to the floor, gnawing and slobbering at the precious morsel.

"He may be blind, but what a nose! Dick can *smell* the pine trees in that painting."

I doubted that. For a moment I wondered if Dick was a reincarnation of Pipsqueak come to wreak more havoc upon my life. Trusting his nose was out of the question.

Henry shrugged and turned away. He opened another door, and out rushed a wave of musty industrial steam, rolling fog-like across our feet and up the dog's stubby legs. We waded through the steam and into the room. My heart was reluctant, my mind ravenous, my fingers tingling with suspicion. Against the far wall, glittering faintly, was a throne flanked with tarnished gold griffins. Above the throne was a mural of factory workers who marched across the walls in servile stride, their ankles chained. The pattern of triangular figures was much like that on the face of the Exchange and evoked the same feeling of disgrace that I had felt there. I searched the parade for some answer. Each youthful bondman drawn in chinless profile, each with a shamefully large nose and a dispassionate tear-shaped eye. No lips, no smile, no obvious expression. They marched to a drumbeat invading the room from invisible speakers, the cadence rising, the rhythm hurried with promised crescendo. From each hip emerged what I mistook to be a mechanical drill, but soon realized was a penis, hugely erect and scrupulously horizontal, entering the muscular thigh of the next in line. Was that it? Was that the reason why men seemed to bond against me? The throne shifted into gear, bumping and grinding up the wall. Henry grinned. He wiped beads of sweat off his brow with a clean white handkerchief. Sarah's good advice shrivelled into flyspeck proportions and then vanished altogether from my thoughts. I blamed her for my predicament and wished back the riot police and the red berets. If only they would come crashing through the styrofoam walls of simulated ancient stone, arrest the tax-evasive Henry and rescue me from my dreams.

I poked at the painted primeval crevices carved into the fake walls and broke off small synthetic chunks. The drum soundtrack quickened and flowed through the spurious cracks. I dropped pieces of the squeaky mould as a trail to follow upon my escape. But blind Dick plodded behind me and gobbled up the crumbs on the sheet-metal floor, which puckered and crumpled as I walked across it. My throat constricted. The arm around my shoulder felt direly coercive. My being there felt painfully unwise. Henry was a pervert, a risk-taker, a man of unlikely means. Everywhere loomed steam engines with useless pistons, cranks, and paddles. Everywhere the thumping sound of pointless levers and machines pumping diddly-squat. The room was full of artifacts from an industrial age gone awry. My eyes confounded by cogged wheels ground into mismeasured grooves, tools lashed together in unworkable combinations, balls joined to chains, and chains to rods. And everywhere the thick fog that harked back to the first smoking factories and their explosive tension.

Henry had rigged the room to no purpose. He had invested in pure endeavour and denied all profit.

The sound was a deafening barrier between my head and my heart. And suddenly I knew why he embraced this mechanical nightmare. It was his personal way of opposing an unstoppable Bay Street and denying the divine right of exchange. It was his stand against industry. And amidst the chaos and noise, it seemed utterly pathetic.

I tried to forget the futile thwack of engine parts and stared over the edge of a vat of oil at the easy rhythm of a dripping hose. The drips formed, fell and vanished in the undisturbed molasses-like liquid. I watched, hypnotized, waiting for the drops to distend, to pull, and finally to reave from the hose and plummet. It was comforting to see the black pearls pass into oblivion, their solitary shape suddenly obsolete, sinking into engine's blood, flammable and insoluble, as if divided from water on principle. I dipped my fingers in the oil, letting the black fluid streak across my knuckles. The cool tacky syrup trickled into the tender webs between my fingers. Then over into my palm I watched it channel along the trenched skin like lava filling ruts and ditches. Henry said something, his voice far away, warped and heavy in the humid air.

"You prefer oil to water?" he asked.

I had no idea what he meant.

"No. I don't think so. Do you?"

He shrugged his shoulders and pointed at the room's centrepiece, a huge wooden wheel resting on edge, peaceful and staid amongst the raging combustions. It sat calm and composed, and perfectly round, while throttles shook with unreleased pressure all around it. "Forget the lubricants and look at this noble wheel," shouted Henry, as he stroked the circumference. "For you Mary, the helm of my mystic ship."

What could I say? There was no denying the wheel's nobility. It had been carved from the cross-section of a gargantuan tree. A tree that had witnessed the passing of human generations, their driving spirits come to naught, their scheming aspirations ending always with a sudden curtain. Henry relished those sudden curtains. He even encouraged them. "Massive floods in the sixties, see," he said, pointing to bands broader than the rest that marked the disasters. I walked over and traced my oily finger over the tightly bound life rings that crossed the spokes like tiny wavelets. Those heedless rings, their insolent growth, while wealth followed poverty, and poverty wealth. I felt the old resentment return toward the trunk's persistence. Here I was, once again, at the side of a memorial to our easy destruction.

Henry fiddled with a leather strap and slumped against a spoke. His face damp and dripping, haggard, and no longer dignified. His grey eyes and red hair muddied brown in the dull foggy light. He smiled, drizzly lips parting. He had hoped for a natural source of energy, something raw and pure to power his wheel. Revolutions were too tame when plugged to a wall socket.

"I wanted something honest and organic. Something that singled out my wheel from the sea of appliances. My first choice was a waterwheel, but that wasn't viable. The water pressure here is almost zero. And windmills are outlawed within city limits."

He had fretted for months, he said, fearing he would fail at the ultimate rotary pleasure. To have come so far and be forced to burn petrol or tap the anti-engines around him.

"I feel a fool for having been so blind to not see the beauty of manpower. What I needed was a special someone to take my helm." A suitable reminder, so he said, that labour was the wellspring. He had launched a city-wide search for the perfect pilot, the person most capable, the one who would spin his wheel of fortune.

"You, Mary. Your awe-inspiring ass, your pungent aroma. This wheel is yours. A symbol of all invention, all progress, and all inventive torture. A helm to beat all others. Spin the wheel, and the strapped body turns, the gut wrenched, the bones released, and gravity defied!"

His jowls swayed as he spoke, his clammy mug rosied with enthusiasm. To describe myself as discouraged would soft-pedal my emotions. He was needy and self-depriving all in one blow. I hated his secretive, anti-social, but simple pleasures. Bay Street's wellspring was more backward than my modest beginnings. All the hoopla was hiding a deep nostalgia for a dirtier mechanical world. Henry squeezed his sweat-soaked hanky in his clamped white-knuckled fist and leapt away from the wheel. He spun round, his feet pivoting, his arms swooping spoke-like churning steam as he imitated the desired effect. His jacket swung up and off his back like a pin-striped billowing cape, his suit pockets bulging with dogbones. Crumbs flew and scattered into the fog, and the wiener dog, sensing the excitement, barked and hobbled about and hurriedly licked the sheet-metal floor.

I left the poor man in mid-pirouette, absorbed in his whirling frenzy and unaware that dog biscuits absconded from his person. I left without spinning the chunky wood helm. Despite my dandelion pledge and my graveyard pursuit, I refused to pilot his soul-searching enterprise. My reasons were not about capital gain, since he had promised impressive paybacks and perks of all kinds. My reasons were about mothers and their spheres of influence. Boat chores had always been precisely apportioned in our family. My being at the helm would breach a well-established order, and I didn't dare encroach on my mother's reign.

And yet no matter how twisted and occult, Henry remained my only Bay Street operator, and I treasured the few terms of endearment we had exchanged. One question cramped my affections, the question that always haunts the chosen, the question as to why me and not another. I walked down his gallery of landscapes, and down his rickety stairs, and never once questioned my own motives. To those I gave free rein, as if my fondness for him were infallible. I doubted only his devotion and wondered whether his predilections were always prankish and irresolute. I wanted to surrender to him, but that would be mutiny.

I walked slowly along the sidewalk, my eyes stinging with King Street dust. I passed the blipping marquee lights of Honest Ed's entertainment emporium. Men in business suits lunched on patios. I stepped over a cross-legged man on a grate, his jacket ruffling like a pitted sail above the sterile subway wind. His bloated wrists rested on his knees, his fingers curled and yellow. At his side was a cardboard box containing pennies and nickels, the small change tossed by rooftop bankers, the pardon donations from passers-by. He remained perfectly still, and I gave him nothing. My feet touched his pavement, grazed the square he had chosen, and suddenly my legs forgot locomotion, my muscles slackened, my tendons went to sleep, and walking required all my concentration. I heaved one foot in front of another, as though yanking string and pulley to raise them. I threw myself forward and staggered like someone suddenly cursed with a crippling illness. I stepped on the cracks between squares until my coordination returned. I walked to the church on the corner, the steeple frail and humble amidst the boasting towers of big business. The building was evidently out of its league. Above the little spire rose the windowed heavens of high finance, which seemed at that moment all too close for my comfort.

It was a lonely church of venerable age, the old yellow stone walls erected with almost too much conviction. The Presbyterian Saint Andrew's had lasted well beyond its ideals; only the husk of stout-hearted fervor prevailed. *Come in for a quiet moment* was the unassuming invitation inside the glass prayer box. After Henry's mystic helm, this simple summons came with welcome relief. I pushed through the heavy doors and entered the house of God, all but expecting banquets of golden fruit. My pupils narrowed in search of saintly distractions and pink and chubby angels of mercy. But everything was grounded and cloistered and unforgiving. The air was all doom and gloom, the dwelling lined with dark wooden pews and somber stained glass, the walls sporting the names and shields and crests of God-fearing fanatics.

I walked down the aisle toward the priest's pulpit, the floor sloping with a slow insidious incline. The heels of my boots were loud on the tiled floor. Too loud for the quiet hall. I tried to step gingerly from toe to toe, but even my soft shuffle sounded brazen. I slid along a narrow pew, suddenly aware of how vastly unsuited benches were to my bottom. I traced my still oily finger over the patron saint's cross, which was carved into each pew and resembled an X. Saint Andrew had been crucified much like I imagined Henry when strapped to his wheel. I counted ten hymn books clustered on the shelf at my knee and for a moment considered opening one randomly and observing whatever rule of conduct I found there. Presbyterians, I reminded myself, believed in predestination. The power of prayer was paltry if cheerless gods condemned as they pleased. Some of us were simply denied grace and salvation without any recourse. The janitor glanced repeatedly in my direction, as if he was the arbiter of such judgment. I found myself whispering with fascination the words, "God has called you to each other," and suddenly, as though commanded, Henry appeared at my side.

"You ran away," he whispered.

"You followed me," I replied.

He sat squarely on my flattened hand, my palm now pressed into the wood bench. I wriggled my fingers and turned my wrist in an effort to free myself. Henry beamed with obvious pleasure, and I instantly yanked my hand out from under him and held it convalescing in my lap. He rocked back and forth on his flat fanny, his grin gone, his eyes narrowed.

"You know it's easier for a camel to go through the eye of a needle than for a rich man to enter the kingdom of heaven." He crossed his legs and leered at the church ceiling. Above us black wood beams curled against the plaster like the bones of a skeletal rib cage. Heaven, it seemed, was a kingdom where all those not of a single unfrayed thread were forbidden. A club to which admission was based on material denial. I pitied the poor camel having crossed a desert only to be spurned for his unusual humps, when the needle itself was made from the ivory of an equally ungainly creature. Heaven, I concluded, was in the habit of splitting hairs. It seemed unfair that Henry would never be elected from the skinny bench to the sacred sunny chamber. He was, after all, a member of the business elite, accustomed to privilege.

"You won't find anything here. That I can guarantee you," he said sternly. He shoved his elegant fingers in his shoe and urgently scratched his sole. His flame-red hair fell into his eyes as he bent over with a burning desire to reach the source of the itch. He sat so closely I could almost see the blue blood pumping through the valley of his deep temple.

"All they offered was a quiet moment," I mumbled apologetically.

"But there's always something else up their sleeve," He stretched his arms out and tugged both of his coat sleeves down over his shirt cuffs. I noticed he had removed his wedding ring. It was obvious that his own motives were often ulterior.

"Like what?" I asked.

His reply was drowned out by the sudden haphazard chords of the organ, sounds that were so discordant and chaotic I wondered if a child had begun slamming the keys. This thunder developed into snippets of harmony started and then abandoned. Waves of bass notes buzzed indistinctly, while the treble rippled as if from an underwater piano. The music soon resonated in the wood benches, cementing the space until every breath inhaled was solid with sound. I glanced over my shoulder and up to the balcony, where enormous pipes were mounted above two small figures. A grey-haired man flapped his arms while his student, a young girl, sat pounding the keyboard and swivelling back and forth, stretching her short legs in order to reach the pedals.

I looked at Henry, who continued to speak words lost to the din. He leaned closer, and still closer, until I could count the broken blood vessels around his eyes. I heard nothing but imagined the rubbery sound of his facial muscles jerked and stretched as he mouthed his breath into phonemes. I watched his tongue touch the top of his mouth, the back of his teeth, the crest of his flat lips. His face was full of sound and movement and empty of meaning. It was a feat of automatism, as if he were a medium for the organ and not his own expression. His lips moved as if pressing bass pedals, his jaw plonking melody, his twitching nostril like a treble key. All his intentions were drowned out by musical movement. I watched his hand on his knee drumming some unknown rhythm of sense and import. I sensed his honesty without understanding him and wondered whether all spoken words were so unnecessary.

The music suddenly ceased, and Henry's raised voice filled the church.

"I'm not offering you a rose garden," he bellowed, then cleared his throat and whispered, "but there are just some things you can't walk away from."

It suddenly seemed to me that beneath his suit was a thick envelope of air insulating his body so that even when dressed he felt naked. His clothes hung too perfectly to be resting on the shoulders of his mortal frame. I wondered if he was all hot air or helium, his body expanding like an overheated money market. I imagined the detached freedom he suffered day in and day out, driving him in search of forces stronger than greed. I saw him sitting at his desk, the Risk Analyst, plucking petals from a daisy and sounding out the chances to buy or sell. His desk drawers were no doubt overgrown with stinkhorns and precious fungi and anything smooth and spongy that might soothe him. I wondered what exactly he had promised his wife and whether she suspected anything.

He leaned forward to whisper. I felt his lips brush against my earlobe, his warm breath tickling the tiny cilia inside my ear. I felt his words cross the drum, travel down the dark tunnel and send pulses of significance into a brain forever addled by adolescent motion sickness.

"What are you afraid of?" he asked.

I looked down at my hands and then into his face, noticing for the first time the thin black rim and the jagged edge of mustard yellow around his eyes. I wasn't afraid of him, of that I was certain.

"The wheel," I answered.

The truth was my mother was sea captain and I was her cowardly crew. The truth was also that tree cross-sections gave me the creeps. The two truths together tapped my chronic syndrome of second thoughts. It occurred to me then that I might pit one fear against the other. Perhaps they were like old caged friends, prepared to leave arm in arm. Dismissing them in pairs might clear the dance floor, and I might yet stack my stunted feelings and achieve some resolve.

"I wouldn't know how to spin it," I admitted.

"Sure you would. It's easy. You're just shy."

"I'm not shy. I'm just not good at pretending,"

His patience was tried. He crossed his arms on his chest, pressed his lips together and peered out from under sinking eyelids.

"No one's asking you to be a movie star."

A flash of limbic memory brought back the dwarf's bidding. He had petitioned me on the subway platform, promising costumes and simulated instant wealth. Like

Henry, he wanted impostors. If sailing under false colours was to be my vocation, then my first calling was Casa Loma.

"Give me a day," I asked, "to think about it."

Casa Loma sat high on the escarpment, shimmering like a mirage in the warm waves of early morning exhaust. The sallow dawn crawled reluctantly up and over the pastry-puff mansion. I followed and stopped to read the plaque halfway up. The castle had been built in this century with the funds from an electricity company, the same company that had electrified Bay Street. The harnessing of random electrons had led to constructing a chivalrous anachronism. Having broken into the atom and tapped its power, having lit the night and exposed everything, the nostalgia for a dark cold medieval castle, harking back to serfdom and fear and trembling, must have filled the sponsor's heart. I suppose the electric charge separated the positive from the negative, and left the rich man wondering how to measure his power and how to leave his mark. In the dissolving atomic world he consoled himself with the perfect compromise to comfort. I stared awestruck at the dumpy towers and flimsy turrets. The portly unshaved stone created a lumpy Plasticine effect with a clean grey tint, as if regularly scoured, polished and buffed. The plaster gargoyles and bulking ramparts were hardly offensive against the ominous amber sky that morning. Another plaque explained how the Bay Street entrepreneur was knighted and widowed, and how his feudal fantasy came to a sad end. A few electrons returned to their preferred orbits, and the man went bankrupt. Ardent auctioning had dispersed most of his belongings.

I entered the great baronial hall, a motley of design and ornament. From various corners came a pre-recorded voice announcing the "Casa Loma Stomp" by the GlenGarry Orchestra. A thumping Big Band tune filled the room with music more martial and rigid than swing. The hallway was clad in elaborate teak and rosewood and led to the conservatory, a round glass room housing exotic plants. Large voluptuous flowers with long thick pistils nestled amongst the flat unusual leaves. Light filtered through a stained-glass dome painted with mauve grapes and black vine. The iron lacework was meant to be the supporting web, but its looping, turning labyrinth seemed unstable, the dark veins like a net ready to fall. I passed through to the library where the walls were lined with imitation books. On the bindings of the painted woodblocks were hand-scrawled titles of the how-to sort.

"You're an extra," said a frazzled assistant of some kind, his voice a hybrid of assertion and query. I yielded, worn out and feeble from thoughts of Henry's wheel and actually quite relieved to be called extraneous. He sent me to the billiards room where the other extras dressed as nameless domestics were stationed. I didn't hesitate. I walked spellbound. My mind was all putty, my will criminally jimmied by any covert command, as though suffering from some frontal lobe disorder. I pulled my maid costume on over my clothes.

"You look fantastic," said the subway trawler who had selected me to play part of the anonymous service industry, not the bombshell he had promised, not the celebrated lead, but a silent ambient background noise, like the sound of running water. The dwarf was a cheat, no question, but why protest his crooked peddling, when to be fair, I was glad for the simple subordinate part. So he was double-dealing, who wasn't? I felt relieved to be given such conventional duties. A handmaid was an honourable profession and preferable to my other options. It felt wholesome after Henry's proposal.

"You think I look good in an apron?" I asked.

"Sure do. But you're standing between me and the doughnuts, darling. Can you just move aside?" He yanked at my skirt and spread his enormous hand over my ass. I stepped away to let him survey the table of lustrous pastries. He picked a doughnut splashed in icing sugar and filled with jam. His chunky fingers grappled at its slippery veneer. He bit through to the centre, his beard spotted with sugary powder. He sucked the sweet dust from his fat thumb and smiled at his carefully selected extras. We were all physical oddballs. All with discrete but noticeable deformities and unstoppable nervous ticks. My satellite ears and orbiting buttocks were just one variation. There was no mistaking us for average inconspicuous people. We stood out like extreme cases, chosen by the clipboard-wielding dwarf, as he haunted the subway platforms, recruiting the alienated and the ugly.

I looked around at my sorry lot. Me and my flawed compatriots scraped off the street, stung with movie-star promises and vexed with flaccid castle plots. Extras of all shapes pinched into armchairs, their feet dangling from legs too short, their swollen heads blue from constricting collars. Monsters made speechless by their life of trial, sticking out like sore thumbs in a billiards room. Was this my final resting place? A member of the collectible oddities? I didn't like it. My gaze shifted to the busty ivory ladies adorning every supporting pillar, the shapely marble flanking the fireplace and the glowing electric log and phoney embers within. Hanging on the wall was the stuffed and mounted head of a stag. Its shiftless glass eyes looked down with ridicule. The antlers looked as if still budding, like the spring branches of a sumac tree. I imagined the deer's four-legged spirit crouched inside the remaining hide, the rest of him carved into venison. He watched the gamesroom, trapped inside his head. No one dared pick up a cue, for fear of being mocked by the hunting trophy. The proprietor must have purchased the head hoping to befuddle his opponents at billiards or darts. The derisive deer hung beside the more dreadful head of a black bear, his thick fur balding in spots. Why, I wondered, had my journey to the city led to this palace of hunting trophies?

"Do you think you belong here?" asked the dwarf, his voice cracked and intimate.

I wanted to say no. I wanted to remove myself from the assembled rejects and assorted plunder. The room was full of carcasses and outsiders disguised as tame domestics. My wholesome role felt counterfeit, but my will was as weak as ever. My resistance grew warbled and unspeakable whenever my tongue grappled with the words. I bit my lip, shrugged my shoulders and gave no other reply.

"You regret leaving him, don't you?"

"Who?"

"Your man."

The world instantly shrunk. Was the dwarf working for Henry? Were all my conspiracy theories justified? I tried to sound casual.

"My man?"

"He's all over you like a cheap suit. Unfinished business. You can't be in the movies all sloppy like that. I pick people who are naked and needy, people without a hope in hell of ever navigating through their shit-heap lives. You've got some other calling, girl. It's written all over you. I'd fire you now if I wasn't obliged to pay you for the whole day."

The man was truly a gifted talent scout.

"I don't know what you're talking about," I lied.

"See that sick flower-garden out there?" He pointed through the window. My eyes followed his stogie-like finger and saw various rumpled rosebushes, their prime long past.

"How many chances you think you got?" he asked.

Maybe he was right. Maybe Henry was my golden opportunity.

"More than one?" I suggested.

Incredulous, he snorted and shook his head.

"A rose is a rose is a rose, honey. One chance only." He guffawed, as if the punchline of some crude joke had been delivered.

Panic crept into my blood. I smiled nervously, pointed toward the door and then walked toward it. My only thought was to escape his discerning judgment. I climbed the grand staircase and entered a room painted in eggshell blue and soft evasive pink, the mantling decorated with cherubs. The magnate's wife had been crippled by a mysterious ailment, which worsened upon taking residence in the castle. Bedridden and worried financially, she must have dreamt of a future where girls were prepared at an early age for the entrepreneurial ups and downs of their husbands. How else to explain her devotion to the Girl Guides? A hallway exhibit attested to her contribution. On a plaque was engraved the maxim: "Girls should be partners and comrades, rather than dolls." The handbook for Girl Guides was described as offering dramatized heroic roles and stories of model behaviour. I kneeled down to read the page at which the book was opened. Courageous Edna had charged into a burning building to save the payroll. "Hurrah! Hurrah!" shouted the onlookers. "Well done, Miss, did you get the money?" they asked. Edna had indeed fetched the money, but she flinched at the publicity, as a good modest girl should do.

The lesson was lost on me. The rewards of self-sacrifice seemed all too obscure. Why martyr myself for one congratulatory moment? I imagined Edna ending up the obedient secretary, committed to the boss in the face of others' accusations, her loyalty beyond the call of duty. I wondered whether my loyalty to my mother was just as absurd.

I left the bedroom suites and floated like a castle ghost through the various rooms and then climbed the spiral staircase that led to the tower. Sparrows beat their wings and bolted back into their favoured cracks. The hefty blocks of stone had been cut and masoned to rise up tightly and close over the crown. Sallow light crept through the square gunholes. I looked out the tiny portal, my little head in the watchtower window. The tawny sky seemed full of sand blown off the lakeshore. The city's ceiling like a hard ochreous beach, as if the polluted lake sediment had shaken off its heavy metals, surfaced and become airborne, only to consolidate above, instead of below. I looked down at the doll-sized pedestrians who glanced up at the yellow sky; they seemed faint-hearted, their necks cranked back onto crooked shoulders. Crowds huddled in bus shelters and under canopies, fearing the hard rain coming. Everything seemed so different, the horizon so frail, the sprawl so tentative, the bricklaying so hollow. Bay Street towers swayed on what was once swamp, their mirrored glass a mere gesture of conceit, their offices increasingly empty as the market continued to fall.

I admit my perspective was presumptuous, even arrogant, but it showed me how temporary and pockmarked the city was. It showed the holes and cracks and breaches. How everything conceived contained the seeds of its own destruction. And it showed this without shame. My heart swelled with a cruel maternal love for the city. And suddenly I pictured my mother on a street corner, drenched and spent, her lips trembling, her hair thick with salt. She fixed her bloodshot eyes on the tower. She wore that familiar look of abandon, when a dead calm held the boat hostage. Around her the everyday buzz of the city flattened into stillness. Her grim weathered hands reached for me. I felt the pressure of her fearful gaze, the gaze that saw flying anchor shanks and other visitors.

The spectre of my seafaring mother shattered the panorama. I moved abruptly away from the window and blushed, my hand on my burning cheek. I left the tower and rambled throughout the castle, oblivious to the rising heat. In the original maid's room, I found a half-empty bottle of whiskey and sat down on a dusty window sill to guzzle the hot, searing medicine. The tourist agency currently operating the building had left the room unrenovated so that guests could fully appreciate the transformation achieved elsewhere. The old brick walls were covered in graffiti. *Sell more ass* stood out in large red print and perfectly chimed with the Girl Guide mottoes on the second floor. Beneath it were the usual territorial declarations about who belonged to whom. Angrier verse surfaced after minutes of staring at the wall. Oblique expressions of violence appeared within the letters of the more commonplace messages. It was a graffiti gold mine. Visitors had scratched obscenities into the stone with coins from their pockets, flattening the rivets on the cog's circumference and working the hard currency for all it was worth. There was no better tool to misuse. The cryptic walls were an unfinished masterpiece. The composition unending, the job never done.

I tipped the bottle back and emptied it. A drunk domestic in a vacant room, blinking at the raging walls, their plaintive scratches always the last sign of dissolution. Affording servants was the inspiration for owning such an unmanageable building, as well as the means for keeping it in order. But I was an unruly domestic. I opened the window and welcomed the fresh breeze. I remembered my mother at the helm, pulling in the sails before the boat met a gust. She always spied the wind rippling the water's surface just ahead of the bow. Every impermanent puff was always off the wind by a constant measure. I wondered whether her boat had grown insensitive, its trudging bottom unscrubbed, its heavy drag dumb to subtle changes in wind direction.

The piercing sound of a fire alarm burst my recollection. Small steel bells pealing at high automated speeds, the startling noise pulsing through the stone and plaster and terrorizing the walls. Already the smell of burning tassels and smouldering carpets, the passage thick with black smoke. Already the raving screams of scaremongers, their cries razing the roof. I stumbled down the stairs, my legs rubbery, my mind steeped in whiskey. The air was hot and low in oxygen, my blood was thin with booze. Grey figures clasped onto prized objects and darted about in panic. I thought of Edna the Girl Guide. She would have rescued some valuable ornament. Resourceful Edna would have won the day. I muttered her name, then choked on a mouthful of smoke and was swept up by the surging wave of terror-struck souls.

The fire had apparently started in the main hall, where a super-watt movie lamp had toppled and burst and ignited the rug. It had then travelled down secret passages and entered various rooms. Flames whipped the library door frame, feeding on fussy wood carvings and embroidered wall hangings. The stag carcass was cremated, its shade set free.

Survivors assembled in the parking lot with piles of ransacked articles at their feet. They watched the fiery spectacle with a cold detachment, safe from its singeing fingers, marking its progress like a performance and applauding its prodigious power to gut from room to room. "Wow!" said one bedazzled observer, his words punctuated by the din of shattered glass. "Holy shit!" said another. It seemed to me that they cheered on the flames, their hearts full of arson, their passion aroused by the picture of disaster. Gasping stragglers appeared in the doorway, but there was no sign of the irregular extras. Would all the oddballs be burnt to a crisp? Victims once and for all? I watched full of horror and delight, thrilled that my survival would distinguish me from them. The fire curled and kicked with a fury. The wind picked up from the lake, raced across the city and up the hill, pumping the flames with a vengeance. The cedar shakes and old elm beams of the stables dissolved into a heavy black smoke that hugged the building like a suffocating fog. The fog thickened and rolled and gave off the strange smell of sweet oranges. Its wisps and eddies obscured the view of the city, but a flock of mottled pigeons flew out and over our heads.

My talent scout stood close beside me. He stroked his beard with stubby fingers. He squinted and grinned and made the ground unsteady. The pavement heaved and swelled, my knees weakened by drink. I gagged on the turbid air and tasted vomit. The little man rocked to and fro with protracted tempo, his heels rising, in turn his toes. His box-head blurred into three separate versions, briefly consolidated, then rent asunder. Time was warped and tortoise-slow. He spoke to a woman with an unlit cigarette, his words long lisps and short crisp consonants. She raised the cigarette to her mouth, the movement painfully prolonged, her snail-like lips slowly puckering around the filter as she bent forward. His arm plodded through space and ended outstretched, offering an exquisite gold lighter. He applied a measured pressure to the lighter's lid, which slid back with a sustained clap, and let loose a husky flame.

My tongue dropped from the roof of my mouth, and the earth was no longer beneath me. I blacked out and fell backwards. My head was suddenly at the wrong end of my body, my sense of up and down undone. I fell back in painful memory, down familiar cement stairs, my limbs flailing at each knock. I remembered as a child falling down the cellar stairs. From the first to the last, every step and concrete edge a crashing blow. Back over front, and front over back, until I hit bottom. A cold basement bottom, damp and dreary, the droning sound of water pumps and bubblers glut the air. My body bruised but unbroken, legs cricked, neck wrenched, and throbbing head on the last step. My inverted mother at the top of the stairs, star-studded, weather-worn, spinning. I blinked to stop her dizzy turning, the flash and twinkling sinking into my retina. She stood upside down on the ceiling, her lips and wrinkled brow reversed, both smiling. Her pupils now setting into rising eyelids like the sun sinking into the sea. Her topsy-turvy world turned on its head. My head.

Firemen carried me to the stone wall. A headache pounded at my temple, my tongue was thick with slag, my ass was sore from falling, and the castle was still burning. My clothes reeked with the acrid smell of smoke, my hair greased as if with creosote. I sat like a traumatized survivor wrapped in an emergency blanket. Asked how it all began, I denied having anything to do with it. I hawked up the acidic surplus of the now unsavoury whiskey and told them it was a freak accident.

Someone handed me a doughnut, rescued from the billiards room, and I crouched against the wall and watched the intrepid firefighters struggling with the billowy flames. They approached and retreated with each burning wave of heat. Both the blaze and the men seemed oddly resolute, a clash between ruthless yellow hydrants and pure destruction. How excited I became, my throat parched with desire, as I watched the wasted torrent of fresh water. How manly they appeared as they straddled their thick hoses like men at a rodeo, riding the water pressure, their rubber gauntlets reining in the coarse spray. How I wished I were a taunting flame doused by their spliced streams as they joined forces against the more persistent. I watched enthralled as they squelched the burning oxygen, each fiery whip snuffed into rising smoke and the fumes dismissed into the morose amber sky.

I pressed my palm against my aching head. The pain was reassuring. It braced a nerve and struck doubt from my mind. I felt the pulsing throb at my temple, proof that I hadn't vanished in a puff of smoke, proof that I had endured a push from the top of the stairs. I could still feel my mother's hands thrust hard into my shoulder blades. Still remember how my back arched involuntarily and my chin shot forward, and I appeared at that moment to be moving of my own volition. Did she think I would take flight and glide gracefully down to land on one knee? My arms never left my side, not even to soften the fall. I plunged head first into my father's aquatic world, where rows of rubbery marine orbs swivelled so as to witness my arrival. My father leapt to my side and rearranged my limbs into some semblance of order before fixing his fierce gaze on the figure at the top of the stairs. "What were you thinking?" he screamed, as though it were only a matter of insufficient reason. But what, I wondered, could possibly have been her motive? She came colossally thumping down and cradled me in her lap, absolving herself with the usual disclaimers. "I don't know what came over me! I wasn't myself," she cried. And I wondered who owned that self-assured shove from the top of the stairs, if not my mother.

I remembered her beloved pet Pipsqueak scurrying down as though driven impulsively toward fallen prey. I lay lame and helpless and coldly examined by the marauding snout of a miniature poodle. I felt the smear of her twitching wet nose against my skin. My father pushed the dog away and dabbed my temples with a soggy clump of seaweed he had taken from a plastic tub. The water slowly streaked my cheek and trickled behind my ears. It felt cool and curative. He placed a wet leafy compress across my forehead; the smooth broad blades were flat and tacky. A few of the less adhesive slithered down to the bridge of my nose. "She's just a girl," he said, shaking his head. "How could you?" My mother raised her hands and gently placed them on his shoulders. I noticed the pale underside of her jaw hanging soft and fleshy above me and wondered whether my sight was shaded by an algae blade or whether my mother's jowls were green with envy. She leaned forward, kissed my father's mouth, and he forgave her.

"You were pushed?" asked the dwarf, as though he surely knew, proving himself to be a talent scout with telepathic skills. It seemed he had read my ambition backwards and traced it to the source. He stared through me and through the wall that I leaned against. His hands were clasped behind him, his pursed lips licked slick and shrewd.

"By my mother," I answered, but he showed no surprise at hearing the source was not so immediate.

"Mothers are like that. They're pushy," he said. "They want the best for their little ones."

He must have had his own bumptious mother to speak so sagely. A black plague of baneful wombs must have swept the nation, a scourge of mothers in crisis, their minds muddled, their mates betrayed. Everywhere that maternal shove of good will gone bad.

"You should send her a memento," counselled the dwarf.

A memento? I had never considered sending her anything. Perhaps a memento mori was called for. Perhaps some quick and easy way to kill her off.

"Like what?" I asked. I poked my finger into a crevice in the wall and rattled a loose chunk of cement. The mortar crumbled and a small stone was dislodged. I weighed the stone in my hand and envisioned my mother at the helm, a wind from nowhere pushing the boom into her back and sending her overboard.

"How about a small something she can show her friends?" he suggested.

"A small stone?" I asked and held mine up for inspection.

He shook his head and lifted his arm away from his torso to reveal an instamatic camera slung from the shoulder. He grinned as though he had just exposed some private part of his anatomy.

"How about a picture of you at the scene of disaster?" he asked.

The pictures of carnage that plastered her bedroom walls came back to me in all their grim exhaustive detail. Documents of sudden misfortune stuck there with safety pins. Vistas undone by destruction in which human figures appeared alien and absurd. I imagined my photograph framed on all sides by her old favourites and relished the thought of the dutiful daughter, neck and neck with other natural disasters. The same Mary who had once been flung across the room would now be flanked by floods and droughts. There I would languish, a victim of circumstance, adored by my mother. For she was certain to cherish the portrait, whether the man with the camera was clairvoyant or corrupt. I noticed then that he fondled the device in a way that suggested his own personal fantasy was at stake. He wore a waggish look as though the camera were stolen and his incentive indecent. But in this he reminded me of more imminent dangers, of pennies from heaven, fungi fanaticism, and futures bought and sold. And suddenly I was overcome with thoughts of Henry, my darling Henry, how near at hand, how foolish to have resisted him. He came to me in his fine woven suits, hungry for something I finally understood. I pictured him waiting beside his mystic helm, waiting to be chastened. And only then did I truly appreciate his offer. For only then was I aware of my family legacy and my future vocation.

I hauled myself up from the ground and tugged at the corners of my blanket, wrapping it tight around my shoulders. The hammering inside my head felt amplified. I shuffled a few feet toward the castle and turned, but my sense of alignment wasn't yet secure, and the whole world spun with me. The smell of burnt drapery and other finery wafted across the parking lot and added to my nausea. "That's fine," said the man from behind the viewfinder. He held the camera with lumpish fingers and elbows barbed like wings at each side. He took three steps backward, then parted his legs and swung his hips a smidgen to and fro. I waited patiently while he shook his head and retraced the few steps he had taken. I thought of Henry's handsome face and how trusting he had looked in the park. I thought of my own poorly photogenic face as the man lowered the camera, licked his forefinger and smudged the lense. I imagined my saliva-streaked image inside the shutters, blurred by bantam air bubbles and blotted out by dirt. I could only assume it was a desired artistic effect. When he pressed the button, the motor droned and out came the polaroid photograph. He tore it from the slit and fanned the air with it. I slid behind him and looked over his shoulder at the liquid silver emulsion still developing as we watched. I liked the thought of my evolving from gooey whirling dross. I liked the way the chemicals formed into the hulking figure in the foreground and the smoking castle behind. And I was glad to see my slowly emerging features were forever blurred by foggy patches where the lense had been besmeared.

"She'll be proud of this," he said and handed it to me.

I compared the picture to the castle, which continued to burn, but was now wet and dripping and looking vaguely embarrassed. The firemen were beating the fiery beast back through the doors. I assumed that a few priceless original ornaments had been consumed: the beautiful oak wainscotting, the antique furniture, the ugly portraits, and the Girl Guide exhibit. The refuse would soon be shovelled into dump trucks and driven away. My portrait, in contrast, captured the ruinous moment and the beleaguered face of a survivor. My clumsy pose and sickened complexion, my look of fear and trembling, my graceless bulk, these together with the shattered glass and the smoke brought about the long-sought-after sense of tragedy of which my mother would indeed be proud.

"Thanks," I said and wedged the picture in my pocket. I was genuinely grateful. We shook hands and he shuffled away, moving amongst the others like a magistrate, offering impartial portraits and demanding nothing in return. I watched as some declined the offer and others accepted. The wind disturbed a pile of ash and set some floating toward me. One shrivelled palm-size flake landed on my thigh. I smudged the scant substance into my white apron and made a heart-shaped stain, a grey stain pressed into the very weave of the fabric. Above me the tarnished sky cracked open a sliver, and tears rolled down my cheeks. I felt giddy and detached, there on the escarpment looking down at the city. I felt endeared to the construction that had choked the lake with industrial pledges, endeared even to Bay Street, which stretched like a tattered red carpet, its thread unravelling, its colour faded, its end chewed on by harbour rats. I pictured my mother's boat anchored offshore. The helm unwatched, the wheel waiting, myself ordained.

The streets broke cleanly from each other, always with a decisive ninety-degree turn. A rare hill caused a twist in the road that was otherwise always flat and straight. I imagined the bulldozers modelled on glaciers that had flattened and filled the swamp. I wondered about the shoreline and the shapely bluffs to the east that had been there before all the storied buildings and the tonnes of concrete. I wondered if every vertical stretch was coupled with an equivalent downward shove.

I walked like a genuine shock victim, hungry and mute, my sense of direction infallible. Each stride a ferocious leap from curb to curb, over air vents, sewers, subway tunnels, past people and parked cars and fire hydrants. Past the ossified Annex homes still in their Queen Anne finery, around Spadina Circle and south through the wholesale underwear district. Past piles of prickly fruit and cheap china and defunct factories until, finally, half-hoping she might yet dissuade me, I arrived at Sarah's oyster bar.

My eyes adjusted slowly to the blue-green algae light. The room was empty of blubbering grey suits as happy hour was yet to come. What remained were the stains of tumescent games, the dampened forms of stacked chairs and the crusty curtains concealing Sarah's peepshow. Only the spent smell of the previous night and a sense that another would always follow. And yet the club seemed far worse without its patrons. They, at least, had lent a certain dignity, the dignity of prude abandon. I much preferred their careful misconduct than the sad, dumpy room in their absence. And despite my wanting to see Sarah, I was angry to find her there, perched on a bar stool.

She was quietly talking to the bartender. The white beam of the bar tracklight lit both his shaved head and her abundant curls, while behind them glittered ice trays, soon to be beds of oysters. I walked slowly across the floor, through the gummy puddles of spilled vodka and fishy effluvia. The sound of her whispered consonants and his guttural sympathy crept across the sticky surfaces. She seemed to be confiding in him. I strained to hear what sounded like solemn personal announcements and heard my own name mentioned. Was it my life story she was telling? I stared into the back of her head and urgently needed to know everything that had ever happened to me. I imagined the truth slithering out like a snake in the grass. I imagined Sarah the mermaid slowly sipping the truth serum from her martini glass. Out would pour secrets and simple explanations, out like seawater from a pummelled stomach. Out like the ugly truth when all else is said and done. And though Sarah had been neglectful at the best of times, I hoped her own misery might move her to give testimony. I wanted her to corroborate, to stamp the polaroid so that I might post it to my mother and confirm all my painful memories. And I wanted her to approve of Henry, not as a man, but as a means to higher ground.

But why was she confiding in the barman? And why would she vouch for me in such lionhearted company? He listened with the kind of rapt attention that would only have baffled me. He wore a tight white tank-top stretched across his massive breast plates and sported two extravagant adjustable arms which pivoted and flexed with forceful expression. And he eyed me suspiciously as I approached.

"Mary, you're here," she said plain-spoken and dopey. "Have you doubled my money yet?" Her eyelids drooped like blue-dusted petals, her vagrant eyes roving the space around me. "No, not yet," I answered, while she tittered and rocked and raised her martini glass, toasting my lack of success. She seemed to have puffed up overnight, her face inflated like a buoyant medusa, her cheeks now bloated, her lips now blurred. The kind of face that launched a thousand fleeing ships, the sea their refuge.

I asked the bartender for water. He took a warm glass from the dishwasher and filled it with crushed ice.

"I've met someone. A man," I said to Sarah.

"What's his name?"

"Henry Gates."

She flipped through a small box of alphabetized business cards and plucked one from which she then read aloud.

"Mr. Henry Gates. 222 Bay Street."

"You know him?" I asked anxiously, hoping she didn't.

"No. I don't think so. I've got lots of these cards. He's probably a seafood fanatic." She laughed and nudged me, "Just like your mother?"

"My mother was . . ." I spluttered empty, not knowing what to say.

"A bitch?" suggested Sarah, laughing. "But Mary, all mothers are saints. Didn't you know?"

I saw my mother in white robe, on barren land. I imagined the pious woman suffering hardships and divine intervention. I wondered if her cruelty was goodness in disguise, but could hardly believe it. If she was a saint, then the hand of God sent me down those basement stairs, and the thought was no more comforting. I felt a pinching pain between my eyebrows and realized I was staring cross-eyed at Sarah. She sat at the end of my nose, her body doubled in two lateral hemispheres, her face swallowed in reversed periphery. Seeing her disfigured was satisfying, as though it proved her version was distorted and her impressions were all wrong.

"Mary?" She touched me on the shoulder. "Are you all right?"

"Fine. Just fine. On my way in fact." I drained the crushed ice from my glass.

"Where to?"

The cold slush filled my cheeks like a winter harbour. My tongue sloshed miniature icebergs over molars and then went numb and frigid.

"Bay Shtreet," I lisped, and without another thought I turned and left the oyster bar behind me. I walked down King Street to my high-risk sweetheart, to the wheel, to a woman's wrath, to my calling. My mother had secured this future for me. Her faith in human frailty, her obsession with forces larger than life, her insatiable taste for lobster. My mind was uncommonly clear and purged of doubt, as though unsettling Sarah's anatomy had finally set me free.

I arrived at Henry's crooked porch, climbed the stairs and stumbled down the gallery of dim landscapes. Each one was a bleak flash of nature bound in a heavy frame. Stopped short by a familiar scene, I swung back to view the cold Atlantic waves crashing onto the shore. Their white cusps curling horse manes, their swell a seventh wave deep. They rolled across the painting, the black water veined with ripples and spray and spotted with oblivious gulls. They slammed into speckled granite rocks that were wet and craggy and veiled in fog. The shore rose on the backs of these rocks, some steep and others gently sloped, like the round bottoms of bent giants. Boulders and chunks of ancient rock were strewn precariously on the barren summits where my father had gone over. I reached out to touch the rock and felt the hardened paint strokes.

Dick nibbled at my boot. The drum soundtrack beat its rising rhythm. I walked to the end of the corridor and opened the door. Again the musty stink of mould, the walls dripping, the air drenched with steam. A series of oil lanterns forged a warm golden glow on the steel instruments arranged without purpose. Henry was strapped to his wheel, strapped and waiting on the massive wooden disc with its century-old grooves wound tight. The wheel of bittersweet fortune. I walked over the crinkling sheet metal, patting my sooty apron, wiping my grimy brow. Henry lowered his eyes demurely. His naked body spread across the diameter, his limbs stretched along thick spokes. Shadows from burning lantern wicks danced across his crotch and crumpled cowardly in a bush of red pubic hair. Leather bands buckled his wrists and left his fingers free. He poked them in the cracks along the perimeter where the bark had once been. I bit my lip, turned the helm hard, and the wheel began to spin.

acknowledgments

The author wishes to thank the Canada Council and the Ontario Arts Council for their financial support during the writing of this book. Thanks also to Tomson Highway, Denise Bukowski, Sarah Davies, Leslie de Freitas and Tom Parker, for their encouragement and editorial advice.